No tears fell for Billington-Smith. No one mourned his passing. During the weekend that preceded his murder he had given every member of his family cause, if not justification, for wishing him dead. His wife ... whom he had humiliated in public; his son ... whom he had disinherited in a violent scene; his son's fiancée ... whom he had actively loathed; his nephew ... who was in financial straits and whom he had refused to help; his sister-in-law ... who, worst of all, was not in the least afraid of him.

Eleven people wished him dead – but which one had partnered death on a morning stroll?

By the same author

THE UNFINISHED CLUE

GEORGETTE HEYER

An Owl Book
HENRY HOLT AND COMPANY
New York

Library of Congress Cataloging-in-Publication Data
Heyer, Georgette, 1902–1974.
The unfinished clue.
Originally published: 1934.
I. Title.
PR6015.E795U5   1985   823'.912   84-19238
ISBN 0-8050-1337-7 (An Owl Book: pbk.)

Henry Holt books are available at special discounts
for bulk purchases for sales promotions, premiums,
fund-raising, or educational use. Special editions
or book excerpts can also be created to specification.

For details contact:

Special Sales Director
Henry Holt and Company, Inc.
115 West 18th Street
New York, New York 10011

First published in hardcover by
E.P. Dutton, Inc., in 1969.

First Owl Book Edition—1985

Printed in the United States of America
3   5   7   9   10   8   6   4   2

THE UNFINISHED CLUE

CHAPTER ONE

IT was apparent to Miss Fawcett within one minute of her arrival at the Grange that her host was not in the best of tempers. He met her in the hall, not, she believed, of design, and favoured her with a nod. 'It's you, is it?' he said ungraciously. 'Somewhat unexpected, this visit, I must say. Hope you had a good journey.'

Miss Fawcett was a young lady not easily discouraged. Moreover, she had been General Sir Arthur Billington-Smith's sister-in-law for five years, and cherished no illusions about him. She shook him briskly by the hand, and replied with perfect equanimity: 'You know quite well it's impossible to have a good journey on this rotten line, Arthur. And how you can say I'm unexpected when I sent an expensive telegram to prepare you both for the joy in store for you—'

The General's scowl deepened. 'Short notice, you'll admit!' he said. 'I suppose you've brought a ridiculous quantity of baggage?'

'Something tells me,' remarked Miss Fawcett intelligently, 'that I'm not really welcome.'

'Oh, I've no doubt Fay's delighted!' replied the General, with a short laugh. 'Though where she is I don't know. She packs the house with visitors, but can't trouble herself to be here when they arrive.'

At this moment his erring wife came down the stairs. 'Oh, darling!' she said in a voice that held a plaintive note. 'How lovely to see you! How are you?'

Miss Fawcett embraced her warmly. 'Hullo, Fay! Why didn't you send a wire to put me off? Arthur's all upset about it.'

The large, rather strained blue eyes flew apprehensively to the General's face. 'Oh, no!' Fay said. 'Arthur doesn't mind having you, Dinah. Do you, Arthur dear?'

'Oh, not at all!' said the General. 'You'd better take her up to her room instead of keeping her standing about in the hall.'

'Yes, of course,' Fay said. 'You'd like to come up, wouldn't you, Dinah?'

This was said a trifle beseechingly, and Miss Fawcett, who wore all the signs of one about to do battle, relaxed, and agreed that she would like to go up to her room.

'I've had to put you in the little west room,' Fay told her. 'I knew you wouldn't mind. We're – we're rather full up.'

7

'Yes, so I gathered,' said Dinah, rounding the bend of the staircase. 'It seems to be worrying little Arthur.'

She had a clear, carrying voice. Fay glanced quickly down the stairs. 'Dinah, please!' she begged.

Dinah threw her a glance of slightly scornful affection, and replied incorrigibly: 'All right, but it's putting an awful strain on me.'

They ascended the remaining stairs in silence, but as soon as the door of the west room was securely shut on them Dinah demanded to know what was the matter with Arthur.

Lady Billington-Smith sank down on to a chair, and put up one of her thin hands to her head, pushing the pale gold hair off her brow in a nervous gesture peculiar to her. 'Something dreadful has happened,' she answered. 'It has upset Arthur terribly.'

'Ha!' said Dinah, casting her hat on to the bed. 'The cook burned his Sacred Porridge, I suppose.'

A slight smile flickered across her sister's face. 'Oh, don't be an ass, Dinah, for heaven's sake!'

'Well, that was it the last time I came,' said Dinah, hunting in her dressing-case for a comb.

'This is much worse. It's Geoffrey.'

'Dipped again?' inquired Miss Fawcett sympathetically.

'Worse than that, even. He's engaged to be married. At least, he says he is.'

Miss Fawcett combed out her short brown locks, and began to powder her nose. 'Barmaid, or tobacconist's assistant?' she asked, as one versed in the follies of young men.

'Neither. She's a cabaret dancer.'

Miss Fawcett gave a crow of laughter. 'Oh, no! No cabaret dancer would fall for Geoffrey.'

'Well, this one has. And it isn't even as though she's English. She's a Mexican.' Lady Billington-Smith allowed this piece of information to sink in, and followed it up by a final announcement. 'And he's bringing her here to spend the week-end.'

'But how rich! how luscious!' exclaimed Dinah. 'I wouldn't have missed it for anything. Has Geoffrey gone mad, do you suppose? Who is the girl?'

'Her name,' replied Fay, 'is Lola de Silva. It sounds awfully improbable, doesn't it? It – it put Arthur off right away. I've had rather a dreadful time with him, because Geoffrey wrote to me, not to his father, and – and asked me to break the news. I'm afraid

Geoffrey's quite infatuated. He seems to think Arthur has only to see this Lola person and he'll fall for her.'

'The joys of being a stepmother,' commented Dinah. 'Is that what Arthur meant when he said that you'd packed the house full of people?'

'Partly, I expect. But he's blaming me for having the Hallidays now, just because he'd rather they weren't here when Geoffrey comes.'

'And who,' asked Dinah, 'are the Hallidays? Kindly enumerate.'

'People we met in the south of France,' replied Fay, a little guardedly. 'He was knocked up in the War, and she's – she's rather pretty, and smart.' She raised her eyes to her sister's face and coloured faintly. 'Well, you're bound to see it. Arthur flirts with her. That's why they're here.'

'More fool you to invite them,' said Dinah sternly.

'You don't understand. Arthur made me.'

Dinah snorted.

'It's no good, Dinah. You're the fighting sort, and I'm not. Anyway, it doesn't matter. He doesn't mean anything serious, and if it keeps him in a good temper I don't mind.'

'Anyone else here?' asked Dinah, abandoning a hopeless topic.

'Yes, Francis. He arrived in time for lunch.'

Dinah grimaced. 'If I'd known he was going to be here I wouldn't have come. What's he turned up for? To touch dear Uncle Arthur? That'll make it a very merry party. Anyone else?'

Fay got up, apparently to rearrange the flowers that stood in a vase on the dressing-table. 'Only Stephen Guest,' she replied. 'He said he'd be here in time for tea.'

'Oh!' said Dinah.

It was a disinterested monosyllable, but it did not seem to satisfy Fay. She looked up into the mirror, and met her sister's frank gaze. 'There's no reason why he shouldn't come here,' she said. 'After all, he's a connection of Arthur's, isn't he?'

Dinah dug her hands into the pockets of her severely tailored coat. 'Who said he shouldn't come?'

'I know what you think.'

'I think you're a blighted ass. Always did.'

Fay tried to remember that she was five years older than Dinah, and failed rather miserably. Her lip trembled; she sank back into the chair. 'It's no use, Dinah. You don't know what it's like, being married to Arthur. You don't know what it is to care for anyone, and never to see them. It isn't as though Stephen and I – as though we ... I mean, I wouldn't, and – and of course he wouldn't, but we can at least see each other sometimes.'

'Is Arthur being noisome?' inquired Dinah, not much moved by this incoherent speech.

'I suppose he's no worse than usual,' Fay replied listlessly. 'It's me. My nerves are all to pieces. Probably there are some women who wouldn't mind his temper and the way he blusters and the things he says. You wouldn't. You'd shout back.'

'No. Delicately nurtured female. Wouldn't have married him,' said Dinah decidedly.

'I was a fool. Only I thought he was different.'

'Personally, I didn't. We knew his first wife walked out on him, and she must have had some reason.'

'Oh, she ran off with another man. It wasn't anything to do with Arthur's temper; or, anyway, if it was, I couldn't have guessed that. Only I was too young. I ought never to have been allowed to marry him. If mother had had any sense ... by the way, where is mother? I haven't heard from her for ages.'

Dinah selected a cigarette from her case and lit it. 'At home, trying a new treatment.'

'Oh, lord!' sighed Fay, momentarily diverted. 'I thought she'd taken up Christian Science?'

'It didn't last. She read a bit in some evening paper about proper dieting, and she's gone all lettucey. Nuts, too. That's why I'm here. There's a filthy beverage you drink for breakfast instead of coffee. I thought not, so I cleared out.'

'Well, I do hope she won't make herself ill,' said Fay.

'Not she. By the time I get back she'll have got religion, or something, and we shall have grace before meals, but not before lettuces, so to speak. As for her having sense enough to stop you marrying Arthur – well, pull yourself together, Fay!'

Fay smiled rather wanly. 'I know. Now, say I made my bed and must lie on it.'

'I shouldn't think anyone could possibly lie on any bed you ever made, ducky. Cut loose.'

'Cut loose?'

Dinah blew smoke rings, one through the other. 'Isn't Barkis willing? I thought he was frightfully willing.'

Fay coloured. 'Yes, but I couldn't. You don't know what you're talking about. I'd sooner die than face the scandal, and the Divorce Court, and all that hatefulness.'

'All right,' said Dinah equably. 'Have it your own way. Do we have tea in this well-run establishment, or are you slimming?'

Fay cast a startled glance at the clock, and sprang up. 'Heaven's, it's past four! I must fly or Arthur will have a fit. He can't bear unpunctuality. Are you ready?'

'I'm ready,' said Dinah, 'but I shall dawdle for ten minutes for the good of Arthur's soul.'

She began in a leisurely way, as soon as her sister had left the room, to unpack her dressing-case, and it was quite a quarter of an hour later when she at last prepared to join the tea-party on the terrace. A slight frown puckered her brow. It did not seem to her that the week-end promised well. Obviously Fay was overwrought and in no condition to manage an ill-assorted gathering; while Arthur, who belonged to that class of soldier who believes that much is accomplished by rudeness, was already in a thunderous mood.

Miss Fawcett had never, even at the impressionable age of twenty, succumbed to the General's personality. He was a well-preserved man, with handsome features and hair only slightly grizzled above the temples. He was large, rich, and masterful, and when he chose, he could make himself extremely pleasant. He was convinced of the inferiority of the female, and his way of laughing indulgently at the foibles of the fair sex induced Fay to imagine that in him she had found the wise, omnipotent hero usually to be discovered only in the pages of romance.

Fay was helpless and malleable, as pretty as a picture drawn in soft pastels, and the General asked her to marry him. He had retired from the army; he wanted to settle down in England. A wife was clearly necessary. Discrepancy of age did not weigh with him: he liked women to be young and pretty and inexperienced.

Nor did it weigh with Mrs. Fawcett. She said that the General was such a distinguished man, and she was quite sure he would be the ideal husband for her little Fay. And since Fay was also sure of it, and neither she nor her mother was likely to pay any heed to the indignant protests of twenty-year-old Dinah, the marriage took place with a good deal of pomp and ceremony, and Fay departed with her Arthur for a honeymoon on the Italian Riviera. She was to discover during the years that followed that a man who had bullied one woman into deserting him and ridden rough-shod over all his inferiors for quite twenty years, was not likely to change his ways thus late in life.

Between him and his sister-in-law there raged a guerrilla warfare which both enjoyed. They disliked one another with equal cordiality. The General said that Dinah was an impudent hussy. Whereas Dinah drove him to the verge of an apoplexy by remarking with an air of naïve wonder: 'What odd expressions people of your generation do use! I remember my grandfather . . .'

The explosion which had cut short this reminiscence had made Fay wince and shrink into herself; it produced in Dinah nothing but a kind of bright-eyed interest.

She was quite ready to spar with the General, if he felt like that, which apparently he did, but it sounded, from what Fay had told her, that there would be trouble enough during the week-end already. She strolled downstairs to tea, whistling softly to herself, still dressed in the severely tailored grey flannel coat and skirt which so admirably became her.

The terrace was at the back of the house, facing south, and was reached either by way of the drawing-room or the billiard-room, both of which apartments had several long windows opening on to it. Fay was seated behind a table which seemed almost too frail to support its expensive and ponderous load of silver ware. An enormous silver tray quite covered it, and the embossed teapot, which Fay had picked up, shook in her weak hold.

As Dinah stepped out on to the terrace a big man in rough tweeds got up from his seat and took the teapot from Fay, saying in a deep voice that somehow matched his tweeds: 'Let me do that for you. It's too heavy for you to hold.'

Dinah recognized Stephen Guest, and smiled. In repose her face had a youthful gravity; her smile dispelled that completely. It was a friendly, infectious smile, crinkling the corners of her eyes. If Dinah smiled you had to smile back, as Stephen Guest did now. His rugged, curiously square face softened. 'Hullo, Dinah!' he said, and went back to his task of pouring out the tea for Fay.

A tall and slender young man with sleekly shining black hair, thin lips under a tiny moustache, and quite incredibly immaculate tennis flannels, got up with the grace of muscles under perfect control, and pulled forward another chair. 'Ah, Dinah, light of my eyes!' he drawled. 'Come and sit beside me, darling, and comfort me.'

'Hullo!' said Dinah discouragingly.

There were two other people on the terrace, to whom Fay proceeded to make her sister known. Basil Halliday was a thin man in the late thirties, with a face prematurely lined through ill health. He had very deep-set, almost sunken eyes and a way of twitching his brows over them that indicated nerves on edge. His wife Dinah regarded with more interest. Camilla Halliday was a pretty woman. She had corn-coloured hair, shingled and perfectly waved, a pair of shallow blue eyes, and a predatory little mouth sharply outlined by scarlet lipstick. She was lounging in a long chair, a cigarette between her lips, and made no effort to get up. Removing the cigarette with one hand, she extended the other towards Dinah. 'Oh, how do you do? Do forgive me, but I'm quite too exhausted to move.'

Dinah noticed that the pointed finger-nails were polished lacquer red. She shook hands, and turned to receive her cup and saucer from Fay. 'What exhausted you?' she inquired.

Francis Billington-Smith, who had exerted himself to bring a plate of sandwiches to Dinah, raised his brows. 'My dear, didn't you hear me ask you to comfort me? I have been ignominiously beaten at tennis. It's what people write letters to the *Daily Mirror* about. "What is wrong with the Men of Today?" So belittling.'

'Oh, but you let me win!' said Camilla, throwing him a glance which Dinah felt to be mechanically provocative.

'Rubbish!' pronounced Sir Arthur loudly. 'No stamina in these modern young men. You play a fine game, Camilla. Pleasure to watch you! Now what do you say to taking me on after tea?'

Camilla smiled up at him. ''Tisn't fair to make fun of poor little me. You know you could give me thirty and beat me with your horribly terrifying service.'

'Oh, come, come!' said Sir Arthur, visibly gratified. 'It isn't as terrifying as that, surely?'

'Why not have a mixed doubles?' suggested Fay in her gentle voice. 'You'll play, won't you, Dinah?' She looked across at her husband, and said timidly: 'Francis and Dinah against Camilla and Basil, don't you think, Arthur? You haven't forgotten that Geoffrey and – and Miss de Silva are coming?'

'Whether they come or do not is not my affair,' said Sir Arthur. 'I may remind you, my dear, that you asked them, and I suggest that it is for you to entertain them when they do arrive. Dinah, you can play with Francis against Camilla here, and me. How will that be, Camilla?'

'You'll have to be very kind to me, then, and take all the difficult balls,' said Camilla. 'But perhaps Miss Fawcett doesn't want to play?'

'As a matter of fact I don't, much,' replied Dinah, accepting another sandwich.

'H'm! I suppose this is a specimen of the modern frankness we hear so much about!' remarked Sir Arthur belligerently. 'Personally, I should have thought that common politeness—'

'You wouldn't,' interrupted Dinah, quite unperturbed. 'You told me last time I came that you'd ceased to expect ordinary courtesy from me.'

'Upon my word—!' began the General.

Camilla laid a hand on his arm. 'Oh, but I do frightfully agree with Miss Fawcett. I know I offend lots of people, I'm so dreadfully outspoken myself.'

'I'm quite sure,' said the General gallantly, 'that you could never offend anyone, my dear lady. But you shall have your tennis. My wife will play instead of her sister.'

'Arthur, really I'd rather not!' Fay said. 'I've got things to do before dinner, and – and one of us must be ready to receive Miss de Silva.'

This slightly tactless reference to his son's betrothed provoked the General into saying with a rasp in his voice: 'I've already told you I've no interest in the young woman, and I don't want her name dinned in my ears all day long. Go and put your tennis shoes on, and for God's sake consider your guests' wishes for once in a way!'

There was a moment's uncomfortable silence. Fay got up, her cheeks flushed, and her eyes downcast to hide the sudden, startled tears. Stephen Guest rose also, his gaze fixed on her.

Camilla gave an affected little shriek. 'Really, you are the most dreadfully masterful man I've ever met!' she said. 'I should be terrified of being your partner now. I know you'd bark at me in that paralysing parade voice of yours every time I missed a shot, and I should be simply petrified with fear. And it isn't I who want to play at all. I'm completely exhausted, and I'd far rather stay where I am, and – now don't be cross with me! Promise you won't be?'

'That's a very easy promise,' said the General.

'Then I'll confess that I'm simply dying to meet the de Silva!' said Camilla audaciously. 'I think it's just too thrilling!'

'Who is this Miss de Silva?' asked Stephen Guest in a low voice.

'Geoffrey's intended,' replied Dinah, finishing what was left of her tea. 'Cabaret dancer. Said to be Mexican.'

'Good heavens! Is he bringing her here? Young fool!' He glanced towards Fay, who had seated herself again behind the tea-table, and added, almost beneath his breath: 'I suppose you realize who it is who will be made to suffer?'

'Let us go and look at the roses,' said Dinah. 'Come on!'

He looked down at her, his eyes still smouldering, but considerably puzzled. 'What?'

'Go and look at the roses,' repeated Dinah firmly, and got up. 'We're going for a stroll in the rose garden, Fay.'

Mrs. Halliday overheard this, and gave her brittle laugh. 'How too romantic!'

'My husband is a very keen gardener,' Fay said. 'You must get him to show you round some time.'

Camilla Halliday sent her a quick look under her lashes, weighing her. 'I should adore it!' she murmured. 'Will you, dear Sir Arthur?'

'Delighted!' he assured her. 'Any time! I can only say that I should like my roses to see *you*.'

Dinah looked back over her shoulder. 'And even that isn't original,' she said pensively. 'Come on, Stephen.'

They descended the shallow steps on to the lawn, and began to stroll across it. Once they were out of earshot Dinah said: 'You were an awful ass to come, you know.'

'Maybe.'

'It's no use trying to shut me up,' said Dinah. 'Ask Arthur. And if you don't mind my saying so, you won't make matters any better by doing the strong, silent man stuff whenever Arthur goes for Fay.'

He smiled rather reluctantly. 'Do I?'

'Rather! Like a western hero.'

'I've been out west,' he remarked inconsequently.

'I should think you were a huge success,' said Dinah with great cordiality.

'Africa too,' he ruminated. 'Then I struck Australia for a spell. It's a great country.'

'So I've been told. Is there anywhere you haven't been?'

'I've knocked round most of the tough spots in this world,' he admitted. 'You learn quite a lot, rolling round.'

'What you don't seem to learn,' said Dinah, 'is a little ordinary sense. It's just dam' silliness to come and stay here. All it does is to make you want to take Arthur into a wide, open space and knock his teeth down his throat. *I* know.'

Stephen Guest's large, capable hands clenched slowly. 'By God, it does!' he said, and drew a long breath.

'Well, you can't go knocking people's teeth out when they're as old as Arthur,' Dinah pointed out.

'I don't know that that would worry me a lot,' replied Guest. 'It wouldn't take much from him to make me see red.'

'Then you jolly well oughtn't to come here.'

'Fay wanted me,' he said.

'Your job,' said Dinah, 'is to make Fay want you much more than that. I've been advising her to run away with you.'

He reddened under his tan, and said gruffly: 'You're a good sort, Dinah. She won't, though.'

'No, not while she can get you to come down here every time she feels like it.'

Stephen Guest considered this. 'I see,' he said presently. 'Thanks for the advice. Don't know that I shall take it.' He paused under an arbour, and frowningly regarded a cluster of pink blooms. 'Ever seen Lola de Silva?'

'That pleasure is yet to come. Have you?'

'M'm.' A gleam of satisfaction shone in his eye. 'Saw her at the Café Grecque once.'

Dinah waited for more, but as Guest seemed to have relapsed into his habitual taciturnity she urged him kindly not to keep anything back.

Thus adjured, he replied: 'Oh, I don't know anything about her! I only thought she'd be a bit out of place here – from what I saw.'

Nothing further could be elicited from him. Dinah gave it up, and led the way back to the terrace.

CHAPTER TWO

IT was not until nearly six o'clock that the sound of a car driving up the long gravel sweep heralded the arrival of Geoffrey Billington-Smith and his proposed bride. Stephen Guest and Basil Halliday had gone into the billiard-room, and through the open windows at the other end of the terrace came the intermittent click of the balls. Fay also had left the terrace, on some murmured pretext. There remained Camilla, languorous in her long chair, holding an idly flirtatious conversation with the General, and Dinah, talking in a desultory fashion to Captain Billington-Smith.

'Would you like me to make love to you, darling?' inquired Francis.

'Do just as you like; I needn't listen,' replied Dinah.

'It seems to be the order of the day,' he said softly. 'You don't like me a bit, do you, my sweet?'

'No, not much.'

He accepted this with his faintly mocking smile, and continued to smoke for a minute or two in silence. 'I'm not entirely sure that I like you,' he remarked presently. 'I've been trying to make up my mind about it. Let us change the subject. This is really very tiresome of Geoffrey, don't you agree?'

'Yes, but it ought to be rather good value. Do you know Lola?'

'I haven't taken her out to dinner, if that is what you mean. I've seen her dance. She wore feathers – not very many of them, but so artfully placed. No, I don't think Uncle will be pleased.' He glanced towards her, and added affably: 'How right you are, darling! Naturally I should be delighted if Geoffrey were disinherited in favour of me, but one must never bank on the future, must one? It is so like Geoffrey to put his father in a bad temper just when I want him mellow. Do not look so warningly at me: neither of them is paying the least heed to us. I am always careful not to offend Uncle.'

'I thought you must have come to make a touch,' said Dinah.

'You mustn't pride yourself on your intuition, however. It was quite obvious. I cannot conceive any other reason for wishing to come here. Or rather I can, of course, but there's a law – Mosaic, I fancy – against making love to one's aunts.'

It was at this moment that the car-wheels were heard. They did not penetrate to the General's consciousness, but in another few minutes Fay came out on to the terrace from the drawing-room and interrupted his *tête-à-tête* with the news that Geoffrey had arrived.

'Well, what of it?' demanded the General. 'Does he expect me to wait for him on the door-step?'

'Arthur – Miss de Silva!' said Fay, on a note of entreaty.

The General turned as his son's betrothed stepped out on to the terrace.

Miss de Silva made her entrance as one accustomed to being received by volleys of applause.

It was not difficult to see why Geoffrey, who was standing smiling nervously and a little fatuously over her shoulder, had fallen in love with her. She was a most striking lady, even beautiful, with enormous dark eyes, an enchanting nose, a lovely, petulant mouth, and clusters of black curls springing from under the very latest thing in hats – a tiny confection, daringly worn over one-half of her head.

Her orange and black and jade suit (though labelled 'Sports Wear' by the genius who designed it) might have been considered by some people to be unsuitable for a drive into the country, nor, on a warm June afternoon, did an immensely long stole of silver fox furs all clipped together, heads to tails, seem really necessary. But no one could deny that Miss de Silva carried these well.

Until her arrival Camilla Halliday had seemed a little overdressed, a little too heavily made up, but no other woman's dress or make-up could appear remarkable when Miss de Silva was present.

The General got up, blinking, and his prospective daughter-in-law at once introduced herself, 'I am Lola,' she said. 'You know me, perhaps, but still I present myself.'

The General shook hands with her, as one in honour bound. 'No, I can't say that I do,' he replied stiffly.

A slightly austere look crept over Miss de Silva's face. 'That is to me extraordinary,' she said. 'But it is seen that you live retired, and I am not at all offended. I have a mind extremely large. It is impossible to offend me. But I must tell you that I find myself in great distraction, and at once the affair must be arranged, if you please.'

'What affair?' said the General, casting a goaded look towards his wife.

'It's all right, Arthur. I've given orders about it,' Fay said placatingly. 'There wasn't room in Geoffrey's car for Miss de Silva's maid, and she is coming by train. Miss de Silva wants her to be met.'

'And if she has not arrived on the train, which is a thing one must fear, for she is a great fool, Geoffrey must go at once to London, for it is quite his fault, and he has behaved with a stupidity which is remarkable, to think that my luggage can be put in his little car.'

'Shouldn't have thought there was the least difficulty about it myself,' said Sir Arthur. 'Ridiculous nonsense!'

Fay, resolutely refusing to catch her sister's eye, laid a hand on

Miss de Silva's arm. 'Please don't worry about it!' she begged. 'I'm sure she will arrive quite safely. I want to introduce you to Mrs. Halliday, and to my sister, Miss Fawcett.' Miss de Silva summed up both these ladies in one cursory glance, and bestowed on them her flashing smile. 'And to my husband's nephew, Captain Billington-Smith,' added Fay.

Francis rose superbly to the occasion and gracefully kissed the fair Lola's hand. 'Need I say that this is a much-longed-for moment?' he said. 'I have had the inestimable pleasure of seeing you dance.'

Miss de Silva accepted this. 'I dance very well,' she stated. 'All over the world people say how well I dance.'

'I'm afraid we don't go in for that sort of thing down here,' said Sir Arthur crushingly. 'Though I've seen the Russians. Marvellous! Most perfect dancing!'

'I dance better than the Russians,' said Miss de Silva simply.

Once more Fay intervened. 'We shall hope to see you one day. But won't you sit down? I'm sure you'd like some tea after your drive, wouldn't you?'

Lola disposed herself in one of the wicker-chairs, and allowed the silver fox stole to fall to the ground. 'I do not drink tea, and it is too late now. I will have instead one little cocktail.'

This was too much for Sir Arthur, growing steadily redder in the face. 'In this house, my dear young lady, cocktails are not served at six o'clock,' he announced.

'Then it is better that Geoffrey shall mix it for me,' decided Lola, quite unruffled. 'I shall not make any trouble for you then, and besides Geoffrey knows how it is I like my cocktail, and that is important too.'

Sir Arthur's voice took on a peculiarly harsh note. 'Cocktails,' he said, 'will be served in the drawing-room at a quarter to eight, and not, let me assure you, one moment earlier.'

At this moment, before Lola, who was gazing at her host in an inquiring and quite uncomprehending manner, could reply, Guest and Halliday came out of the billiard-room, and a diversion was thus created. Under cover of fresh introductions Dinah whispered to Geoffrey that he must take Lola into the house. She had discovered that her week-end was to be a strenuous one, but she was not the girl to shirk an obvious duty. Since Geoffrey seemed incapable of moving Lola from the terrace, she announced that she was sure she had caught the sound of a car. 'It's probably your maid,' she told Lola. 'Shall we go and see?'

'Ah yes, that I must see at once,' agreed Miss de Silva. 'For if it is not Concetta, Geoffrey must instantly go to find her.'

'Yes, of course,' nodded Dinah, and shepherded her into the house. Geoffrey followed, bringing the silver fox stole.

'The future Mrs. Billington-Smith,' murmured Francis, taking a cigarette from his flat gold case.

The General rounded on him. 'Hold your tongue, sir!'

'Of course, I think she's *too* marvellous!' said Camilla, giggling. 'But I do utterly understand how you feel, Sir Arthur. I think it's terribly sweet of you to let him bring her.'

'He won't bring her a second time,' said the General grimly. 'Brazen, painted hussy! Cocktails! Fay, you'll kindly make that young woman understand that in this house my word is law! I don't want to have any unpleasantness, so I'm warning you! You asked her here, and I'll thank you to see that she conforms to the rules of the place. Now I don't want to hear another word on the subject, and I'm sure your guests don't either. Come, Camilla, let me take you round the gardens: the roses are at their best, I flatter myself.'

Once inside the house Dinah tried to explain to Lola. At first Lola could not be brought to heed anything beyond the fact that Concetta had not yet arrived, but when it had been made plain to her that the train from London was not due at Ralton Station for another ten minutes, she consented to postpone Geoffrey's departure a little longer, and to go up to her bedroom with Dinah.

'It is very well thought of,' she approved. 'Geoffrey has been very selfish to bring me in an open car which will not take my luggage, and perhaps I am untidy from the wind. I shall arrange myself, and Geoffrey shall bring my cocktail up to me. And there must not be any gin, Geoffrey, but absinthe, for gin is a thing that makes me completely sick.'

'I shouldn't think there's any absinthe in the house,' said Dinah. 'Still, I daresay Finch will think of something. I'll carry the fur, Geoffrey: you attend to the drink question. I wonder which room you're having, Miss de Silva? We'd better inspect.'

Happily there was a housemaid on the landing who had just finished unpacking Miss de Silva's advance baggage, and she was able to direct them. She eyed Lola with the envious admiration she accorded only to film stars, and when Dinah saw the results of her unpacking she was not surprised. The dressing-table was loaded with innumerable toilet jars, scent flagons, brushes, rouge-pots, and powder-bowls, all with opulent enamel fittings. A *négligée*, very like the one worn by Dawson's favourite star in her last film, was laid reverently over a chair, and in the big mahogany wardrobe was hanging an evening frock that might have come straight from Hollywood.

'Oh, I'm sure she's on the films!' Dawson breathed to Mrs. Moxon in the kitchen. 'You never saw anything to equal the dresses she's got. Oh, they're lovely, Mrs. Moxon! they are really! She's like Lupe Velez, that's who she's like. Oo, I wonder if it could be her, under an assumed name – you know how they do?'

'Films!' snorted Mrs. Moxon, banging the rolling-pin on the board with unnecessary force. 'She's one of them good-for-nothing cabaret girls, that's what she is. And when you've been in service a bit longer nor what you have, Joan Dawson, you'll have more sense than to go goggling at her sort. Get out of my way, do!'

Upstairs in the sunny bedroom Miss de Silva had thrown the *négligée* on to the bed, tossed her hat after it, and sat herself down at the dressing-table, anxiously surveying her face in the mirror. 'It is terrible!' she announced, and snatched the lid from one of the powder-bowls. 'It is not polite to make a complaint, and therefore I say nothing, for I have very good manners, I assure you, but it should not be permitted that a man should demand of anyone that they motor in an open car. Naturally there must be a wind. I am not unreasonable, and I do not expect there to be no wind, but Geoffrey should have a car which is not open and which will take Concetta as well.'

Dinah curled herself up on the window-seat, frankly enjoying Miss de Silva. 'I know,' she said sympathetically. 'Men are so thoughtless, aren't they? I don't suppose he explained about his father either.'

'But no: you mistake,' Lola corrected her. 'It is all explained to me. He is of a type difficult to manage. That one sees.'

'Yes,' said Dinah, 'but – but I'm afraid Geoffrey's father is a little more than difficult.'

'There is no need that I should disturb myself,' replied Lola, attending carefully to her eyelashes. 'I do not know where is Geoffrey, and why he does not bring me my cocktail?'

There did not seem to be much hope of impressing upon Miss de Silva the need to deal tactfully with her host, so Dinah, never one to waste time in pursuing lost causes, abandoned the subject, and asked curiously: 'Are you very fond of Geoffrey?'

She was right in supposing that Lola would not in the least resent so personal a question. Lola replied with great promptitude: 'Naturally, I love him extremely. I love very often, you understand, and always passionately. It is not so with the English, I find, for you have in general very cold hearts. It is not at all so with me. I have a very warm heart, very profound.'

A knock on the door interrupted her. Geoffrey appeared carrying a tray, with glasses and shaker on it. 'I say, we shall have to keep this dark,' he said. 'Father would have a fit if he knew. Darling, I'm so frightfully sorry, but there's no absinthe.'

The look of rigidity which Dinah had noticed before instantly possessed Lola's face. 'But it is to me incomprehensible that when you know that I wish absinthe in my cocktail you do not at once arrange it, my dear Geoffrey. Perhaps it is that you do not concern yourself with what I like, but only with what you like?'

'It's sickeningly careless of me, sweetheart,' Geoffrey apologized. 'Of course I ought to have brought a bottle down with me, but when I get near you I clean forget everything else. Darling, do forgive me, and just taste this mixture. Finch made it, and he's sure you'll like it.'

'I do not know Finch, and it is not at all clear to me how it is that he can know what I like. I am quite unhappy, quite wounded that you can love me so little you wish to make me sick with gin.'

'There isn't a drop of gin in it, Lola. I swear there isn't! Of course I wouldn't give you gin. Good God, if anything happened to you through my fault I should be fit to shoot myself!'

'Well, I will taste your cocktail,' Lola said, relenting, 'Because I do not wish to make trouble, and I see that through the fault of your papa this house is not well-run. But when you have told him that I wish absinthe he will attend to it. Only you are to tell him with tact, my dear Geoffrey, for I do not desire him to feel uncomfortable.'

Dinah gave a sudden gurgle, hastily choked, and began to pour out a delicately pink liquid from the shaker. Lola looked inquiringly at her, but she shook her head. 'Nothing. I only coughed. What do you call this roseate mixture, Geoffrey?'

Inspired, Geoffrey said: 'It's a brand-new cocktail, a super-cocktail, made for the most beautiful creature in the world, and I'm calling it La Lola.'

Lola was so much pleased by this compliment that she held out her hand to Geoffrey, and said that it was a pretty idea, and he should tell her how the cocktail was made so that she herself (supposing that she liked it) could adopt it. After two cautious sips she said graciously that it was quite agreeable, and would be a very good cocktail indeed if a little absinthe were added.

Then the missing Concetta erupted into the room with many voluble ejaculations delivered in a foreign tongue. She was followed by a train of dress-boxes, and Lola at once became extremely animated, and ordained that everything should be unpacked at once, and her bath prepared, and a certain box of powder found immediately.

'I think we'd better leave her now,' Geoffrey said reverently. 'You'd like us to clear out, wouldn't you, darling?'

Yes, Lola would like them to go at once; it was terrible that her trunks had arrived so late; there was no time at all to make a suitable toilette for dinner.

Geoffrey signed to Dinah to go, and followed her, very softly closing the door behind them.

On the landing Dinah leaned against an oak chest, and rather thoughtfully regarded him. A lock of his long, fair hair hung over his brow, and his face was flushed with nervous excitement. He was a handsome, slightly effeminate youth with large eyes, and a mouth that quivered a little when he was at all agitated. He affected a style of dress which was considered by his set to be artistic, and was addicted to large-brimmed hats, polo-sweaters, and pleated dress shirts. He had always been delicate, a subject in his boyhood to nerve-storms, which were the dread of all who came in contact with him. He was frightened of his father, and except amongst his chosen intimates he was not very popular with other men. His air of highly strung fragility, and a certain charm of manner, however, appealed to a great many women, and quite a number of sympathetic matrons felt a distinct desire to mother him.

Not being of these, Dinah felt no such desire, but she was sorry for him, and treated him with a mixture of forbearance and bracing common sense.

He turned to her now in his impetuous way, and stammered:

'Isn't she wonderful? Isn't she lovely? Have you ever seen anything so enchanting as the way she looks at one?'

'Never,' said Dinah accommodatingly.

'I knew you'd say so! I knew you'd only to set eyes on her! There are hundreds of men absolutely mad about her, and she's going to marry me! I tell you, Dinah, I can hardly believe it's true. Everything's changed for me; I feel like a different person since she said yes.'

'I expect you do,' agreed Dinah.

'Of course you know she's simply throwing herself away on me.' Geoffrey said anxiously. 'I mean, her career, and all that, because she's practically a genius at dancing – everybody who knows anything at all about it says so. It's the most ridiculous rot for Fay to talk about Father not liking it. Why, when he realizes—'

'Look here, Geoffrey,' interposed Dinah, 'I expect it's all just as you say; in fact, I can see Lola's a stupendous person; but you ought to pull yourself together. It's no use waffling about your father in that idiotic way, because you know perfectly well he's a stinker, and he won't realize anything at all.'

Geoffrey's face fell. 'But now he's *seen* her? I knew it would be no good just telling him, but when he sees her for himself, and talks to her – why, she'll twist him round her little finger! She can twist anybody!'

'She won't twist Arthur,' said Dinah flatly. 'She isn't in the least his type. Besides, he's got off with the Halliday wench.'

'Who?' asked Geoffrey vacantly.

'The blonde woman. You saw her on the terrace.'

'Oh, did I? I don't know. I was looking at Lola. She has a way of dropping her eyelids, Dinah—'

'Stop being maudlin!' commanded Dinah. 'She's got a way of saying the wrong thing too, and that's the way Arthur will notice, let me tell you.'

'But you don't understand!' said Geoffrey. 'She's utterly natural. That's part of her fascination.'

'All I can say is that it didn't seem to be fascinating Arthur – noticeably.'

Geoffrey's underlip began to quiver. 'If Father tries to stop it – if he's foul to Lola – if he's beast enough to – well, look *out*, that's all! He's been rotten to me ever since I was a kid, and if he thinks he's going to muck up my life now by refusing to consent to my marrying Lola – not that he can do it, because he can't – but if he does – well, I shall do something *desperate*, and he may as well know it!'

'Don't get so excited,' said Dinah severely. 'Do you think there's any hope of persuading Lola to do the shy violet act? I know it's a bit late in the day, but it might keep him fairly cool. I'm chiefly concerned for Fay. You know, it really is rather asinine of you to bring Lola down here, and it'll all react on Fay. Can't you have a talk with Lola? I did try myself, but I daresay you'd be able to do it better. Tell her what'll go down with Arthur and what won't.'

'I couldn't possibly,' said Geoffrey. 'She'd be most frightfully hurt. She simply wouldn't understand. Of course you're only a girl, and probably you wouldn't see it, but Lola's the type of woman who drives men absolutely mad about her.'

'Well, if she goes on as she's started, I should say she'd drive Arthur mad enough to be put into a looney-bin,' said Dinah with asperity, and withdrew to her own room.

CHAPTER THREE

IN their several bedrooms at the Grange eight people were engaged in dressing for dinner, and perhaps only one of these bore a mind untroubled by worry, or vexations. That one was surely Miss Lola de Silva, and even she experienced feelings of slight annoyance at finding that not only had she to share her bathroom with Miss Fawcett and Mr. Guest, but that it was unprovided with a shower, further proof of Sir Arthur's incompetence.

Stephen Guest, occupying the bathroom after her, found it full of steam, rather damp underfoot, and redolent of an exotic perfume. It repulsed him; he found it impossible to enter the bath until he had washed any lingering taint of scent away, and since he was never one to require another to wait on him, he performed this disagreeable task himself. It did not improve his temper, which was already gloomy.

He had loved Fay for two years, at first in silence and from a distance, but with the unwavering tenacity of the very taciturn. With the exception of an incident in his youth, there had been no other woman in his life; he knew, beyond need of averring it, that there would never be another. For Fay, so fragile and helpless, he had all a naturally rugged man's devotion, and without attempting to put such feelings into impassioned words he had long made up his mind that there could not be – indeed, must not be – anything that he would no do for her.

Accustomed during a life spent largely, as he himself said, in the tough spots still remaining in the world, to grasping what he wanted with a strong hand, he found himself now enmeshed by a net of conventions. This he would have torn ruthlessly down for his own ends, but he served not them, but Fay, and she had a shy woman's respect for conventions. To come as a guest into her husband's house and to remain passive in sight of her unhappiness was a greater test of his power of self-control than anyone merely observing his doggedly calm front could have imagined. He came because Fay wanted him. He did not accuse her even in his heart of selfishness; he was untroubled by qualms of conscience; if he could persuade her to it he would steal her from under her husband's very nose, and never, in the future, look back with the least sentiment of remorse.

But she seemed as far as ever from consenting to a step that seemed to her so dreadful, and ahead lay a week-end likely to be worse than any he had spent at the Grange. As he wrestled with a collar stud he wondered how best he could help Fay, whether by monopolizing Lola, a prospect that filled him with alarm, or by trying to interpose his own solid person between Sir Arthur and the immediate scapegoat of his wrath. He thought perhaps Dinah would help: she was a good sort, Dinah.

Dinah too, slipping an evening frock off its hanger, foresaw a stormy week-end, but an irrepressible sense of humour prevented her from looking forward to it with unreasonable dread. Saving only her protective affection for Fay she could have enjoyed the situation provoked by Geoffrey, and would have sat with folded hands, as an appreciative onlooker. But since Fay, incapable of fighting her own battles, would be the chief sufferer it behoved her to do what she could, even if the best she could do was only to draw Sir Arthur's fire.

Stalking through the communicating door between his room and Fay's, Sir Arthur was, in his own phrase, clearing the air. Every annoyance of this disastrous week-end was Fay's fault, from the unwelcome arrival of Dinah to the ill-assorted party assembled for dinner in half an hour's time. Anyone but a fool would have had the wit to wire regrets both to Dinah and to Guest. No one but a fool would have invited the Vicar and his wife to dine on this of all evenings.

She faltered that the invitation had been given a week before; he snarled at her, and she thought, with a frightened leap of her heart, that he looked at her almost with dislike. She was wrong. He did not dislike her; he was even, in a contemptuous way, fond of her, but she had lost her charm and become instead of the blushing, adoring girl he had married, a shrinking, exasperatingly virginal woman who tried nervously to placate him, and whom it was impossible not to bully. Her worst crime in his eyes was that she had brought him no children, no promising son to console him for the disappointment of Geoffrey, that thorn in his flesh, child of the wife who had dragged his name through the mud twenty-one years ago, running off with some worthless civilian who had not even married her when it was all over.

There was his nephew too to annoy him. He was fond of Francis; Francis had gone into the Cavalry, just as all decent young fellows should, and his colonel spoke well of him. He wore the right clothes, looked a sahib, rode to hounds, and was a good man to ask down for a day's shooting. No damned humanitarian nonsense about Francis; he came of the right stock, not a doubt of that. But he was extravagant; seemed to think his uncle had nothing to do but to pay his debts. That would have to be stopped. If Master Francis had come to beg he would be taught a sharp lesson for once.

He could not blame Fay for Francis's visit. Francis had arrived without invitation. It irritated him that Fay should be blameless. He asked her why the devil she could not put some stuff on her face as other women did instead of going about looking pasty and colourless.

If Geoffrey and Francis and Dinah had only chosen some other week-end he would not have minded so much. But he had looked forward to the Hallidays' visit, and it was all spoiled. He had no objection to Guest's presence. Guest could sit and adore Fay as much as he liked; she was too damned chaste to let harm come of that; knew which side her bread was buttered on, too. He would have entertained Fay while her husband engaged in flirtation with Camilla. She was a seductive little woman, Camilla; out for what she could get, probably, but ready (or he was much mistaken) to pay for what she wanted. That husband of hers was a dull dog. Hadn't the sense to get a man's job, and blamed the War for it. Just

27

like this damned puling generation, always grumbling at fate; no guts to 'em; he'd like to have a few of 'em in his old regiment.

And Basil Halliday, unhappily brushing his coat, trying to think that his dress trousers were not so shiny after all, was despising Sir Arthur – hating him too, the libidinous old swine – and wondering what Camilla was up to. She couldn't like the man; of course she couldn't like him. It was just her way to flirt with anyone who was handy, and it was no use worrying about that. It wasn't that he didn't trust her. Lord, hadn't she stuck by him when, God knew, she'd had chances enough to chuck him over? But he did wish he hadn't let her persuade him into coming down here. It was all very well to talk about free board and lodging, and naturally he saw the force of that argument, for that was the way one lived nowadays, making oneself agreeable to people for the sake of a dinner that hadn't been prepared by a slut of a cook who ruined everything she touched. If you liked soft living and pretty things you had to swallow your pride to get them when you were saddled with a rotten crock of a husband who couldn't earn more than five hundred a year if he lived to be ninety. He didn't blame Camilla; only this bloody soldier, with his money-bags and his loud voice and his greedy hands longing to paw her was surely coming it a bit thick. The man was stupid, too; one of those officers – he'd seen a lot of them during the war – who thought the whole world was bounded by the British Army.

He cast a worried glance towards the door that led out of the dressing-room into the bedroom, where Camilla sat before the dressing-table, making up her face. He could just see her, absorbed, plucking a hair from the thin line of her brows. He didn't know what was in her mind; didn't like to ask. There was a little nagging ache behind his eyes. If he said anything to Camilla now it would lead to one of their frequent quarrels. Better to keep quiet; not play the jealous husband.

Camilla was making an elaborate toilet, determined to put Lola in the shade. She had chosen to wear the pink chiffon frock which wasn't paid for yet, but which might be soon – with luck. It had bands of pink sequins that glittered when she moved, and was cut very low across her breasts. Really it was rather too low; she had to pin a piece of silver lace inside it. All the other women would know that it was the wrong frock to wear at a country dinner-party, but she didn't care what the women thought. The General would like it; it would make him want to fondle her (amorous old idiot!) and he could if he felt like that. It was a damned nuisance that this wretched cabaret dancer had turned up, putting the old boy in a bad temper. She'd need to handle him carefully, leading him on, listening to his ghastly stories about India, which always began 'When I was at Peshawar,' or Wellington, or some other damned place, and always ended with a hearty laugh. She'd have to give him a chance to mess her about a bit. She rather hated being kissed by men with toothbrush moustaches, but it couldn't be helped, and anyway in these days, when half the men you met arrived at kissing terms within half an hour, you soon got over that kind of squeamishness. In a way he was fairly easy to deal with. That was the best of these conceited men. She'd only got to play up to him for him to start hinting at things, and if she couldn't touch him for something handsome then she must be a pretty good fool. Only she'd have to take care not to let him give her some rotten trinket. Jewellery was no good these days; you got nothing for it, and God knew if she didn't lay her hands on solid cash soon she'd be in a nasty mess.

If only Basil would be sensible, everything would be all right. But he'd been looking like a sick herring the whole afternoon, poor old thing, and it would be just like him to get into one of his jealous rages and muck the whole show. He ought to know by now that her head was screwed on the right way. The trouble with him was that he'd got a lot of pre-war ideas about women and honour. It was rather sweet of him, of course, but utterly pathetic in these hard times. Damn! it was ten to eight already, and she hadn't done her eyelashes. Oh, well, they'd have to stay as they were: no sense in putting the old man's back up by being late for his filthy dinner-party.

Downstairs, in the long white-panelled drawing-room, Fay, drilled into punctuality, had been awaiting her guests since twenty minutes to eight. She was looking tired, but pretty, in a flowered frock that was like the chintzes on the chairs – cool, and mistily tinted. Stephen Guest had come into the drawing-room behind her. She smiled at him, that wistful smile that tore at his heart, and put her hands to arrange his tie – a lamentable bow, already askew.

'Dear Stephen!' she murmured, the hint of a tender laugh in her voice. 'Why don't you buy one with broad ends? It would be so much easier to tie.'

He couldn't bear it when she stood so close to him, looking up at him with her gentle blue eyes. Suddenly he put his arms round her, holding her tightly to him. 'Fay, you've got to come to it. We can't go on like this. I'm only a mortal, you know.' His voice was thickened and rough, his mouth was seeking hers.

'Please don't, Stephen!' she said faintly. 'Oh, please don't! Arthur – the servants. Stephen, be kind to me; be patient with me!'

He let her go, breathing rather fast, his square face flushed. 'See here, Fay! You love me, and I love you. We're all hedged in here by these God-darned conventions. One of these days things'll get too much for me, and I'll go plumb through the lot of them, and there'll be one fine show-down. Can't you make up your mind to face the music, and come away with me? We won't stay in England – the Lord knows I've had enough of the place. Too much stiff-shirt and kid gloves about it. I'll take you any place you say. We won't defend the case; you don't need to set foot inside the Divorce Courts.'

'I couldn't. It's wicked of us! I oughtn't to have asked you to come, only I wanted you so. Dinah thinks it was rotten of me, and she's right. It *is* rotten; only if I'm never even to see you I might as well be dead.'

At sight of her distress the angry colour in his face died. He took her hand and patted it clumsily. 'I'm sorry. Didn't mean to upset you, dear. You've got enough to worry you without me adding to it. Only, we've got to find some solution, haven't we? But we won't talk about it now. I'm just here to be leaned on, and to help you any way I can.'

Her eyes filled. 'You're so good to me, Stephen. I'm a rotter to let you waste your life for my sake.'

He would have answered her, but Sir Arthur's voice sounded in the hall, and in another moment he had entered the room, followed by Finch, with a tray of cocktails which he set down on a table against the wall. Somewhere in the distance an electric bell rang, and Fay said with forced brightness: 'I expect that's the Chudleighs. They're always on time.'

It was not the Chudleighs, however, but Mrs. Twining who was presently announced.

Mrs. Twining was a widow who might have been any age between forty-five and sixty. She lived rather less than five miles away and was a frequent visitor at the Grange. She said that, having been acquainted with Arthur for so many years, she considered herself a privileged person. She was in the habit of making this observation with a faintly mocking lift of her arched brows, but the General, possibly because he knew her so well, usually refused to be drawn.

When she first took up her abode in the neighbourhood she was eyed a little suspiciously. She was so perfectly dressed that naturally people felt that she might not be quite the type of person one wanted to know. She was obviously in comfortable circumstances, but she seemed to have no tangible roots. This was presently explained by the knowledge that she had spent the greater part of her life abroad, some of it in India, where she was understood to have buried the late Colonel Twining, and some of it in well-known military stations like Egypt and Malta. All this was perfectly respectable, and when it was made apparent that she was on terms of long-standing acquaintance with Sir Arthur Billington-Smith several ladies called upon her. She was found to be perfectly well-bred, though rather clever, and was in due course accepted by all the best people.

She came in now in her graceful, assured way, and shook hands with Fay, saying lightly: 'I am so glad that I am not late after all. I am told that every clock in my house is wrong, so I feared I might arrive to find you at dinner. How do you do, Arthur?'

'You remember Mr. Guest, don't you?' Fay said.

'Yes, perfectly,' replied Mrs. Twining, smiling at him. 'He told me a great deal that I didn't know about the western States.'

'I hope I didn't bore you?' said Stephen, rather conscience-stricken.

Mrs. Twining sat down in a *bergère* chair, letting one hand rest upon its arm. 'No. You interested me, Mr. Guest. Till then my knowledge of that part of the world had all been culled from various films it has been my misfortune to see. I never felt that they were really reliable.'

The entrance of the Hallidays and Dinah interrupted Stephen in his assurance that the films Mrs. Twining had seen were probably quite inaccurate. Francis came in a minute later, looking rather sleeker than before, and Sir Arthur began – while his wife performed introductions – to hand round cocktails. He took up a commanding position in front of the empty grate, when Francis relieved him of this duty, and set the ball of conversation rolling by remarking that it didn't look as if they were going to get any rain yet;

he didn't know about Julia's garden, but his own wanted it badly.

Every one had some contribution to make on this subject, from Camilla, who begged Sir Arthur not to wish for rain till Monday, to Stephen Guest, who observed that the country needed it.

Geoffrey slipped guiltily into the room in the middle of this discussion, but if he hoped to make his tardy entrance unnoticed he was disappointed. His father stood facing the door, and said in a bluff voice, through which lay an unmistakably threatening under current: 'A trifle late, my boy, aren't you? We were ready to receive our guests in my young days.'

Geoffrey coloured angrily. It was just like Father to treat him as though he were a schoolboy in front of a roomful of people. He mumbled: 'Sorry!' and walked over to the cocktail tray.

Sir Arthur said sharply: 'Good God, sir, where have you left your manners? Say how do you do to Mrs. Twining!'

Geoffrey grew redder than ever. 'I didn't see you, Aunt Julia. How do you do?'

Mrs. Twining patted a chair beside her. 'Come and sit down, Geoffrey. It seems a long time since I saw you. I hear you are engaged to be married?' Something between a snort and a scornful laugh from the General made her turn her well-coiffed head. 'I beg your pardon, Arthur?' she said smoothly.

'Time enough to talk of being married when he's done cutting his second teeth,' said the General, moving away towards Camilla.

'The Reverend and Mrs. Chudleigh,' announced Finch from the doorway.

The Vicar and his wife came in.

The Rev. Hilary Chudleigh was a man of late middle age, with a gentle austere countenance, and a permanent stoop to his shoulders. He had been vicar of the parish for only four years. The best years of his life had been spent working in the worst slums imaginable, and it was only when his health at last cracked that he consented to accept a living in the country. He was not really fitted to be a country vicar, for he disapproved of fox-hunting and pheasant-shooting, and was not at all fond of social intercourse. The General said that he was a namby-pamby fellow with a bee in his bonnet. The Vicar said, sadly but with conviction, that the General was living in sin. If it had not been for the arguments of his wife, and the advice of his very tactful bishop, Mr. Chudleigh would never have set foot inside the General's house. He did not recognize divorce. This, not unnaturally, was apt to produce a somewhat strained atmosphere on the rare occasions when, in duty bound, he visited the Grange. He had tried once to bring Sir Arthur to a realization of his error. The result had not been happy, and it had taken six months to heal the breach. Left to himself, the Vicar would never again have approached Sir Arthur, but he was not left to himself. His bishop came to lunch one day, and was more tactful and persuasive than ever. The Rev. Hilary, who was growing old and rather tired, saw that the situation was too difficult for him to cope with. The bishop apparently recognized divorce and remarriage, and the bishop pointed out that Sir Arthur was not only one of the more influential landowners in the district, but a churchwarden as well. It seemed one could not ostracize rich men who occupied front pews every Sunday, contributed to the church restoration funds, and took leading parts in parochial meetings.

So he gave way, troubled in his conscience, and at least three times a year he and his wife dined at the Grange. It was certainly a little unfortunate that one of these dinners should occur when Miss de Silva was in the house. It annoyed the General very much to think that the Rev. Hilary (who had the impertinence to condemn his morals) was to be brought face to face with the abominable young woman Geoffrey had had the effrontery to bring down to the Grange. Lola would give the fellow a fine handle; she would give Mrs. Chudleigh something to talk about too, for weeks to come.

Mrs. Chudleigh was engaged at the moment in shaking hands with Fay, and explaining how she feared they might be a little late on account of their having walked up from the vicarage this lovely evening. She was a thin woman of about fifty, with a weather-beaten complexion, and hair of that pepper-and-salt variety that might in her youth have been almost any colour. Kindly people said that she must have been pretty once, but she had not worn well, and did nothing now to improve her appearance. She wore pince-nez, despised face powder and curling-tongs, and had a genius for acquiring frocks made according to the last fashion but one. Her weak-sighted eyes had a trick of peering, which gave her an inquisitive air, and she had a voice that had probably, in her girlhood, been a childish treble, and had become, in the process of time, merely sharp.

Both she and her husband refused cocktails, but the Vicar accepted instead a glass of sherry, remarking to Dinah that he had

33

never learned to like the modern *apéritif*. His mild gaze travelled to Camilla, who was talking to Francis, and had given vent to her rather empty laugh. He blinked a little, as well he might, for the pink sequins sparkled dazzlingly as the light caught them, and inclined his head a little towards Dinah. 'I am afraid I did not catch that lady's name,' he said apologetically. 'My wife tells me that it is quite a tiresome failing of mine, but I am a little deaf, you know.'

'I think most people mumble introductions,' replied Dinah. 'That is Mrs. Halliday.'

'Ah, indeed?' The Vicar looked at Camilla with renewed interest. 'I knew a Halliday once. A dear fellow; we were at Lincoln together. But I dare say he would be no relation.'

The sound of the grandfather clock in the hall striking the hour penetrated to the drawing-room. The General consulted his wrist-watch, as though to verify it.

'You see, we were not late after all, Hilary,' said Mrs. Chudleigh, with an air of self-congratulation.

Dinah slipped unobtrusively towards Geoffrey, who was standing moodily behind Mrs. Twining's chair. 'If you don't want Arthur to start making gobbling noises, go and hurry your betrothed,' she said in a urgent undertone.

Geoffrey spoke from a wider experience of Lola. 'She's always late,' he said simply.

Mrs. Twining turned her head. Her cool grey eyes held a gleam of amusement. 'Of course!' she said softly. 'Gobbling noises!'

Dinah blushed. 'You weren't meant to hear that, Mrs. Twining. But he does, you know.'

'He always did,' replied Mrs. Twining. 'Geoffrey, my dear, I really think you would be wise to take Dinah's advice. Already this party seems to me to be showing signs of wear.'

'It wouldn't be any good,' said Geoffrey. 'She doesn't like to be hurried.'

His voice, breaking a momentary lull in the noise of conversation, attracted the attention of Mrs. Chudleigh. She came towards him immediately, various gold chains which she wore about her neck chinking together as she moved. 'Why, here is Geoffrey!' she exclaimed, holding out her hand. 'I actually didn't see you. I must really have my glasses seen to. And how are you? What a long time it seems since we met!'

'Yes, I've been in town,' said Geoffrey, shaking hands.

34

'Very busy with your writing, I expect,' nodded Mrs. Chudleigh. 'I read a little verse of yours in a magazine not so long ago. Of course I didn't understand it, but it was very clever, I'm sure. I used to scribble verses myself when I was young – not that they were ever good enough to be printed. We used to write them in one another's autograph albums, but I believe that has quite gone out of fashion.'

Geoffrey, who perpetrated, very seriously, fugitive poems without rhyme or (said the uninitiated), reason, shuddered visibly and mumbled something in his throat.

'You must tell me all about yourself,' invited Mrs. Chudleigh paralysingly. 'I expect you meet a great many interesting people up in London and have quite a gay time with all your writing friends.'

The General's voice interrupted her. 'I don't know how long your – fiancée – intends to keep us waiting for dinner, but I should like to point out to you that it is now ten minutes past eight,' he said with awful emphasis.

At that Mrs. Chudleigh's eyes gleamed with interest, and she said: 'Well! So you're engaged to be married, Geoffrey! I had no idea! And is your fiancée actually staying here? This is quite an occasion, then! An engagement-party!'

'Nothing of the sort!' said Sir Arthur, who had been betrayed into divulging Lola's identity through his inability to bring himself to utter her confounded outlandish name.

Mrs. Chudleigh looked sharply from him to Geoffrey, scenting discord. 'Well, I am sure this is a great surprise,' she declared. 'Quite unexpected! I am most anxious to meet her, though I feel quite sorry for her having to enter a roomful of people all staring at her.'

The door was flung open; there was just a moment's pause, sufficient to allow every one time to turn their heads, and Miss de Silva swam into the room.

It was easy to see what had made her late. Her raven locks, which she had worn earlier in the day in ringlets low on her neck, had all been curled and frizzed into a stiff mass up the back of her head to form a sort of halo for her face. She was made up in the Parisian style – a dead white with vivid red lips and heavily blacked eyelashes. She wore a frock of black velvet rising to a point at the base of her throat and held there by a diamond collar. It fitted her like a glove; it was utterly plain, with a long train lined with scarlet, and no back at all until her trim waist was reached. A quantity of diamond (or, as Mrs. Chudleigh strongly suspected, paste) bracelets glittered up each arm, and in one hand she carried a fan of cock's feathers dyed scarlet. She was arresting, magnificent, and quite incongruous, and her appearance rendered her host speechless.

'I am late, that is certain,' she announced, 'but I shall not be blamed, because it was the fault of Geoffrey, who was so stupid to bring me in a little car that would not take my luggage. And I do not drink cocktails with gin: they are to me quite abominable. So there is not the need to wait any longer for dinner, and I do not disarrange any one at all.'

The Vicar bent towards Dinah's ear, and, with an intonation of incredulity, inquired in the peculiarly penetrating whisper ot all deaf persons: 'I beg your pardon. Did I understand you to say that it was Geoffrey's fiancée?'

'Yes,' said Dinah, carefully averting her gaze from Mrs. Chudleigh's stiffening form. 'Er – yes.' Then she unwisely allowed herself to look at Sir Arthur, and felt uncontrollable laughter bubbling up. She retired hastily into the background.

Fay was introducing Lola to the assembled company with an air of spurious brightness. Mrs. Twining said in her faintly drawling way: 'My dear, I am sure there is no need to introduce Miss de Silva, for we must all have heard of her, and of her dancing.'

'It is true,' agreed Lola affably. 'I am very famous, not only in England, but everywhere.'

'Dinner is served, my lady,' said Finch, enacting Providence from the doorway.

The General wheeled round, and, still speechless, offered his arm to Mrs. Twining.

Behind them, in sedate couples, the rest of the guests walked in to dinner.

The dining-room lay at the end of the hall, and was on the opposite side of the front door to the study. It was a large, somewhat sombre apartment, with mahogany furniture and crimson hangings. A number of dark-looking oil paintings in very massive gilt frames hung on the walls, and to one of these, unfortunately placed in her direct line of vision, Lola took instant exception. It depicted, with faithful verisimilitude, a large assortment of garden produce, scattered most unsuitably round a brace of pheasants and a dead hare. Lola had hardly seated herself when she caught sight of this masterpiece, and she at once uttered an outraged cry and got up again. 'Ah, but it is impossible that I should sit opposite to that picture, which I find entirely disgusting. There is a dead animal with blood on it, and I shall immediately faint if I must look at it.'

'It's only a hare, darling,' said Geoffrey, feeling that it was for him to smooth over this breach.

'But naturally I can see that it is a hare. I am not blind. And I must tell you that to see a hare is extremely unlucky. I am already quite upset, but I preceive that it is not possible to remove such a big picture. It will be better if I sit where I cannot look at it.'

The General found his voice. 'Upon my soul!' he burst out. 'Do you imagine, young woman, that I am going to remove my pictures to please—'

Dinah sprang up. 'All right,' she said hurriedly. 'Change places with me, Miss de Silva.'

Lola walked composedly round the table and sat down between Francis and the Vicar. 'So it arranges itself,' she said.

The Vicar, who had turned round to study the offending picture in all its detail, addressed her with an interested and more kindly light in his eye. 'You do not like things to be killed, Miss de Silva? I am sure we must all sympathize with you.'

'I do not mind that they should be killed, but I do not at all like to see a picture of a dead hare with blood on its nose when I am to eat my dinner,' replied Lola firmly.

Since the Vicar was a vegetarian and a pacifist this remark was not a happy one, and he drew back, disappointed and perturbed. His wife, always his champion, bucklering him against the world with a kind of fierce protectiveness, at once entered into the discussion and said across the table: 'We do not all consider it folly to disapprove of bloodshed, I can assure you, Miss de Silva. A great many people today consider *all* bloodshed to be wrong.'

'In my country,' said Lola, applying herself to her soup, 'we do not think that.'

'Lola is a Mexican, you know,' confided Geoffrey, seated next to Mrs. Chudleigh.

'A Mexican!' echoed Mrs. Chudleigh. 'Oh, dear me! Of course that would account for it. Such a dreadful country! One feels that something ought to be done about it, but then they're all Roman Catholics, aren't they? And so Miss de Silva is a dancer, I think you said? On the stage, of course? Well, I always say it takes all sorts to make a world, and I hope I am sufficiently broad-minded ... I see you have Mr. Guest staying with you again. He is quite a frequent visitor, is he not?'

Fay, overhearing this remark, coloured faintly, and lost the thread of the Vicar's painstaking conversation. Beyond him Lola was recounting the tale of her triumphs to Francis, while Camilla Halliday, seated on his left, sought doggedly to capture his attention. The General addressed himself solely to Mrs. Twining and Mrs. Chudleigh, but occasionally sent a smouldering look down the table towards Lola. Stephen Guest said nothing in particular; Geoffrey listened in adoring silence to what Lola was saying to his cousin, and Dinah pursued a futile conversation with Basil Halliday.

It was not a comfortable dinner-party, and at times it was in danger of becoming quite cataclysmic, as, for instance, when Lola produced a tiny Russian cigarette between the entrée and the bird, and requested Francis to light it for her. The General looked daggers at his wife, and since she felt herself powerless to intervene, began to say in his most unpleasant voice: 'Would you have the goodness to refrain—'

'A foreign custom, my dear Arthur,' interposed Mrs. Twining, and took her own case out of her bag. Under her host's astonished glare she drew out a cigarette, and placed it between her lips. 'A match, please,' she said calmly.

'What the devil's the matter with you,' Julia?' demanded Sir Arthur. 'Since when have you taken to that disgusting habit?'

She raised her brows. 'You ought to know by now that I am eminently adaptable,' she said. 'Ah, thank you, Mr. Guest. So kind of you.'

Mrs. Chudleigh gave a shrill laugh. 'I must say I did not expect to see you smoking at table, Julia,' she remarked. 'We live and learn. I wonder what Hilary would have to say to me if I were suddenly to light a cigarette in the middle of dinner?'

'Oh, every one does it nowadays,' Geoffrey assured her. 'I do myself, you know.'

'In this house,' said his father, 'you do nothing of the kind, let me tell you!'

'I'm sure it can't be good for you,' Mrs. Chudleigh said earnestly. 'I always say tobacco is the curse of the modern generation. It goes through all classes. You would hardly believe it possible, but I actually discovered a housemaid of mine smoking in her bedroom once. I had suspected that she did, and I managed to catch her red-handed!'

This recollection was received by Geoffrey in gloomy silence, but provoked Camilla, who was ruffled by her failure to lure Francis away from Lola, to say lightly: 'Poor wretch, why shouldn't she? Live and let live is my motto!'

'Indeed!' said Mrs. Chudleigh, her eyes snapping dangerously. 'We all have our own ideas, of course. Personally I always consider myself directly responsible for the moral *tone* of any servant under my roof.'

'Moral tone?' repeated Camilla. 'It sounds as though she were going to have a baby, or something.'

Mrs. Chudleigh turned quite scarlet and sat very straight in her chair. 'Really, if you will excuse me, I think it is time we ceased this conversation, Mrs. – er – Halliday. No doubt I am old-fashioned, but there are some subjects *I* was brought up to consider unfit for dinner-table discussion.'

As she enunciated this speech with great precision, it not un-naturally caught the ears of nearly everybody in the room. There was a moment's awkward silence. Lola's voice filled it. 'And I must tell you that when I danced in Rio I had a success quite enormous, and a man shot himself outside my hotel, which was a compliment of the most distinguished, and also,' she added practically, 'very good publicity, in Rio.'

'How very romantic!' said Fay, in a shattered voice. 'Do have a salted almond, Mr. Chudleigh!'

The Vicar was regarding Lola in shocked amazement. 'My dear Miss de Silva, you speak very calmly of this dreadful tragedy! It must surely have appalled you to know that this unfortunate man had committed the terrible sin of taking his own life for – one might almost say – your sake!'

'Yes, truly I was sorry for him,' agreed Lola, 'but I had my picture in all the papers, and one is forced to think of these things.'

'Talking of newspapers,' said Stephen Guest, coming staunchly to the rescue, 'I saw a queer thing in one the other day. . . .'

With one accord those at the bottom end of the table turned gratefully towards him, greeting his laboured reminiscence with extravagant enthusiasm.

'You see!' said the General to Mrs. Twining, in a furious under-tone. 'Insufferable! In my own house! The young whippersnapper

39

having the damnable effrontery to bring the woman here. Not by *my* invitation, mark you! Well, I flatter myself it will be the last time my fine son makes a fool of himself under this roof! I've no doubt you'll have a great deal to say on his behalf. You're very fond of taking his part, aren't you? But I don't want to hear it! Do you understand? I don't want to hear it!'

'Perfectly,' said Mrs. Twining. 'I always did understand you, Arthur, and you have not changed in the least.'

The General's already high colour darkened. He opened his mouth to retort, and became aware of Mrs. Chudleigh, avidly listening to his confidences. By a superhuman effort of will he changed what he was about to say into a rasping cough.

The long dinner seemed interminable, but it came to an end at last, and Fay rose, and the women went out in procession.

The worst *must* be over, thought Dinah, bringing up the rear. But all the same when they reached the drawing-room she walked over to one of the open windows, and drew back the curtains, saying: 'It's a gorgeous night. Do come on to the terrace, Miss de Silva!'

'Dinah,' said Mrs. Twining emphatically, as Lola followed Miss Fawcett out, 'deserves a good husband and I hope she finds one.'

'What a ghastly reward!' remarked Camilla, busily powdering her face. 'I didn't know there were such things.'

Mrs. Chudleigh, who had not forgiven her for her behaviour at dinner, said with a steely brightness: 'That is a very cynical remark, and one that I am sure I hope you don't mean. I am proud to say that *I* have a husband who is *more* than good.'

'You are fortunate, Emmy,' said Mrs. Twining dryly. She moved towards the sofa, and sat down, disposing her long skirt with one practised hand. 'Well, Fay, I am sorry for you, but you may console yourself with the reflection that Geoffrey is not, after all, your son. For once, I am almost sorry for Arthur. A most unnerving young woman.'

'But it is dreadful!' exclaimed Mrs. Chudleigh, her eyes gleaming through her glasses. 'To think of that poor boy in the clutches of such a woman! You must forgive me, Lady Billington-Smith, but I feel *most* strongly on the subject, and I do trust that *some* effort will be made to rescue him from such a disastrous entanglement! In my position as a clergyman's wife I do feel that I have some right to speak. And my husband and I have always been most fond of

Geoffrey. I am sure we should both of us be quite distressed to think of him ruining his life like this.'

'I don't think you need worry,' said Mrs. Twining. 'Long experience of Arthur induces me to think that he will place every conceivable obstacle in the way of the marriage.'

'Well, I must say I hope he will manage to stop it,' said Mrs. Chudleigh. 'But one can't help feeling that it needs *tact*. I am sure Hilary would be only too glad to have a little talk with Geoffrey.'

'It's very kind of you, but I think it would be much better to let it die a natural death,' replied Fay with quiet dignity.

Mrs. Chudleigh gave a tight-lipped smile. 'Ah, you are young, Lady Billington-Smith, and naturally optimistic. I am afraid I have lived too long in the world to share your optimism. From what I can see of that woman she exercises a Fatal Fascination for men. Of course, if you admire that bold kind of good looks, I suppose you might call her pretty. Personally, I never trust people with brown eyes, and I should not be at all surprised to hear that she was no better than she should be. And you heard for yourself what she had to say. Really, I was never more shocked in my life! About that unfortunate man who committed suicide.'

'I hope you are not suggesting, Emmy, that Geoffrey is likely to follow his example?' inquired Mrs. Twining, idly surveying her rings.

'If you don't mind my saying so, I shouldn't think he'd have the guts,' said Camilla negligently.

Mrs. Chudleigh's thin bosom swelled. 'If by that expression – which, I must confess, I imagined till now to be confined to schoolboys' use – you mean that he would not have the *courage*, I am afraid you betray your ignorance of human nature, Mrs. Halliday. Not that I wish to imply for an instant that Geoffrey would even contemplate doing such a dreadful thing.'

'Surely we are taking this a little too seriously?' suggested Mrs. Twining. 'I for one am not led to suppose that Miss de Silva's affections are of a very permanent nature. I wish you would tell me, Fay, what you do to your roses to make them so much more perfect than mine.'

'It isn't me,' Fay answered, sitting down beside her. 'Arthur looks after the garden, you know. He is very keen on it.'

'Ah, yes, of course,' said Mrs. Twining, watching Camilla stroll out on to the terrace. 'My dear, will you allow a very old friend of your husband to suggest that if you can induce him to take this affair calmly it might be a very excellent thing?'

'I know,' Fay said unhappily. 'I – I will try, only – it isn't always easy – when Arthur's annoyed – to – to manage him, you know.' She flushed a little, and turned with relief as Dinah came in through the French window. 'Oh, darling, there you are! Did you manage to make her understand at all?'

'It isn't possible,' said Dinah despairingly. 'We shall have to make up our minds to it. She's going to be the life and soul of the party.'

'Oh, dear, how awful! What on earth shall I do?' demanded Fay helplessly.

'You can't do anything. I warned her there'd be bridge, but she says it will be better if we dance to the radio.' She paused, and delivered her final bombshell. 'And she thinks Francis looks as though he could tango, and she is going to do an exhibition tango with him for us all to watch. And I should think,' concluded Miss Fawcett thoughtfully, 'that it'll be pretty lush, what's more.'

CHAPTER FOUR

MISS FAWCETT, awaking betimes on Monday morning, flirted for a while with the idea of staying in bed to breakfast. Her better self won, however, and she got up in time to breakfast at half past eight, thus deliberately courting a *tête-à-tête* with the General, ever an early riser.

This act of heroism was induced by the events of the week-end. Someone, Miss Fawcett thought gloomily, must try to smooth the General down before he actually flung his son out of the house.

Her prognostications on Saturday had not been false. Miss de Silva had indeed been the life and soul of the party, even going so far as to offer to perform a dance for the edification of the assembled company. Only the General's rigid notions of Christian conduct had prevented him disowning his son the first thing on Sunday morning.

But in spite of the fact that Sir Arthur's principles forbade him to quarrel on the Sabbath, Sunday had not been a happy day. Yet every effort was made to please the General. With the exception of Lola, who, it appeared, never rose before eleven, the whole party went dutifully to church, and Francis, who had blandly announced that Geoffrey's lamentable lack of tact was interfering with his own schemes, made elaborate arrangements for the rest of the day. He banished Geoffrey and Lola on an expedition to Clayton-on-Sea, provided his uncle with every opportunity of flirting with Camilla Halliday, and ended the day by inviting his uncle (by this time almost mellow) to recount some of his Indian experiences. By the time Lola and Geoffrey returned from Clayton-on-Sea the air was thick with shikaris, chuckkas, Pathans, Sikhs, sahibs, bazaars, mahouts, and jinrickshas, and the General midway through an anecdote about a fellah who was a Gunner, a minor Rajah, and a Kabul pony.

But from the moment of Miss de Silva's appearance the General's amiability waned. It was plain that Geoffrey had made an attempt to impress upon Lola the necessity of placating his father, for she broke into the anecdote just as the *sais* was shampooing the Kabul pony's legs before the first chukka, and announced her firm intention of talking to Geoffrey's papa. The General was a ruthless conversationalist, but he was no match for Miss de Silva, whose twenty-three years in the world had provided her with a larger stock of egotistic reminiscences than he had acquired in all his sixty summers. Russian grand dukes, Polish counts, Spanish anarchists, and Mexican bandits took the place of the Pathans, and the Sikhs, and the Gurkhas, and the scene shifted with bewildering rapidity from Rio de Janeiro to New York, Paris, London, and Monte Carlo, the saga being strung together by the principal *motif* of Miss de Silva's amazing successes in these different cities.

By supper-time the General was in a state of bottled-up emotion that seemed to put him in danger of explosion at any moment. The sight of his son watching Miss de Silva with an expression of rapt, uncritical admiration was the last straw. The sanctity of the day prevented an immediate outburst, but, as the house-party, in various stages of nervous exhaustion, went limply in to supper, he informed Geoffrey that he had just one or two things to say to him, and would see him in his study at half past nine next morning without fail.

Therefore Miss Fawcett arose betimes.

On her way to the bath she passed Fay's room, and the sound of a military voice upraised in furious monologue induced her, as soon as she had dressed, to visit her sister before she went down to breakfast. She found Fay weeping hysterically over the brushes on

43

her dressing-table and put her back to bed and dosed her with aspirin. As far as she could gather from a choked and incoherent explanation, Fay had tried to persuade the General not to take his son's engagement too seriously. Whereupon it seemed (but the story was lost in a maze of sobs, I-saids and he-saids) that Sir Arthur had not only called his wife a soft-headed, meddlesome fool, but had laid the blame of every mishap occurring within the last five years at her door, and declared his intention of cutting Geoffrey off with a shilling immediately after breakfast.

Miss Fawcett recommended her sister to pull herself together, promised to order a tray to be sent up to her room, and went off downstairs to have it out with the General.

She found him eating a solitary breakfast, and wasted no time in skirmishing preliminaries. 'Look here, Arthur,' she said forcibly, 'you've been upsetting Fay. That's a cad's trick, and you know it.'

The General bent upon her the famous glare that had caused so many adjutants to shiver in their shoes, and said menacingly: 'Will-you-have-the-goodness-to-mind-your-own-business?'

'No,' said Dinah, 'I will not. You've been throwing your weight about ever since I entered this house, and now it's my turn. If you want to bully anybody, try bullying me! It wasn't Fay's fault that Geoffrey got himself engaged to Lola, and it isn't fair to take it out of her just because you're feeling sore. I quite see that it's very annoying for you to have to put up with Lola, but, good Lord, Arthur, you don't suppose it'll last, do you?'

'That's enough!' thundered the General. 'By God, haven't I enough whining and puling to put up with from your damned fool of a sister without having your impertinence added to it?'

'No, you haven't,' replied Miss Fawcett. She sat down at the table and resolutely forced herself to speak without rancour. 'Do try and be sensible, Arthur. You'll look utterly silly if you throw Geoffrey out; you will really. And you know what he is. He's quite likely to go and do something idiotic if he gets into one of his worked-up moods.'

Sir Arthur banged his fist on the table with such violence that all the crockery shuddered. 'He can go to the devil his own way!' he barked. 'A fine son he is! What did he do at Eton? Slacked! No good at games, no good at his work! Delicate! Faugh! What did he do at Oxford? Got himself into a mess with a girl in a tobacconist's shop, that's what he did at Oxford, and a damned fool I

44

was to buy her off. What's he doing now? Wasting his time with a set of long-haired nincompoops and disgracing my name! That's all he's doing, and it's going to stop. Do you hear me? It's going to stop!'

'They can probably hear you all over the house,' said Dinah calmly. 'Cutting Geoffrey off with a shilling won't stop him disgracing your name; it's much more likely to make him do something worse. But I'm not particularly interested in his affairs, or, in fact, in anyone's except Fay's. You may not realize it, but you're fast driving her into a nervous breakdown.'

'Nerves!' ejaculated Sir Arthur with a scornful crack of laughter. 'That's all you modern women think about – nerves! My God, I've no patience with it!'

'All right,' said Dinah, a gleam in her eye. 'Put it like this, since you will have it! If you go on making Fay's life a hell for her you'll find yourself with another wife who's deserted you!'

The General's face grew purple; his eyes protruded; words jostled one another in his throat.

'In the meantime,' said Dinah, picking up her knife and fork, 'I'm sending for the doctor to come and prescribe a tonic for her.'

Anything the General might have been moved to say in answer to this was put a stop to by the entrance of Francis and Stephen Guest. They were followed in a few minutes by the Hallidays, who also betrayed signs of ruffled tempers. Basil Halliday was looking strained, and kept glancing towards his wife with a mixture of anger and entreaty in his sunken eyes; Camilla was faintly flushed, and talked and laughed in a determined manner that seemed to Dinah to be largely defiant.

It had been decided that, since the only through train to town in the morning left Ralton Station, six miles away, at ten minutes to ten the Hallidays were to put off their departure until after lunch. Camilla reminded Sir Arthur that he had promised to take her over to the keeper's cottage to see a litter of springer pups. She said that she was dying to see them, and pouted prettily when he told her that he must first drive in to Ralton on business.

The pout and the look that went with it had the effect of making Sir Arthur unbend a little. He surveyed the charmer with the eye of an epicure, but it would have taken more than Camilla's wiles to interfere with the routine which governed his life. Assuring her that he would take her to see the puppies before she left, he explained that, the day being the first of the month, he had to go through his accounts, and draw a cheque to pay all the wages and the household bills before he could do anything else.

'Method, my dear Camilla! I pride myself upon being methodical. The Army teaches one to lay down certain rules and to stick to them. I pay all the staff, including the outdoor servants, regularly as clockwork, directly after lunch on the first day of the month. My wife has to have her household books ready for inspection by nine o'clock in the morning. Then I find my total, go to the bank, draw what money I want, and by tea-time the whole business is finished. No hanging about, no paying wages every other day of the month. No. I fix a regular pay-day and stick to it, and in that way, Camilla, I know to a farthing what is being spent in the house. It's the only way.'

It seemed to Camilla an appalling way, but she said brightly: 'I call that such a good idea! I know I'm dreadfully unbusiness-like myself. I wish you could teach me some of your method, Sir Arthur.'

He rose, smiling indulgently down at her. 'Oh, we don't expect the fair sex to be business-like! Never met a woman yet who had any notion of method, and, by Gad, I hope I never do! Now what is the time? Nine o'clock! Very well, then. I shall leave for Ralton at ten, and I shall be back here at eleven, and you and I will go off to see the pups. How will that be?'

'It's too sweet of you!' said Camilla. 'I shall be all ready to the tick, just to show you how methodical I *can* be!'

Francis got up. 'I shall have left before you get back from Ralton, Uncle,' he said. 'Are you busy just now? I should like to have a word with you before I go, if I may.'

Sir Arthur looked at him rather grimly. 'H'm! If you think it worth while I can spare you five minutes; not a moment more.'

They left the room together. Stephen Guest bent towards Dinah. 'Is Fay staying in bed to breakfast?' he asked in a low voice.

'Yes,' replied Dinah matter-of-factly. 'She's not feeling frightfully fit. She doesn't sleep well, you know.'

Basil Halliday raised his eyes from his plate. 'I'm sorry. I know what it is to suffer from insomnia. It would be much better if we left by the nine-fifty, Camilla. We can easily catch it. Lady Billington-Smith won't want us hanging about all the morning.'

'Oh, we can't possibly!' said Camilla quickly. 'Of course, I'm dreadfully sorry about Fay, but do beg her, Miss Fawcett, not to bother about us in the least.'

'Camilla, I would prefer to catch the nine-fifty,' said Halliday, the fingers of his right hand working a little.

Camilla paid no attention to this, and, observing a pulse throbbing in Halliday's temple, Dinah interposed: 'There's no need for anyone to hurry away on Fay's account. She'll be down presently. Stephen, are you catching the morning train?'

'No,' he said, after a moment's deliberation. 'I think I'll wait over till the afternoon.'

Dinah got up. 'Well, I'll go and see if Fay wants anything done for her,' she said, and went out.

Stephen followed her, and stopped her as she was about to go up the stairs. 'Just a moment, Dinah.'

She glanced sharply round at him, and saw that his face was more than ordinarily grim. 'Well?'

He came to the foot of the staircase, and laid his hand on the rail. 'Fay's upset?' he demanded abruptly.

'She's all right. For goodness' sake don't you start being dramatic! Why on earth don't you go by the train you said you were going by?'

'I'm seeing Fay before I go.'

Dinah sighed. 'I suppose you heard Arthur making himself felt before breakfast.'

'Yes, I did hear him,' replied Guest in a level voice. 'And I don't leave till I've seen Fay.'

'All right, you needn't be so emphatic about it. But it's no use thinking you'll get her to run away with you, Stephen, because she won't. I know Fay, and she's just the sort of person who'd rather be a martyr than start a scandal.'

He looked at her for a moment. 'Maybe you're right,' he said, and turned away, pausing by the hall table to pick up a newspaper.

Dinah found her sister fairly calm, but very pale and heavy-eyed. She was speaking to Mrs. Moxon, the cook, when Dinah came in, and started nervously at the sound of the opening door. Since the between-maid had been sweeping the landing when it happened, the entire indoor staff knew by this time that the General and her ladyship had been having words again. There was an air of dark sympathy about Mrs. Moxon. She said: 'You leave it to me, m'lady,'

47

and 'I *was* going to speak to you about that Janet. But there, it'll do some other time.'

She departed presently, full of good intentions about the remains of the joint, and spread the news below stairs that her ladyship was looking like death so that it made her heart fair bleed to see her. She further expressed a desire to give His-High-and-Mightiness a piece of her mind. 'Let him come poking his bad-tempered nose into my kitchen, that's all, Mr. Finch!' she said delphically.

Upstairs Fay smiled wanly at her sister, and said: 'Sorry to make such a fool of myself. I don't think I can be very well. I probably need a change or a tonic, or something.'

'Yes, that's what I told Arthur. I propose to ring up your doctor, if you'll tell me what his name is.'

'I have Dr. Raymond, but I don't know that—'

'Then we'll send for him,' said Dinah. 'It'll put the wind up Arthur. By the way, Arthur's quite determined to cast Geoffrey off. He's the sort of man who'd cut off his nose to spite his face and then argue that it looked better that way.'

Fay raised herself on her elbow. 'Dinah, I'm terribly worried about Geoffrey. It's all very well for you – you're not his stepmother; but I feel it's my duty to try and stand between him and Arthur. And if Arthur turns him out it'll look as though I'd been working against him.'

'Don't confuse the issues,' said Dinah. 'Let Arthur turn him out. He'll take him back again fast enough.'

'That's just what he won't do!' Fay said urgently. 'You think Arthur's just a joke. He isn't. He's dreadful. Right down inside him he's hard; hard as nails, Dinah! He likes to hurt people, and bully them, and make their lives a misery for them. And if once he says he won't have Geoffrey in his house again it'll be final. I tell you I know what I'm talking about! Haven't you heard Arthur say that when he says a thing he means it, once and for all? That's true. He does mean it. He thinks that's being strong and iron-willed. He'd do anything sooner than go back on what he's once said.'

'Steady!' recommended Dinah. 'You keep cool. Shall I tip the wink to the Halliday wench to pour oil? I rather loathe the idea, but she does seem to go down very smoothly with him.'

A look of distaste crossed Fay's face. 'I think I'd rather you didn't,' she said. 'I mean – no, I can't confide in a person like that. I'd better get up. Stephen hasn't gone, has he?'

'No,' said Dinah shortly. 'I wish he had.'

As she descended the stairs again five minutes later she was met by Finch, with the information that Mrs. Twining was on the telephone, and would like to speak either to her ladyship or to Miss Fawcett.

The only extension of the telephone which the General had allowed was to his own study, so anyone else wishing to use the instrument had to do so in the hall, quite the most public place that could possibly have been chosen.

Dinah picked up the receiver. 'Hullo? Dinah Fawcett speaking.'

'Good morning, my dear,' said Mrs. Twining's voice tranquilly. 'I am merely curious, you know. How have you weathered the week-end?'

'Well, it's all pretty grim,' said Dinah.

'I was afraid perhaps it might be. Arthur had such an irreligious face in church. Has he disowned poor Geoffrey yet?'

'I think he's doing it now,' replied Dinah, with a glance down the long hall to the study door, from behind which came the sound of a loud voice booming and roaring.

There was a slight pause. 'I see,' said Mrs. Twining thoughtfully. 'Do you know, I think I will come and have a little chat with Arthur.'

'Do you think you can do anything with him?' asked Dinah hopefully. 'Fay quite definitely can't.'

'I have no idea,' said Mrs. Twining. 'I think I have a little – a very little – influence over him. Tell Fay that I will look in at lunchtime. Good-bye, my dear.'

Dinah put the receiver down as Finch came into the hall through the door that led to the servants' wing. 'Mrs. Twining will be here for lunch,' she said. 'I think perhaps I'd better do the flowers for Lady Billington-Smith. What is the time, Finch?'

The butler stepped back to get a view of the grandfather clock. 'It is just on the quarter, miss. To be exact, I should say it is sixteen minutes to ten, since I believe we are a little fast.'

'We should be,' murmured Dinah. 'Has Captain Billington-Smith gone, do you know?'

'No, miss. Captain Billington-Smith was with Sir Arthur until twenty minutes past nine, and has, I believe, gone up to his room.'

'Oh, well, I suppose I'd better wait to see him off,' reflected Dinah, and wandered into the morning-room, a somewhat gloomy apartment behind the study with windows that faced, inappropriately, west.

She sat down to glance through a picture paper, and had just passed from 'Dramatic Outburst in Court' by way of 'Boy Hero Saves Kitten's Life' to 'Four Killed in Air Liner Disaster' when a door was slammed violently, and hasty footsteps passed the morning-room and went up the stairs two at a time.

Geoffrey, thought Miss Fawcett. What does a helpful spinster do now? Nothing. (Answer adjudged incorrect.)

The grandfather clock began to whir alarmingly, and presently struck ten in the brittle manner peculiar to all genuine models. Simultaneously, the General's voice was to be heard, demanding in stentorian tones why the devil that fellow Peacock hadn't brought the car round yet. 'When I say ten o'clock I mean ten o'clock, and the sooner you all realize that the better it will be for you!' he rasped.

Dinah did not catch the butler's quiet answer, but in about half a minute Peacock apparently arrived with the General's car, for the echoes of a harangue on punctuality delivered on the doorstep reached her ears. Miss Fawcett reflected that to live continually with that over-loud, nagging voice might conceivably wear down nerves less delicate than her sister's.

It ceased at last, and gave place to a prodigious series of explosions from the car, and a jarring of gears too hastily changed. Miss Fawcett emerged from the morning-room in time to hear Peacock, still standing in the porch, say sullenly to Finch: 'Good place or not, I'm giving in my notice when he pays me, and that's that.'

Shortly before half past ten Francis came down the stairs in a leisurely fashion. It was never an easy matter to read the thought behind his eyes, and Dinah, frankly surveying him now, was unable to decide whether he had succeeded in his mission to Sir Arthur or not. A not very pleasant smile curled his thin lips, and when he caught sight of Dinah he remarked in his usual languidly cynical way: 'Such a pathetic sight, my pet. Do go up and look. My poor little cousin waiting on the mat outside Lola's door! He looks just like the Weak Young Man Driven to Despair in a Raffles play. I am quite sorry to be leaving, for the party is beginning to be almost amusing. Do say good-bye to Fay for me, and thank her for a perfectly bloody week-end. Do I kiss you, or not?'

'Not,' replied Miss Fawcett decidedly. 'Good-bye. Try not to get had up for speeding. Arthur's very hot against that about now.'

Upstairs, Geoffrey, regardless of appearances, had flung himself down on a chair against the wall on the landing, and was sitting with his elbows on his knees and his head in his hands awaiting Miss de Silva's pleasure. Miss de Silva, like Sir Arthur, held to certain fixed rules, one of these being an immovable resolve not to be disturbed by anyone but the faithful Concetta until eleven o'clock in the morning. She had already intimated to Geoffrey, through Concetta, her mouthpiece, that it was impossible, quite impossible, to admit him into her room, so there was nothing for him to do but to wait, which he did, under the sympathetic eye of Dawson, engaged in turning out Captain Billington-Smith's late bedroom. Dawson was stirred to the depths of her romantic soul by Geoffrey's pose of utter dejection, but she did not really want his troubles to vanish. She had a passion for drama, and had already in her mind condemned Geoffrey to be shot through the head by his own hand. As she folded sheets and shook up pillows she was silently rehearsing the evidence she would give at the inquest. Miss Joan Dawson, *'a slim, youthful figure in a brown dress and close-fitting hat'* – her new black crinoline straw which Ted liked was nicer, really, but they always wore close-fitting hats – *'gave her evidence in a low, clear voice. . . .'*

Peckham, the head housemaid, came up the back stairs with her starched skirts crackling to give due warning of her approach. There was no nonsense about Peckham; she never went to the pictures, or kept company with a boy, or weaved stories about her employers. She knew her place, knew it far too well to cast more than one detached, incurious glance at Geoffrey, still holding his head in his hands. Her brisk, severe voice cut through all lurid imaginings, like a sharp pair of scissors ripping up lengths of gossamer. 'Now then, Dawson, are you going to be all day over one room? Pick up those sheets and take them along to the linen basket; I'll finish this off, thank you.'

Camilla Halliday came out of her bedroom at the back of the house, and opened her eyes rather at sight of Geoffrey. She was wearing a large hat, in readiness for her trip to the keeper's cottage. It had a becoming tilt to its brim, and she knew that it made her look young and appealing. She went towards the head of the staircase, but paused before going down, and said, with a kind of tolerant, half-scornful concern: 'You look pretty rotten. Are you ill, or something? Has anything gone wrong?'

Geoffrey raised his head, and gave a bitter laugh. 'Oh, nothing! I've only had my whole life ruined!'

'Help!' said Camilla. 'As bad as that? I suppose there's nothing I can do?'

'No one can do anything,' said Geoffrey. 'Not that I want anyone to try. I at least have my *pen* left to me, and after the things that have been said to me today I wouldn't enter this house again if Father begged me to on his bended knees. In fact, I won't answer for myself if I have to see him again.'

'Oh, well!' said Camilla, shrugging her shoulders. 'If there's nothing I can do I think I'll be going downstairs.' It's just my rotten luck, she thought, that ghastly fool of a boy putting the old man's back up just when I want him in a good mood. O God, I suppose I shall have to let him gas about India again, and slobber all over me.

Then she heard the General's voice in the hall, and the weary, discontented look vanished as though by magic from her face, and she ran down the remaining stairs, calling to the General: 'Oh, Sir Arthur, you really are too terribly punctual for words! How *can* you manage it? I think you must be some kind of wizard. And I meant to be on the doorstep waiting for you, just to show you!'

Geoffrey heard his father say, with ponderous playfulness: 'Ah, you won't steal a march on me in a hurry, fair lady! I told you I should be back on the stroke of eleven, and here I am, you see, all my business done, and entirely at your disposal just as soon as I've deposited this little packet in my safe.'

The door of Miss de Silva's room opened, and Concetta appeared. 'It is permitted that you see the Signora now,' she said kindly.

There did not seem to be very much reason why Geoffrey should not have seen the Signora at any time during the past half-hour, for she could not have been in the throes of her toilet since she was still in bed when he at last entered the room.

She was wearing a very low-cut elaborate nightgown, and her black curls, though brushed till they shone, had not been crimped into any of the styles of coiffure that she affected.

Geoffrey stopped short just inside the room, gazing at her hungrily. 'God, how lovely you are!' he said, a trifle thickly, and plunged forward to the bedside, grasping at her.

Lola submitted to his rather greedy embrace with a smile of satisfaction. She allowed him to kiss her, on her mouth, and her throat, and up her white arms, but she did not betray any sign of being much stirred by his ardour. She seemed to find it pleasant but incidental, and as soon as she was tired of it she pushed him away, though quite gently, and said: 'It is enough. In a minute Concetta will come back to dress me and you must at once go away. And I must tell you that I have not slept at all, not one instant, because it is impossible that I should sleep when cocks are permitted to crow all night. It is a thing that I find very badly arranged, quite insupportable.'

'Darling!' Geoffrey said, trying to seize her hands. 'I ought never to have brought you! But you shan't spend another moment in this house. I'm going to take you away at once, my poor angel!'

'But what are you talking about? It's not at all sensible. Naturally I shall spend a great many moments in this house, for I am not dressed yet, and besides, I do not go away until I have eaten lunch,' said Lola, always practical.

'I know a little place on the road to town where we can lunch,' began Geoffrey.

'I, too,' said Lola coldly. 'I prefer that I should eat my lunch here.'

'I won't eat another meal in this house! I couldn't!' said Geoffrey, with suppressed violence. 'I may as well tell you, Lola, that I've had the hell of a row with Father. In fact, it's all over between us two, and I hope I never set eyes on him again!'

Miss de Silva regarded him with sudden suspicion. 'What is this you are saying?' she demanded. 'But tell me at once, if you please, for I do not at all understand you!'

'We've quarrelled – irrevocably!' announced Geoffrey, giving a somewhat inaccurate description of the one-sided scene enacted in the study at half past nine. 'Of course it was bound to come. We're oil and water. I've always known it. Only I did think that Father—'

Miss de Silva sat up. 'You are talking quite ridiculously, my dear Geoffrey. It is not oil and water, but, on the contrary, oil and vinegar. I am not so ignorant that I do not know that. But I do not see why you must quarrel with your papa for such a stupid reason, which I find is not a reason at all, in fact, but a great piece of folly.'

'You don't understand, darling. I said we were oil and water – not vinegar. It's an expression – an idiom.'

'It is entirely without sense,' replied Lola scornfully.

'It means we don't mix. Well, anyway, it's just a saying. It doesn't really matter. The point is that Father's behaving like an absolute cad. Simply because you're a professional dancer he's trying to do everything he can to stop us being married. I simply hate telling you this, darling, because I'd die sooner than let you be hurt. But there it is. He's one of those hide-bound, utterly disgusting Victorians. One simply can't argue with him. He's always hated me. I expect it's because of my mother. She ran off with some other man when I was a kid. I don't really know much about it, but I believe there was a perfectly ghastly scandal at the time. Anyway, Father's been an absolute beast to me all my life – it's a pity he didn't have Francis for a son, though as a matter of fact he wouldn't think so jolly well of him if he knew some of the things *I* know about him – and this is just the last straw. Because nothing would induce me to give you up. He needn't think I care about his filthy money. Money simply means nothing to me, and in any case I happen to be able to write, and though he chooses to sneer at my work there are other people who know far more about it than he does who think I'm going to go a long way. I couldn't help smiling when he talked about me starving in the gutter for all he cared. Of course he'd never believe that anyone could make any money by writing, but he'll just see, that's all!'

Lola, who had listened to this rambling speech in complete and unusual silence, relaxed once more on to her bank of pillows, and said in a thoughtful voice: 'It is true that your papa is a character extremely difficult, not at all sympathetic. It will be better perhaps if I do not marry you.'

Geoffrey stared down at her, startled and incredulous. 'Lola! You can't think that I'd give you up! Good God, I'm mad about you! I adore you!'

'It is very sad,' agreed Lola. 'I myself am quite in despair. But it is not sense to marry if you have no money. One must think of these things, though certainly it is very disagreeable.'

He snatched at her wrists. 'Lola, you can't mean that! Lola, don't you care for me? What does it matter about the money, if we love each other? I'll make money, I swear I will! You can't say you won't marry me!'

'Certainly I love you,' replied Lola with composure. 'I love with great passion always, but I am not at all a fool, and it is plain that

54

if you have not a great deal of money it is impossible that we should marry. And I will tell you, my dear Geoffrey, what I have been thinking, that perhaps it is better that I do not engage myself to you, for I am quite young, not at all *passée*, and besides, I find that I do not wish to live in the country where there is no absinthe, no shower in my bathroom, and cocks that crow all night so that I cannot sleep.'

'But we shouldn't live in the country! We could live anywhere you liked!' Geoffrey said desperately.

'I like always to live in the best places,' said Lola with simplicity. 'And I must tell you, please, that you are hurting me.'

His grasp on her wrists tightened. 'Lola, you're saying it to tease me! You don't mean it! Oh, my God, you couldn't be so cruel, so utterly heartless!'

The beautiful brown eyes flashed. 'It is not I who am cruel, let me tell you, but entirely you, my good Geoffrey, to wish me to marry you when you have not any longer any money!'

'But Lola, I'll make money! I know I can make enough for us to live on! It won't be a fortune, but we'll manage somehow.'

'I find that you are being completely selfish. You do not think of me at all,' said Lola austerely. 'It is quite necessary that I should have a great deal of money, a fortune, as you say. And I wish that you will instantly let go of my arms, because though I do not make complaint you are hurting me excessively. And then you will go away so that I may dress myself, and after I have eaten my lunch, but not in the least before, you will drive me back to London.'

He sprang up; his face was very white, his lips trembling incontrollably. 'I can't *believe* it! I can't *believe* it!' he stammered, his voice breaking on a dry sob. 'I can't give you up! I tell you I can't, I won't!'

'It is for us both a great tragedy,' agreed Lola. 'But your papa—'

The death-like pallor grew. 'It's all his fault!' Geoffrey gasped. 'Ever since I was born – and now *this*—! devil, devil, devil!' He dashed his hand across his eyes, and stumbled over to the door. 'He's ruined my life, and my happiness, and taken you away from me – God, I can't bear it!' He wrenched open the door and rushed out, almost colliding with Dawson, a breathless and entranced auditor on the landing.

*   *   *

'... and "Out of my way!" he says, just like that, and he gave me a push that sent me up against the wall – Oo, Mrs. Moxon, you wouldn't believe what a push he gave me; it's a wonder I didn't fall over, it is really! And then he went off down the stairs, without one backward look, and out of the house, with no hat nor nothing, and leaving the front door open behind him, which Mr. Finch'll bear me out is the solid truth!'

CHAPTER FIVE

At a quarter to twelve the General's voice was once more to be heard in the hall, this time shouting for his wife. He and Camilla had just returned from their inspection of the litter of springer puppies, and, whether by her desire, or his, it had become necessary for her to take back to town with her some of his famous roses.

Fay, who had only just emerged from her bedroom, and was in consultation with Peckham upstairs, at once hurried down. 'I'm here, Arthur,' she said in her fluttering way.

'Oh, there you are! I want Camilla to have some roses to take home with her,' decreed the General. 'Tell Lester, will you? Where is the fellow? I thought I'd made it plain that I wanted the front lawn mowed this morning? I suppose you've taken him off that job to do something for you that could quite well be done tomorrow. It's always the way! As soon as my back's turned—'

'I haven't told him to do anything,' said Fay wearily. 'I haven't even seen him.'

'Then where the devil is he?' demanded the General, balked. 'I must say I do think you might see that the servants do their work when I'm out!'

'If you had told me, Arthur—'

'Oh, don't let's have any argument about it!' begged Sir Arthur. 'Though I should have thought— However, doubtless I was wrong. Find out what the fellow's doing, and tell him to cut Mrs. Halliday a couple of dozen blooms.'

'It's most awfully sweet of you,' said Camilla. 'I do hope it isn't any trouble?'

'Trouble? Good gracious me, it's no trouble at all, my dear Camilla. It's a pleasure. Only wish the roses were more worthy of you!'

Camilla gave her empty little laugh, and said archly: 'Now you're

56

trying to flatter me, and I won't listen to a word you say! Thank you terribly, Fay – it *is* good of you to bother! I'll just run up and take my hat off.'

The General watched her go up the stairs, and became aware of his wife, still standing beside him. Since his conscience pricked him slightly, he naturally felt annoyed with her for being there. 'Well, don't hang about looking like seven bells half struck!' he said irritably. 'You might at least try to behave pleasantly to your guests. And kindly understand that if anyone wants me before lunch I'm busy, and don't want to be disturbed. I've wasted quite enough of the morning as it is. Look at the time! Ten to twelve, and as far as I can make out you're only just up! I wonder what my mother would say if she were alive today and could see the way you modern women lie in bed till all hours!'

'Oh, don't, don't,' Fay cried out suddenly, putting her hands to her head. 'I can't bear it! You're driving me out of my mind, Arthur!'

The General stared after her, as she turned and hurried away towards the garden-hall. 'More nerves!' he said, with a short laugh, and walked into his study, and shut the door loudly.

It was just as well that he did not know that Miss Fawcett, who had spent the morning 'doing the flowers', had already robbed the rose-garden of its choicest blooms. Now, conscious of rectitude, she had joined Stephen Guest on the terrace, and subsided into a deep wicker-chair beside him.

'I call it more than a little sultry,' she remarked. 'No *double entendre* meant, I assure you. Does my nose want powdering?'

'It looks all right to me,' said Guest, giving it his consideration.

'I mistrust your judgment profoundly,' said Dinah. 'However, I don't think I can be bothered to go upstairs. Though I have noticed that it's becoming quite the done thing in this house to make your face up in the full view of— Oh, hullo, Mrs. Halliday! How were the puppies?'

'Sweet,' said Camilla. 'I adored them. Don't say I've butted in on a *tête-à-tête*! Where's Basil?'

Stephen Guest, who had risen politely, looked vaguely round. 'I don't know,' he answered. 'I think he went into the billiard-room. Shall I go and see?'

'Oh no, don't bother, thanks,' said Camilla, seating herself. 'We are a small party, aren't we? I always think the Monday after a weekend is frightfully depressing, don't you? I mean everybody leaving, or packing, or something. I suppose it's much too early for a cocktail?'

'It's about twelve,' said Dinah, consulting her wrist-watch.

This hardly seemed to be an adequate answer to the question. Camilla gave a short sigh, and said: 'Oh, well!' and began to drum her fingers on the arm of her chair.

The arrival of Mrs. Twining, a few minutes later, created a diversion. She came through the drawing-room out on to the terrace, looking, as usual, cool, and perfectly dressed. 'I told that inestimable Finch that I'd announce myself,' she said. 'Good morning, Mrs. Halliday. I have had to go to Silsbury, Dinah. Such a bore, but you see that is why I am so early. It did not seem to be worth while to go home again.'

Dinah shook hands with her. 'Won't you sit down? I think I saw Fay going towards the rose-garden a minute or two ago. I'll go and tell her you've arrived.'

'Let us both go and tell her I have arrived,' said Mrs. Twining. 'I should like to see Arthur's new standards. Mine have not done at all well; I believe it is the soil.'

'Do you really want to see rose trees?' Dinah asked bluntly, as they walked across the lawn to the yew hedge that shut off the rose-garden.

'Not in the least, my dear. I want you to tell me just what has happened today. There is that peculiar and plague-stricken quiet about the house that usually means that there has been a great deal of unpleasantness.'

'Well, there has,' admitted Dinah. 'There's been a row with Fay, and then a sort of skirmish with me (but that was my doing), and then what sounded like a really super-row with Geoffrey. I don't know what happened exactly, but Francis said that Geoffrey was looking pretty sick.'

'I always felt that Sunday's forced abstinence was putting too great a strain on Arthur,' remarked Mrs. Twining thoughtfully. 'Where is Geoffrey now?'

'Well, I don't really know. He *was* outside Lola's door at half past ten. He may be in her room. To tell you the truth, Mrs. Twining, I'm not awfully interested in his troubles, except when they affect Fay.'

'Why should you be?' said Mrs. Twining. 'I am sure I am not surprised. It was so extremely stupid of him to bring that remarkable young woman of his here. But I don't think we must let Arthur cast him on the world.'

Dinah glanced curiously at her. 'You're very fond of Geoffrey, aren't you?'

Mrs. Twining had stooped to smell a great crimson rose. 'Too full-blown to pick. What a pity! No, my dear, I don't know that I should describe myself as being very fond of Geoffrey. I knew him when he was in his cradle, however, and I have always been sorry for the boy.'

'Did you know his mother, Mrs. Twining?' asked Dinah. 'I've often wondered.'

Mrs. Twining put back a trailing rambler with her gloved hand. 'Have you, my dear? Yes, I knew her quite well.'

'What was she like? Arthur never mentions her, you know, and there isn't even a photograph.'

'When Arthur puts people out of his life,' said Mrs. Twining, with a faint smile, 'he does it very thoroughly. She was generally thought to be pretty.'

'I don't really blame her for leaving Arthur, but it was rather rotten of her to leave Geoffrey,' reflected Dinah.

Mrs. Twining passed through the gap in the hedge again on to the lawn. 'Yes, it was, as you say, rotten of her,' she replied. 'But whatever she did that was rotten, or foolish, she had to pay for. Tell me, is Arthur in, do you know?'

'Yes, I think he must be. Oh, there is Fay, coming away from the vegetable garden! *Fa-ay!*'

They waited for Fay to catch up with them. She gave her hand to Mrs. Twining, saying: 'It's so nice of you to have come, Julia. Things are being — a little difficult. Perhaps if you spoke to him Arthur might listen.'

'Listening is not his speciality, but I will try,' promised Mrs. Twining. 'Where is he?'

'Oh, it would never do if you disturbed him before lunch!' said Fay, looking quite flustered at the bare thought of such a thing. 'He's writing letters in his study.'

They ascended the steps on to the terrace. Stephen Guest pulled up a chair, his gaze on Fay's face. 'Come and sit down,' he said. 'You look done up.'

She pushed the hair away from her forehead. 'I've got a headache. It's nothing.' Her voice was forlorn; as she sat down she raised her eyes fleetingly to his, and he saw that they had filled with tears. She tried to smile, and said in a low, unsteady voice for his ears alone: 'It's all right, Stephen. Really it's all right.'

Mrs. Twining was talking in her pleasant way to Camilla Halliday; Dinah was wondering what had happened to Geoffrey and his Lola, when Finch came on to the terrace to tell Fay that Mrs. Chudleigh had called, and would like to see her.

'Oh dear!' said Fay involuntarily; then, recollecting herself, she added: 'Ask her if she will come out on to the terrace, please.'

'Blast and damn!' said Dinah. 'What on earth can she want?'

'Dinah darling!' expostulated Fay.

'That's a lady who's mightily interested in other people's business,' said Guest. 'I can't say I like the type myself.'

'She wants me to give a talk at the Women's Institute,' said Fay. 'I said I'd let her know, only I forgot.'

'Mrs Chudleigh!' announced Finch.

The Vicar's wife stepped briskly out on to the terrace, and sent one of her quick, peering glances round. She looked rather hot and more than a little crumpled in a tussore coat and skirt, and a burnt-straw hat of no particular shape; and she wore in addition to these garments a blue shirt blouse, dark brown shoes and stockings, and a pair of white wash-leather gloves. She shook hands with Fay, nodded to Mrs. Twining and to Dinah, and favoured Camilla with a stiff little bow. 'I'm so sorry to come bothering you, Lady Billington-Smith, but you know I always say I do all my unpleasant tasks on a Monday! It is the Children's Holiday Fund, and I know you are always so good and generous in giving towards it.'

'Don't you ever shirk your unpleasant tasks?' inquired Camilla, with an air of patronage amounting to insolence.

But Camilla was no match for the Vicar's wife. 'No, Mrs. Halliday, never!' replied Mrs. Chudleigh in a steely voice. 'I hope that I should never shirk any duty, however unpleasant.'

'God help us, we're for it again!' murmured Dinah to Stephen Guest.

Camilla was looking a little foolish, and had given a half-laugh, and shrugged her shoulders.

'Do come and sit down over here, Mrs. Chudleigh!' Fay intervened. 'Of course my husband and I are only too glad to subscribe to the Fund.'

Mrs. Chudleigh accepted the chair indicated, which was placed on the outskirts of the group, and said that she must not stop, for that would make her late for lunch. 'And Hilary is so absent-minded that he would never think to begin without me,' she said, her face softening as it always did when she spoke of her husband. 'I really only came to beg, and to ask you whether you are going to address us on Friday? You said you might give the Women a little talk on Gardens, and I'm sure it would be much appreciated. Only when you did not let me know,' she added with a significant look, 'I wondered whether perhaps you have rather too much on your hands just now?'

Fay coloured. 'No, I should be pleased to speak, if you think it would interest the Club. But you know I'm not very good at giving lectures.'

'Then we shall consider that settled,' said Mrs. Chudleigh, ignoring the last part of this speech. 'I see you still have some of your guests remaining with you. You will be glad, I expect, to have the house to yourself again. If you will allow me to say so, you are not looking at all the thing, Lady Billington-Smith.'

'I have a slight headache,' acknowledged Fay. 'The week-end has been – a little trying, as I'm afraid you were made to realize on Saturday.'

'That dreadful young woman!' Mrs. Chudleigh said, drawing in her breath sharply. 'I assure you I felt for you. A very difficult situation to deal with. I take the greatest interest in *every* member of Hilary's Parish, high or low, and I have been most distressed to think of Geoffrey, who is such a *nice* boy, being caught by – really, I must say an adventuress! But you know, Lady Billington-Smith, young people, and especially what I call highly-strung young people, sometimes need very careful handling. You must forgive me, but from what Sir Arthur said at the dinner-table I gathered that he was very much enraged.'

'Yes,' Fay said, helpless under this flood of words. 'My husband is very angry indeed.'

Mrs. Chudleigh shifted her chair rather closer. 'How very unfortunate! I was afraid it must be so. I suppose there is no truth in the story that is going round the village that it has actually come to an open breach?'

Fay's heart sank. She said rather feebly: 'I can't imagine how such a story could have got about.'

'You know what servants are,' replied Mrs. Chudleigh darkly.

'Always ready to gossip! The baker's man told my cook that *your* kitchen-maid had told *him* that the General had quarrelled *violently* with Geoffrey this morning. Of course, personally, I never pay any heed to what servants say, but I feel I know you so well, Lady Billington-Smith, that it is really my duty to let you know what is being said. And if there is no truth in it, I shall be only too *glad* to contradict the story whenever I hear it.'

A nerve in Fay's head was throbbing unbearably. She got up. 'Mrs. Chudleigh, I'm afraid I can't discuss the matter with you. Geoffrey has very seriously angered his father. I don't know what is going to come of it, so I'm not in a position to tell you anything. You must forgive me if I seem rude, but I – I am a little upset.'

Dinah, obedient to a signal from Stephen Guest, who had been watching Fay with a troubled frown, turned her head, saw her sister's look of exhaustion, and promptly went to the rescue. 'What is this club that Fay's going to lecture to, Mrs. Chudleigh?' she inquired, sitting down in Fay's vacated chair. 'I'd no idea she could lecture!'

She listened to Mrs. Chudleigh's explanation with an air of intelligent interest, and heard not one word of it. Basil Halliday had just come out of the billiard-room, and was approaching the group with his hands thrust into his coat pockets, and his lined face rather pale and set. He jerked a bow to Mrs. Twining, and sat down near to her. Dinah saw him look at his wife for an instant, and then away again.

'I wondered what had become of you,' Camilla remarked.

'I've been indoors,' he said curtly.

Heavens, what a party! thought Dinah. It only needs Geoffrey doing his highly-strung act to make it complete. Even Lola would be a relief.

Stephen Guest was feeling in his pockets. Halliday said mechanically: 'Tobacco? I've got some.'

Guest got up, shaking his head. 'Thanks, I think I'll fetch my own, if you don't mind.' He went into the house, and Dinah thought, with an inward grin: Getting too much for poor old Stephen; really, it's more like a home for mental cases than a house-party.

Mrs. Chudleigh's voice recalled her wandering attention. 'Your sister looks far from well, Miss Fawcett.'

'Anyone who had to live with my brother-in-law would look far from well,' said Dinah with incorrigible outspokenness.

'The General is not an easy man to manage, of course. Naturally we all know that. I am afraid this distressing affair of Geoffrey's has been too much for your sister.'

'Well,' said Dinah, of intent, 'it's a fairly rotten position for her, isn't it? Geoffrey isn't her son, and she can't do anything to stop Arthur disowning him, and everybody who doesn't know her – not people like you, of course – will at once think that she's been doing the wicked stepmother.'

'It is a pity,' said Mrs. Chudleigh, 'that Lady Billington-Smith is so much *younger* than the General.'

'I entirely agree with you,' said Dinah cordially.

Mrs. Chudleigh folded her lips in a rigid line, and rose. Fay, observing her, said: 'Oh, must you go, Mrs. Chudleigh? Won't you stay and join us in a cocktail?'

'Thank you, I never touch anything before dinner-time, and then very rarely,' replied Mrs. Chudleigh forbiddingly. 'Now please do not dream of coming with me! Perhaps you will send me your subscription to the Fund, for I should not think of troubling you to give it to me when you are busy entertaining your guests. Dear me, it is actually half past twelve already! I must indeed hurry if I am not to keep Hilary waiting. Really, there is no need for you to go with me, Lady Billington-Smith. I will take the garden way, if I may, and that will save going through the house. *Good*-bye, I hope your headache will be better soon – though I do not think that I should recommend *cocktails* as a cure!' She smiled rather acidly, bowed to the rest of the company, and went off down the steps to the lawn, and across it to the path that led to the drive.

Camilla Halliday barely waited until she was out of hearing before she said: ' "For this relief much thanks"! I'm sorry for poor old Hilary.'

Mrs. Twining looked her over. 'You need not be,' she said calmly. 'Emmy Chudleigh is entirely devoted to her husband.'

Camilla reddened angrily under this second snub she had received in less than half an hour. Luckily Finch came on to the terrace at that moment with a tray of cocktails, which diverted her attention. Mrs. Twining, having disposed of Camilla to her satisfaction, turned to Basil Halliday, and in the blandest manner started to talk to him. Fay lay back in her chair with her eyes half shut, and Dinah, feeling that Camilla had been harshly, though justly, used, asked her how she managed to tan so evenly. This being a conversational gambit after Camilla's own heart, she at once revived, and became most voluble. Within the space of ten crowded minutes Dinah learned just how one could acquire that particular shade of golden-brown so much admired; what oil to use, and what to avoid; how one sunbathed on the Riviera; and which shade of lipstick one ought to use when the tanning process was completed.

Then Stephen Guest reappeared, and Camilla at once transferred her attention to him. 'You're very nearly too late for a cocktail!' she said. 'Come and sit down beside me. Are you going on the three-ten like us, or are you one of the idle rich, with a car?'

'No, I don't run a car,' he replied. 'I shall be on the train all right.' He stretched out his hand towards the table and picked up his glass.

'Hullo, have you cut yourself?' inquired Halliday, leaning forward in his chair.

Guest glanced quickly down at his hand. There was a smear of blood on his shirt-cuff. 'Yes,' he replied. 'That's what kept me. I was opening one of those darned tobacco tins. I got the lid stuck, and like a fool tried to tear the top off.'

'Oh, I know! aren't they awful?' said Camilla. 'You mean the sort you have to twist round, to cut that stupid tin-stuff? Have you put anything on it? You ought to paint it with iodine, you know. I have a friend who got a septic hand through just that sort of thing. Do let me look at it!'

'It's nothing,' Guest said, pulling down his cuff.

Fay had opened her eyes. 'Stephen, have you really hurt yourself? Do please put something on it! Let me see!'

Guest drank his cocktail and set the glass down again. 'Shucks, Fay! as we say out west. It's only a scratch.'

Mrs. Twining glanced at her watch. 'Fay, my dear, it is very nearly one o'clock, and high time Arthur was made to emerge from his monk-like seclusion. I will take my courage in both hands and beard him in his den.' She rose as she spoke, smiled reassuringly at Fay's doubtful look, and went into the house.

Stephen Guest moved over to a chair beside Dinah. 'I gather she means to try her hand on Arthur?' he said in an undertone.

'Yes, that's why she came,' Dinah replied. 'Heroic attempt, but I don't myself think she'll get much change out of him.'

'No, I should say she wouldn't,' said Guest in his deliberate way.

Mrs. Twining was not absent for long. In little more than five minutes she had returned, and stood in the window, very white and breathing unevenly. 'Fay ... Mr. Guest ... !'

Guest got up quickly, looking at her with narrowed eyes. 'Is anything the matter, Mrs. Twining? You look kind of queer.'

'Yes,' she said faintly. 'I feel – a little sick. Arthur ... I went into the study ... Arthur is there – dead.'

'*Dead?*' The shocked cry came from Fay.

Mrs. Twining moistened her lips. 'Murdered!' she said. She took a step forward, putting out her hand to grasp a chair back, and they saw that her glove was wet with blood.

CHAPTER SIX

FOR a moment no one moved or spoke. Then Stephen Guest broke the startled silence. 'Dinah, look after Fay,' he said, and strode past Mrs. Twining to the window.

'I'll come with you,' Halliday said, in a queer, strangled voice. As he brushed by her chair he heard his wife stammer: 'But who— Oh, it's too awful! I don't believe it!'

Finch was just coming out of the dining-room when the two men crossed the hall. Guest said: 'There's been some kind of an accident, Finch. You'd better come along.'

The butler laid down the tray he was carrying. 'An accident, sir? I hope not Mr. Geoffrey, sir?'

'No. Sir Arthur,' replied Guest, walking towards the study door.

It was shut, just as it had been all the morning. He opened it, and went in.

The room seemed very quiet. The General was seated at his desk. He had fallen forward across it, with his head on the blotting pad, and one arm stretched out over a litter of bills and invoices. The other hung limply at his side. A curious Chinese dagger lay on the floor by the chair, its blade sticky with blood. There were no signs that any struggle had taken place. The room, a square, severely furnished apartment, was almost painfully tidy. A saddle-bag chair stood beside the empty fireplace; some bookshelves of the expanding variety filled one wall; there was a small safe behind the door, and, next to it, a filing cabinet. The desk stood in a central position, facing the French windows looking on to the drive. These stood open, apparently of design, since each half was bolted to the floor to prevent slamming in any sudden draught. On the west wall another long window was securely fastened, the dun-coloured net curtains being drawn apart to admit the maximum amount of light to the room. The General was sitting in a swivel chair with a low rounded back, and placed against the wall were one or two straight chairs with leather seats. There was a Turkey carpet on the floor, and several trophies hanging on the walls. The desk itself was a large, knee-hole writing-table, with drawers. An electric reading-lamp with a green shade stood on it, the telephone, a brass ink-stand, a blotter, a sheaf of accounts, a couple of pens, and a pencil which seemed to have slipped from the General's fingers. On the floor, within reach of the General's hand, was a waste-paper basket, half-full of torn and crumpled sheets of paper.

All three men had paused for an instant in the doorway. The butler said in a hushed voice: 'Good God, sir!' He went forward with Guest, and bent over his master's still form. 'Sir Arthur!' Then he raised his head, and looked from Guest to Halliday. 'Stabbed!' he said, as though the thing were barely credible.

'Yes,' said Guest unemotionally. 'Stabbed in the neck – with this, I guess.' He bent to pick up the dagger at his feet.

'Don't touch that!' Halliday said quickly. He had not moved from the doorway, where he had stood transfixed, staring at the General's body, but he took a quick step forward now and caught Guest's arm. 'There may be finger-prints.'

Guest straightened himself. 'I was forgetting. You're right.'

'Are you sure he's dead? Can't we do anything?' Halliday demanded shakily. 'This is too ghastly!' He put out his hand, hesitated for the fraction of a minute, and then resolutely laid it over the slack one lying on the desk. 'He's not cold.'

'He's dead all right,' Guest answered.

The butler, who was looking rather pale, but still quite composed, moved across to the windows, and carefully shut and bolted them and drew the net curtains across. He pulled a handkerchief from his pocket and passed it over his face.

'Feeling queer?' Guest asked.

'No, sir. Thank you. It gave one rather a turn for the moment. It seems so sudden. Quite unexpected, as one might say. I take it, sir, you will be ringing up the police station?'

'I suppose we ought to do that at once,' Guest answered, and picked up the instrument.

'I say, this is an appalling business!' Halliday said. 'Of course the police must be sent for, but I'm thinking of Lady Billington-Smith.'

'Pardon me, sir, but has her ladyship been apprised of the – the accident?'

'Good God, yes! everyone knows. It was Mrs. Twining who found him.'

'Oh dear, dear!' said Finch. 'It is not, if I may say so, a sight for a lady.'

Stephen Guest was speaking into the mouthpiece of the telephone. 'I'm speaking from the Grange, from General Sir Arthur Billington-Smith's ... Yes. There has been an accident ... Yes, to the General. He's dead ... No, not a natural death ... You'll be up right now? ... All right.'

'What are we to do?' Halliday asked. 'We can't leave him like this!'

'I think, sir, if I were to lock the door of this room it would be the best thing,' said Finch. 'With your permission I will do so, and keep the key until the police arrive.'

'Yes, you'd better,' agreed Guest. He cast a cursory glance down at the dead man. 'Nothing for us to do here. We'd better be getting back to the women-folk.'

At that moment a bell shrilled in the distance. Finch frowned slightly. 'I think that is the front door, sir. If you will come now I will lock the room up before I answer the door.'

'Never mind about that yet. Go and get rid of whoever it is,' Halliday said.

The butler looked at him. 'Yes, sir. If you will excuse me, I should prefer to see all locked up first.'

Guest walked across to the door and took out the key, which was placed on the inside. 'All right, Finch. I'll lock up,' he said briefly.

'Very good, sir,' Finch said, and went out.

'Give me the key!' said Halliday. 'I'll do it. You get back to Lady Billington-Smith.'

Stephen Guest fitted the key in again on the outside of the door. 'That's all right. I shouldn't keep on looking at him, if I were you. Not a nice sight.'

'No,' Halliday said with a shudder. 'Horrible!'

Finch came back and addressed himself to Guest. 'It is Dr.

Raymond, sir, come to see her ladyship. I was wondering whether we should not inform the doctor of what has happened?'

'Yes, by all means,' Guest answered. 'Is he in the hall? I'll go out and speak to him.'

The doctor was a burly man of about forty, with a cheerful manner and twinkling blue eyes. He was just pulling off his driving gloves when Guest came out of the study.

Guest said: 'Good morning, doctor. My name's Guest. Would you mind coming into the study a moment?'

'Certainly,' said Dr. Raymond, looking somewhat surprised. 'But I came to see Lady Billington-Smith. Is anything wrong?'

'Yes,' said Guest bluntly. 'Sir Arthur has just been discovered, dead.'

The doctor's smile vanished. 'Sir Arthur *dead*? Good heavens! I'll come at once.'

When he stood inside the study and saw the General's body, his face changed. He shot one quick, searching look from Guest to Halliday, and then went up to the desk and bent over the still form there. He glanced up, and said in a curt, impersonal voice: 'Do you know when this happened?'

'We're rather expecting you to tell us that,' replied Guest.

Dr. Raymond lifted the General's hand gently and tested the reflex action of the fingers. The three other men stood silently waiting for him to finish his brief examination. Presently he straightened himself. 'Have the police been notified?'

'As soon as it was discovered,' replied Guest.

Halliday moved away from the door. 'Have you formed any opinion as to when it could have been done, doctor?' he asked.

'It would be very hard to say with any exactness,' the doctor answered. 'Certainly within the last hour. Now if I may I should like to wash my hands, and then I think I had better see Lady Billington-Smith. She knows, of course, of this – tragedy?'

'Yes, she knows,' Guest said. 'Halliday, you might take the doctor along to the cloakroom. Nothing further you want to do here, doctor? Then Finch can shut the room up.'

Halliday took him aside a moment. 'Look here, Guest, hadn't you or I better take the key? I mean – one can't be too careful, you know.'

'I don't fancy you need worry about Finch,' said Guest. 'Still, you may be right. Doctor, will you take charge of the key till the police come?'

Outside they met Dinah, who had just come out of the drawing-room, looking rather pale but otherwise herself. 'I say, this is pretty ghastly, isn't it?' she said. 'Mrs. Twining's been telling us how she found him. What has got to be done? Can I help at all?'

'Keep everybody quiet,' recommended Stephen. 'This is Doctor— Don't think you told me your name, doctor?'

Dinah's face lightened. 'Oh, good! My sister's feeling pretty bowled over, Dr. Raymond, and I should think a strong brandy-and-soda wouldn't do Mrs. Twining any harm. In fact, that's what I came to get.'

'I'll see Lady Billington-Smith in one moment,' Raymond promised. 'You're Miss Fawcett, I expect? If you'll lead the way, Mr. – Halliday, isn't it? – I can just have a wash.'

Dinah waited until he and Halliday had gone; then she turned to Guest again. 'Stephen, this is going to be awful,' she said. 'It'll mean the police, won't it?'

' 'Fraid so,' Guest replied. 'It'll mean, unless I'm much mistaken, that no one will be catching that three-ten up to town. Think you can cope with the women?'

Finch gave a discreet cough. 'If I might make a suggestion, sir, I could serve luncheon quietly in the dining-room now, for the visitors.'

'It seems rather ghoulish,' said Dinah dubiously. 'Still – I suppose, one's got to eat, and anyway it would get Lola and Camilla out of the way.'

'Has Lola come down yet?' inquired Guest.

A reluctant grin destroyed Miss Fawcett's gravity. 'Yes, she has. I don't want to be flippant, but – but she's being rather good value. Only, of course, very trying for Fay. She seems to have made up her mind to be arrested for the crime. Camilla's merely hysterical. What I can't make out is where Geoffrey has got to. There's no sign of him, and it's already half past one.'

Halliday and the doctor came back at that moment, and Dinah broke off to conduct Dr. Raymond into the drawing-room.

Fay was seated beside Mrs. Twining on the sofa, her hands clenched nervously together in her lap, her eyes unnaturally wide, as though she had caught a glimpse of some horror. Mrs. Twining, on the other hand, was as composed as ever, if a little white. Camilla Halliday was wrenching at a handkerchief, saying over and over again: 'I can't *believe* it! I simply can't believe it!' Lola, seated in a high-backed arm-chair, was looking bright-eyed and heroic. As the doctor came in, she was saying with great complacency: 'For me this is an affair extremely terrible. It is known that the General – whom, however, I forgive, for I am a very good Christian, I assure you – has been most cruel to me. Certainly the police must ask themselves if it is not I who have stabbed the General.'

Fay gave a shiver, but her fixed stare into space did not waver.

'Here's Dr. Raymond,' Dinah said, taking charge of the situation. 'Mrs. Halliday, Lola – will you come into the dining-room now? Dr. Raymond would like to see my sister alone, and – and – I think Finch is serving lunch.'

'Lunch!' Camilla cried wildly. 'How can you be so awful? I should be sick if I had to *look* at food!'

Mrs. Twining got up. 'Nonsense!' she said. 'You must try not to let your feelings run away with you, Mrs. Halliday, and to help as much as you can by behaving quite normally.' She exchanged a somewhat forced smile with Dr. Raymond, and led the way to the door.

Before she had time to open it, a cry from Lola stopped her. 'Ah, *Dios!*' Lola exclaimed, and pointed dramatically to the window.

Geoffrey stood there, looking hot and dishevelled and nerve-ridden.

'Geoffrey! Where on earth have you been?' said Dinah involuntarily.

He passed a hand across his brow. 'What's that got to do with you?' he said. 'I don't know. Miles away.' He became aware of their eyes staring at him, and said sharply: 'What are you all looking at me for? It's nothing to do with you where I've been, is it?'

Dr. Raymond stepped up to him, and took him by the arm. 'Steady, young man. You're a bit over-done. Sit down. Something rather shocking has happened. Your father has been – well, murdered, I'm afraid.'

Geoffrey looked blankly up at him. 'What? Father's been *murdered*?' He blinked rather dazedly. 'Are you going potty? I – you don't *mean* it, do you?' He read the answer in the doctor's face, and suddenly got up. 'Good God!' he said. His mouth began to quiver; to their dismay he started to giggle, in helpless, lunatic gusts.

'*Well!*' Camilla gasped. 'I *must* say!'

'Stop that!' Raymond said harshly. 'Stop at once, Geoffrey: do you hear me? Now control yourself! Quite quiet!'

'Oh, I c-can't help it! Oh God, d-don't you s-see how f-funny it is?' wailed Geoffrey. 'Your f-*faces*! Oh, d-don't make me laugh!'

Dinah vanished from the room, to reappear in a few moments with the brandy decanter and a glass. The doctor and Mrs. Twining were standing over Geoffrey, who had grown quieter, but who was still shaking with idiotic mirth.

Dr. Raymond looked up. 'Ah, thanks. Not too much – yes, that's enough. Now Geoffrey, drink this.' He put the glass to Geoffrey's lips, and almost forced the spirit down his throat.

Geoffrey coughed and spluttered. The laughter died. He looked round the room, and moistened his lips. 'Sorry. I don't know what happened to me,' he said in an exhausted voice. 'Hul – hullo, Aunt Julia! What are you doing here? Who murdered Father?'

'We don't know, my dear,' Mrs. Twining said quietly. 'Dinah, if you'll take Mrs. Halliday and Miss de Silva into lunch, I think I'll stay here till Geoffrey feels more himself.'

Dinah promptly held open the door for the other two to pass out. Under her compelling gaze they did so, but once in the hall Camilla gave a shudder, and declared her inability to pass the study-door. She was with difficulty induced to overcome this shrinking, and entered the dining-room in the end grasping Dinah's arm.

Both Guest and Halliday were seated at the table. Guest was stolidly eating cold beef and Halliday, opposite to him, was making a pretence of eating. They rose as the three women entered the room, and Guest pulled out a chair from the table. 'That's right,' he said. 'Come and sit down, Mrs. Halliday.'

Camilla disregarded him, but made a clutch at her husband. 'Oh, Basil, isn't it awful? I feel absolutely frightful! What will the police do? Will they want to see me?'

Basil Halliday removed her hand from his coat sleeve. 'There's nothing for you to feel frightful about, Camilla. It hasn't got anything to do with you. Sit down, and pull yourself together.'

Camilla burst into tears. 'You n-needn't talk to me in that un-kind way!' she sobbed. 'You don't seem to realize how upset I am. I mean, I was only *with* him a little while ago. What will the police ask me? I don't know *anything* about it!'

'Of course not. We neither of us know anything. All we have

to do is to answer any questions perfectly truthfully,' said Halliday, putting her into a chair. 'That's right, isn't it, Guest?'

'I should think so,' Guest replied. 'Can't say I know much about the procedure.'

Miss de Silva eyed Camilla austerely. 'I do not find that there is reason for you to weep,' she announced. 'If I do so that is what may be easily understood, since Sir Arthur was the father of Geoffrey. But I do not weep, because I have great courage, and, besides, I do not choose that my eyes should be red. There will be reporters, and one must think of these things, for it is a very good thing to have one's picture in all the papers – though not, I assure you, with red eyes.'

This speech had the effect of stopping Camilla's rather gusty sobs. She said: 'I can't think how you can be so callous! And please don't ask me to eat anything, because I simply couldn't swallow a mouthful!'

'Just a little chicken, madam,' said Finch soothingly at her elbow, and put a plate down before her.

Dinah had seated herself beside Stephen Guest, and was mechanically eating a morsel of chicken. It seemed curiously tasteless, and rather difficult to swallow. She felt as though she were partaking of lunch in an unpleasant nightmare, where everything was topsy-turvy, and familiar people said and did ridiculous things that surprised you even in your dream. She asked, 'Have the police come?' and thought at once how odd that sounded, quite unreal, as unreal as the thought of Arthur, murdered in his own study. It was the sort of *macabre* thing that happened to other people, and was reported in the evening papers, making you wonder whatever they could be like who got themselves into such extraordinary cases. Things like this just didn't happen in one's own family. It was no good repeating to oneself that it *had* happened; one just couldn't realize it.

'Yes, they arrived about five minutes ago,' Guest was saying. 'Four of them. They're in the study now. They'll want to interview Fay first, I expect. Is she very upset?'

'Well, naturally it's a frightful shock,' Dinah said. 'I've left Dr. Raymond and Mrs. Twining with her. She seems more stunned than anything. Geoffrey's there too,' she added.

Camilla raised her head. 'I never saw anything *like* the way Geoffrey took it!' she announced. 'It takes a lot to shock me, but I

72

must say that about finished me. He just *laughed*! However badly he'd quarrelled with poor Sir Arthur I should have though he could at least have *pretended* to be sorry.'

'Hysteria?' inquired Guest, lifting his brows.

'I'm sure I don't know. All I can say is that he came in looking quite wild. I was absolutely terrified. I thought he'd gone mad or something.'

'It is for Geoffrey a good thing that his papa is killed,' said Lola thoughtfully. 'Naturally I cannot marry him when he has no money, but that is quite different now, and he will have a great deal of money, and also he will be Sir Geoffrey, which I find is better than Mister; more distinguished.'

'Sorry,' said Dinah, 'but Arthur wasn't a baronet. Geoffrey will have to go on being Mister.'

Miss de Silva appeared to be much chagrined by this piece of information, and slightly indignant. 'I should prefer that I should be Lady Billington-Smith, like your sister,' she said firmly. 'I do not understand why Geoffrey is not to be Sir Geoffrey. It seems to me quite incomprehensible, but perhaps it will be arranged. I will speak to Geoffrey.'

Suddenly Dinah knew that she too was going to break into hopeless laughter. She bit her lip, and tried to choke down the impulse.

The watchful Finch came round the table and poured some wine into her glass. 'A little burgundy, miss,' he whispered.

Dinah gulped it down gratefully. Really, Finch was wonderful: like a sick-room attendant.

Camilla, on whom food and drink seemed to have had a reviving effect, had launched into an exclamatory and rambling discussion of the morning's events with no one in particular. Her husband tried to stop her. 'It's no use asking who could have done it: we can't possibly know,' he said angrily. 'The less we talk about it the better!'

The footman came into the room from the hall, and murmured something in Finch's ear. He was a young man, and looked somewhat scared, as though all these dramatic proceedings were to him a fearful pleasure.

Finch nodded, and went round behind Guest's chair. 'The Superintendent would like to see you now, sir,' he said in a low voice. 'In the morning-room, sir.'

Dinah, overhearing, was irresistibly reminded of a dentist's

73

waiting-room. Your name was spoken in a sepulchral voice, and out you went, feeling a little sick at the pit of your stomach.

Stephen Guest was not long gone. He came back into the room after perhaps ten minutes, and nodded to Halliday. 'They want you next,' he said. 'Just taking statements. Apparently they can't do much till the Chief Constable turns up from Silsbury. I understand he's bringing the police surgeon along with him.'

Halliday got up jerkily, and went out.

'What did they say? Will they want to see me? Do they know who did it?' asked Camilla.

Guest picked up his table-napkin and sat down again. He glanced rather contemptuously across at Camilla, and replied briefly: 'Not yet. I expect they'll want to see everyone.'

'Where's Fay?' asked Dinah. 'Have they finished with her yet?'

'She's gone up to her room. They saw her first, I think. I spoke to Mrs. Twining. She said Fay wanted to be alone. Going to lie down, and would rather no one came up. I'm afraid there's no chance of any of us getting away today. Will that affect you, Miss de Silva?'

'At the moment, and because I choose, and not at all for any other reason, I rest,' said Lola with dignity. 'Certainly I do not go away, but I think it will be better if I change this frock that I am wearing, for it is green, as you see, and I am quite of the family, so that I must put on a black dress. And I remember that I brought with me a black dress that is extremely chic, moreover.'

'As a matter of fact, I was wondering what one ought to wear,' said Camilla. 'I mean, it doesn't seem quite right to be going about in colours, does it? Only I simply never wear black, and I can't say I want to buy anything, because it isn't as if it would be the least use to me afterwards, you see.'

Dinah felt herself to be incapable of entering into this discussion, and turned instead to Guest, who was spreading butter on a cheese biscuit in a leisurely way that seemed rather incongruous. 'Have they found out anything, Stephen?' she asked softly.

'I don't know,' he replied. 'They aren't giving much away.'

Dinah sighed, wishing that he would be a little less laconic. In a moment or two Halliday came back into the room. He said in an unnaturally calm voice: 'They want you, Camilla. You've got to tell them just what you were doing this morning, you know. It's only to check up on your movements, so don't get fussed and say a whole lot of things that aren't in the least relevant.'

'Oh, Basil, I wish you'd come with me!' said Camilla. 'Won't they let you? I simply hate going alone. I know they'll ask me all sorts of questions I don't know anything about.'

'Then say you don't know! For God's sake don't behave as though you were frightened!' he said roughly. 'There's nothing at all for you to be frightened of, I keep on telling you!' He held the door for her to pass out, and shut it behind her with a snap. He came back to his chair, and reached out a hand for his tumbler. 'This is a bit serious for me,' he said. 'I suppose you know I seem to have been the last person to have seen Sir Arthur alive?'

Dinah stared at him in surprise. Lola, who was carefully peeling a peach, paid no heed. Stephen Guest folded up his napkin. 'No, I can't say I did know,' he replied. 'Well, I was,' Halliday said. 'As a matter of fact I had – not exactly a row with him, but – well, call it a disagreement. One doesn't quarrel with a man in his own house; that goes without saying. It's rather unfortunate, as things have turned out.' He glanced across the room to where Finch was standing. 'I understand you heard me talking to Sir Arthur, Finch. You seem to have given the police the impression that we had a violent row.'

'That was not my intention, sir,' replied the butler gently. 'When I was asked if I had heard anyone with Sir Arthur at any time between twelve o'clock and one, I could not do less than tell them the truth.'

'You needn't have told them we were quarrelling,' said Halliday. 'It was no such thing. However, it doesn't really matter, only that it puts me into rather an awkward position.'

'I am extremely sorry, sir,' said Finch.

Camilla came back looking flustered. 'Thank goodness that's over!' she said. 'They want you now, Miss de Silva. Basil, if we aren't allowed to go home we'd better see about our things being unpacked again. I must say, I can't see why we should have to stay here. It's getting absolutely on my nerves, having all these policemen hanging about. There's one in the hall now. I suppose they're afraid we shall try to escape!'

'I seem to be reserved for the last,' remarked Dinah, when the Hallidays had gone. 'I do wish they'd hurry. I want to go up to Fay.'

'I fancy, miss, that you will not be required to make a statement,' said Finch, coming to her elbow with the coffee-tray. 'I understand that you were on the terrace the entire time.'

'Yes, I suppose I was,' reflected Dinah. 'Does that mean I'm not a suspect?' Even as she said the words she wished that she had not. She got up. 'I'll take my coffee upstairs with me. I think this is all getting rather beastly. I hadn't thought of that before. Not even when Mr. Halliday told us about being the last to see Arthur. It didn't seem to mean anything in particular, somehow. I suppose every one of us is more or less under suspicion.'

'I shouldn't worry, if I were you,' said Guest, opening the door. 'Don't let Fay worry either. See?'

The afternoon was surely the most interminable ever spent at the Grange. It seemed to Dinah as though it would never end. The feeling of unreality grew. Fay remained shut in her room, and would admit no one; the Hallidays had also chosen to stay upstairs. Dawson was sobbing noisily as she went about her work. Geoffrey seemed unable to sit still; and Stephen, who sat perfectly quietly in the billiard-room and read the paper, seemed just as unnatural by reason of his very calm. Lola, after a protracted interview with the dazed but suspicious Superintendent, had announced that it was important that she should rest between lunch and tea, and had gone upstairs for that purpose. Mrs. Twining remained in the drawing-room with Geoffrey, and Dr. Raymond had been permitted to depart as soon as his statement had been carefully transcribed.

The Chief Constable, Major Grierson, arrived just before half past three in a large car with the Divisional Surgeon, a sergeant in plain clothes, and a photographer. He was a worried-looking man of about fifty, with a quick, fussy way of talking, and what appeared to be a chronic catarrh. He kept on dabbing at his thin nose with a ball of a handkerchief, and his conversation was punctuated by sniffs. He was met by the local Superintendent, and by Dinah, who happened to be in the hall when he arrived. He said: 'This is a terrible business. Shocking, shocking! Knew the General quite – er – well. You're his sister-in-law? Quite. Now Superintendent, if you are ready . . . !'

He, and the doctor, the photographer, and the plain-clothes man, who turned out to be the finger-print expert, all followed the Superintendent into the study, and remained there for a very long time.

At half past four Fay came downstairs. She had changed into a black frock, which had the effect of enhancing her pallor. Her eyes still had that strained, dilated look, as though they were haunted, but her manner was carefully controlled. She took her usual place behind the tea-tray, and said with an effort: 'It was nice of you to stay, Julia. I'm afraid it has all been very – very horrid for you. I find I can't quite realize it yet. It doesn't seem to be *possible,* somehow. Have they – have they finished yet? Did they find anything to show – to give them any clue, do you know? I feel so certain myself that it must have been someone from outside. The windows were open, after all, and – Arthur made a great many enemies. Don't you think so, Julia? Don't you, Dinah?'

Geoffrey set down his cup and saucer with an unsteady hand. 'I suppose you mean you think I did it?' he said. 'Well, it may interest you to know that I wasn't anywhere near the house.'

Fay looked distressed. 'Oh no, no, I didn't mean that!' she said. 'Of course I didn't mean that!' She looked up as Stephen Guest entered the room, and in that fleeting moment Dinah read the dread in her eyes. Then Fay said quietly: 'Ah, here you are, Stephen. I was just going to ask Geoffrey to tell you tea was ready.'

The Hallidays came in at that moment. Camilla had solved the problem of dress, apparently to her satisfaction, by putting on a brown frock instead of the pale blue one she had worn all the morning. She looked as though she had been crying, and seemed rather subdued.

There was nothing subdued about Lola, who presently sailed into the room dressed in the deepest of mourning. Any stranger entering the room would certainly have taken her for the widow, and not Fay. She wore a long, trailing robe of some dead-black material, without any ornament at all, and carried a handkerchief with a deep black hem. Where she could have found such a thing at a moment's notice Dinah could not imagine. She was forced to the conclusion that either it must belong to the faithful Concetta, or the inky border had been hastily stitched to an ordinary white handkerchief.

'I am quite upset,' she announced. 'You can feel how my heart is beating, altogether too fast. I have seen that they have taken away the corpse of Geoffrey's papa. It has made me feel extremely sad, quite overcome. And I must tell you that it is very painful to me that these policemen who stand in the hall should stare at me as though they think it is I who have stabbed Geoffrey's papa. I have told the fat policeman that he cannot at all prove that I am an assassin, but he is, I think, a fool, since he will only open his mouth like a fish, and not answer me when I speak.'

Her auditors were spared the necessity of replying to this address by the entrance of Finch, who came to tell Fay that the Chief Constable would like to speak to her and to Geoffrey.

They both went out, Geoffrey saying: 'I wonder what he wants to see me for? I suppose, though I hadn't thought of it before, that now Father's dead I'm the head of the family. I suppose that's it.'

The Chief Constable was looking more worried than ever. The Superintendent, who was standing beside him, with his thumbs tucked into a belt of quite enormous span, had a profoundly dissatisfied look in his eye, and stared hard at a painting over the fireplace in a glassy way that gave the impression that he had entirely dissociated himself from any subsequent proceedings.

The sight of Fay made Major Grierson dab his nose a great many times in succession. He said: 'Ah, Lady Billington-Smith! Quite. Er – a very bad business. I assure you I – er – feel for you most deeply. Now, Mr. – er – Billington-Smith, we have come to the conclusion, the Superintendent and I – yes, yes, Superintendent! We have come to the conclusion, as I say, that this is a case where it will be – er – advisable to call in Scotland Yard.'

'Scotland Yard?' repeated Geoffrey. 'Do you mean we've got to have detectives down? But I say – I mean, is that absolutely necessary?'

The Superintendent brought his aloof gaze down from *The Fighting Téméraire*, and bent it sternly upon Geoffrey.

Major Grierson's manner became still more impersonal. 'I should not, Mr. Billington-Smith, do anything that was in my – er – opinion unnecessary. Now you will understand, of course, that no one must enter the room where the – er – in short, the study. Quite. The Superintendent will leave two of his men – er – on duty. I understand that you have guests in the house. None of these must leave until after the – er – visit of the Yard Inspector. Yes, Superintendent, what is it?'

'In the matter of Mrs. Twining, sir,' said the Superintendent woodenly, 'who, if agreeable, desires to return to Blessington House, which same being her residence in the vicinity.'

'Mrs. Twining, yes. Well, I think in the case of Mrs. Twining, since she lives close – er – at hand, there would be no objection. She will understand, of course, that she must hold herself in – er readiness to be here to answer any further questions which the Yard Inspector may wish to put to her. Naturally.' He dabbed afresh at his nose. 'And – er – one other matter, Mr. Billington-Smith. The Inspector will want to see the – er – safe in the study opened. That should be done by your – er – late father's solicitor. Perhaps you will arrange for him to – come down for that purpose. I think that is all at – er – present.'

'Yes, but surely it can't be necessary – I mean, it'll be a most awful nuisance having to stay cooped up here with a lot of policemen on guard,' objected Geoffrey. 'I shouldn't have thought it would be so frightfully difficult to find out who murdered Father – not that I'm criticizing, of course, but—'

Fay pressed his hand. 'Geoffrey, if Major Grierson thinks it necessary, of course – of course it must be done,' she said almost inaudibly. 'We – we quite understand, Major. And you want my husband's solicitor to come down. Yes, I – see. Geoffrey, you'll telephone to him, won't you?'

CHAPTER SEVEN

INSPECTOR HARDING, of Scotland Yard, arrived at Ralton shortly before two o'clock on Tuesday afternoon, and drove straight to the police station. Here he was awaited by Superintendent Lupton and Sergeant Nethersole. The Superintendent, who was fifty years of age, with scant grey locks, a red and somewhat fierce face, and a waist measurement of fifty inches, looked forward to Inspector Harding's advent with considerable hostility. It was not that he really wanted to handle this case up at the Grange. He would not go so far as to say that he thought it beyond his powers, but he could see that it was going to mean a lot of work, awkward work too, what with the General having been a big pot in the neighbourhood, and her ladyship giving away the prizes at the Police Sports only a week ago – not that he held with all these sports, and football teams and he didn't know what beside. They hadn't had them in his young days in the Force, and nobody need think he was going to en-courage the young chaps in his division to waste their time over such-like nonsense, because he wasn't. A quiet set-down in a cosy bar with a mug of beer had always been good enough for him in his off-time, and still was, though naturally as you got older you needed more than one mug of beer. But that was neither here nor there, and whether he approved of sports for the police or not, it would be an awkward job handling this case, a very awkward job it would be. But that wasn't to say he wanted one of those sharp Yard chaps poking his nose into everything, and trying to teach him his business. If he saw any signs of uppishness he'd put Mr. Inspector Know-All in his place pretty quick, and no mistake about it.

Sergeant Nethersole, an earnest and painstaking man of thirty-seven, awaited Inspector Harding's arrival with quite different feelings. He was a diffident person, very anxious to make his way in the Force. It had never fallen to his lot to work with the Yard till now, or, in fact, to encounter anything more exciting in his career than a few road accidents, and two cases of burglary. These offered very little scope for a man with ambition, and when he found that he had been detailed to assist Inspector Harding in his inquiries he was very much gratified, and made up his mind closely to observe the methods of detection employed by one of those clever London chaps. He was a large man, with a somewhat wooden face. His round blue eyes had a trick of staring fixedly at any handy object whenever he was thinking particularly deeply. He was slow of utterance, and slower still to wrath. No one could ever remember to have seen Sergeant Nethersole give way even to a momentary annoyance, and, unlike the Superintendent, he never bullied his subordinates.

When the Inspector arrived, and was conducted to the Superintendent's Office, the Sergeant got up out of his chair, and stared at him unwaveringly for quite two minutes. He had not the least desire to offend; he was merely getting to know Inspector Harding. His gaze might appear bovine, but his methodical mind was absorbing a number of facts about the Inspector.

Not at all what he had expected. That was the first thing he thought. One of these public-school men, he rather fancied. You could always tell. A quiet-mannered chap, good steady pair of eyes that looked at you fair and square. I like a chap who can look you in the face, thought the Sergeant, never realizing that there were few with nerves hardy enough to meet unflinchingly his own stare.

He wasn't one of these testy old-stagers, either, nor yet a whipper-snapper. He'd be about his own age, he wouldn't wonder. Just the sort of chap to handle the nobs up at the Grange, being, as you could see, one of the gentry himself. He didn't know how it would be, working with him, he was sure, but on the whole he was bound to say he liked the look of him.

The Inspector walked across the room and shook hands with the Superintendent. 'Good afternoon, Superintendent. I hope I haven't kept you waiting,' he said. Then he turned, encountering the gaze of Sergeant Nethersole, and shook hands with him too, giving back stare for stare.

Well! thought the Superintendent, that's what we're coming to, is it? Nice set-out when they take to sending down la-di-da Percies from the Yard. A fat lot of use he'd be, all stuffed up with a college education, and like as not trying to come the lord over everybody. Not but what he spoke nice enough, quite respectful and polite, but you never knew.

'Well, Inspector Rarding,' he said patronizingly, 'so you've come down to take over the case for us!'

'Not to take it over, surely, Superintendent? I understand that you are in charge of the case.'

The Superintendent's eye became a shade less frosty. 'That's right,' he said. 'Naturally, me being Superintendent of the district, it's my business to have charge of the case. But of course I'm not as young as I was, and me and the Chief Constable, we put our heads together and came to the conclusion that what we wanted was some-one to lend a hand, it being a lot to ask of a man of my years to take on a case like this one single-handed. That's how it is.'

'My instructions are to give you all the assistance I can,' said the Inspector. 'I understand it's rather an awkward case for a local man to deal with.'

Really, that was very handsomely spoken, very handsomely spoken indeed that was. 'Well, that's where it is,' said the Super-intendent, thawing almost visibly. 'It *is* awkward, and that's the truth. Now, what we'd better do is to get down to it right away; you and me, and Sergeant Nethersole here, whom I've detailed to work with you while you're on the case.'

'Right,' said the Inspector, and drew up a chair and sat down.

The tale which the Superintendent began to unfold was neither concise nor easy to be followed, but the Inspector seemed to grasp its main outlines, and except for one or two interruptions when he asked apologetically to have some point more fully explained, he heard it more or less in silence.

The Sergeant, seated with his large hands clasped between his knees, thought: Lupton's getting beyond it, that's what. Fair rigmarole it must be to anyone not acquainted with the General and his family. What's he want to go reading bits out of all them statements for? Jumping from one person to the other without making it plain who any of them are, instead of telling the Inspector, quietlike, the facts of the case, and leaving him to read the statements for himself. Patient sort of chap he seems to be; picks up points pretty quick too.

Inspector Harding allowed the Superintendent to talk himself out. Then he said: 'I see. Let's be sure that I've got the main facts right – I'm afraid the identities of the various people in the case are a bit beyond me at present. General Billington-Smith entered his study at ten minutes to twelve. At five minutes past twelve the butler went through the hall to the front door, and heard what he took to be a quarrel going on between the General and a member of the house-party.'

'Mr. Ralliday,' nodded the Superintendent. 'Unhealthy-looking gentleman, he is. What I call fidgety, if you know what I mean. Very much on the jump, I thought to myself. No occupation, which is fishy, if you look at it that way. Lost his job, if you ask me.'

The Inspector waited until this excursion into the realms of conjecture was over. Then he said: 'And he, I think you said, admits that he did enter the study somewhere about twelve o'clock, and had a disagreement with the General, on a subject which he prefers not to disclose. He doesn't know when he left the study, but thinks he was not there more than a quarter of an hour at the most. He then went up to his room, and joined the rest of the party on the terrace about ten minutes later. So far as you know, he was the last person to see the General alive. A few minutes before one o'clock Mrs. – Mrs.' – he glanced down at one of the many sheets of paper laid before him – 'Mrs. Twining went to fetch the General to join the party on the terrace for a cocktail. According to her story she found him dead at his desk. She bent over him, saw that he had been stabbed, and that there was nothing she could do, and returned to the terrace to break the news. Have I got that right?'

'You've got it right as far as it goes,' replied the Superintendent disparagingly. 'But there's a lot more to it than that, I can tell you. You've left out the movements of all these visitors staying in the house for one thing.'

'Until I've had time to read the statements over carefully I think

I'd better confine myself to the main outline, Superintendent. May I see the doctor's reports?'

The Superintendent hunted through a sheaf of documents, and handed two typewritten sheets of foolscap across the desk. 'Here you are. You'll want to have the photographs too,' he added, producing these.

'Thanks.' Inspector Harding took the prints, and laid them down, without raising his eyes from the report in his hand. He read in silence for a minute or two, while the Superintendent and the Sergeant watched him. Then he looked up. 'I see. He was stabbed from behind as he sat at his desk, with a Chinese dagger used by him as a paper-knife, the knife entering the neck below the right ear, and severing the carotid artery. Death, in the opinion of' – he consulted the first report – 'Dr. Raymond, occurring within a minute, possibly less. No finger-prints?'

The Superintendent shook his head. 'No, that's just what makes it difficult for us. Nowadays people are so knowing, what with story books about murders and I don't know what besides, that they're up to all the dodges. Whoever done this murder took care to wear gloves. That's all this talk of Progress leads to, putting people up to them sort of tricks,' he said bitterly, and opened a drawer in the desk, and extracted from it the Chinese dagger. 'That's it. Exhibit No. 1,' he said. 'Nasty thing to keep lying about, I call it.'

The Inspector took the knife, which was a thin blade set in a carved ivory handle, and held it for a moment in his hand. 'Very nasty,' he agreed, and gave it back.

'Exhibit No. 2,' proceeded the Superintendent, handing over a sheet of note-paper. 'Found under the deceased's hand, like as if he might have written on it just before he died.'

'That's interesting,' said the Inspector.

'Well, I don't know so much about that. The Divisional Surgeon, *he* holds to the opinion that Sir Arthur wouldn't have had time to write anything after the blow was struck. On the other hand, Dr. Raymond thinks that he could. That's what it is with doctors. What with one saying one thing, and another arguing it could have happened different, you never know where you are. And it doesn't seem to me to lead anywhere, that bit of paper. Well, I mean, look at it!'

The Inspector was looking at it. Scrawled in pencil across a half-sheet of engraved note-paper was the word 'There'. There was no more; the faint pencil mark tailed off, as though the pencil had dropped suddenly from nerveless fingers.

'To my mind it doesn't lead anywhere,' grumbled the Superintendent. 'There what? The way I look at it is this: Supposing Sir Arthur was starting out to write something when suddenly he gets stabbed from behind? There's nothing to show he wrote it *after* he'd been stabbed.'

'Except that the word is scrawled crookedly across the paper,' suggested the Inspector. 'I should like to keep this, if I may, Superintendent.'

'Oh, you can have it,' said the Superintendent generously. 'It's about all there is to have, what's more. Not but what something may turn up, because the Chief Constable was very set on having nothing disturbed in the room where the murder took place, so there hasn't been what I call a proper search.'

'I see. And about the position of the study: I understand it is in the front of the house, facing on to the drive?'

'That's right. On the right of the front door as you go in, it is, there being what they call the morning-room behind it, then the stairs, and beyond them the drawing-room, which is a big room along the back of the house, next to the billiard-room.'

'The terrace, I take it, is also at the back of the house? Then the study is at a considerable distance from it? No chance of any noise in the study reaching the ears of anyone on the terrace?'

'Oh dear me, no,' said the Superintendent, with a tolerant smile for one as yet unacquainted with the dimensions of the Grange. 'It's a very big house. What you might call a mansion. Very well off, Sir Arthur was, and did himself proud.'

'And these windows,' pursued the Inspector, consulting one of the photographs. 'Were they open, or shut?'

'Wide open, the front window was. The one on the west side the General never had open, it being right opposite the door, and him not liking a draught. It was the butler shut the windows after the crime was discovered, which, properly speaking, he shouldn't have done.'

'No footmarks outside?'

'No, but that doesn't mean anything either, when you come to think of it. There hasn't been any rain since I don't know when, and the ground's as hard as a rock. 'Tisn't as though there was a flower-bed by the window either. Well, naturally, there wouldn't be, because it's one of them french windows, as you can see for yourself. There's just a bit of grass, and then the drive, which is gravel. Whoever it was that murdered the General might have come in through the window without leaving any trace, or, on the other hand, he might have come in by the door, and no one the wiser.'

'That makes it rather difficult,' said the Inspector. 'Is it known whether the General had any enemies?' He looked up from the photographs as he spoke, and saw that both men's faces had relaxed into broad grins. His own rather grave grey eyes smiled faintly. 'Oh! Have I said something funny?'

'Well, Inspector Rarding, you've pretty well hit the nail on the head, that's what you've done,' said the Superintendent. 'I don't suppose, if you was to search the whole county, you'd find anyone who'd got more enemies than what Sir Arthur had. I don't mind going so far as to say that if you set out to find somebody who'd got a good word to say for him you'd have a job.'

'That's a fact,' corroborated the Sergeant, in a slow, deep voice. 'You'd have a job.'

It was at this moment that the Chief Constable walked into the room.

'Ah, Superintendent, I see the Inspector has – er – arrived. No doubt you have put him in – er – possession of the facts. Inspector Harding, isn't it? Very glad you have got down here, Inspector.'

The Inspector had risen, and turned to face the newcomer. Major Grierson, who had held out his hand, looked at him extremely sharply, and said: 'Dear me, surely we have – er – met before? Your face is very – er – familiar, yet for the moment I cannot exactly call to – er – mind where we have met. Do you, by any chance, remember meeting me?'

'Yes, sir, I remember you perfectly,' answered the Inspector, shaking hands. 'We met in Bailleul.'

'Why, of course, of course!' exclaimed the Major. 'Harding! Dear me! Yes! You were attached to Colonel – er – Mason! Yes, yes! Well, this is a surprise! But what are you doing in the Police Force? You were – wait, I have it! You were reading law at – er – Oxford!'

'The War rather knocked that on the head, sir, so I joined the Police Force instead.'

'Well, well, well!' said Major Grierson.

The Inspector moved to the desk, and put down the photograph he was still holding in his left hand. 'Superintendent Lupton has just been giving me all the facts of this case, sir,' he said. 'It looks like being a bit of a teaser.'

The Major's face clouded over. 'Very bad business. Nasty – er – case, Harding. I felt at once it was – er – a matter for Scotland Yard. Too many people in it. Have you read the – er – statements?'

'Not yet, sir. I was going to suggest to the Superintendent that he should let me take them away with me now, so that I can study them before I go up to the Grange.'

'By all means! Certainly! A very good – er – plan, Superintendent. Don't you – er – agree?'

The Superintendent, who had viewed with disfavour the meeting between the Major and Inspector Harding said that he had no objection, but that in his opinion the sooner the Inspector went up to the Grange the better it would be.

The inspector looked at his wrist-watch. 'Then shall we say in an hour's time? That will make it half past three.'

'Yes, yes, do just as you – er – think best, Harding,' said the Major. 'Where are you – er – putting up?'

'At the Crown, sir, if they have a room,' replied the Inspector.

'You could not do better,' approved the Major. 'I'll put you on your – er – way.'

Outside the police station he button-holed the Inspector in a confidential manner, and warned him that the Superintendent was rather a difficult man to deal with. 'Between ourselves – er – Harding, not quite the man for this – er – business. Naturally – quite realize you must have – er – a free hand. But if you *could* manage to – er – keep on the right side of him, as it were— But I've no doubt you – er – will do your best.'

'I will,' promised the Inspector.

'And when we've – er – finished with this case you must come out and – er – dine with me, and we'll have a yarn. I shan't keep you now. You've got a tough – er – job there. Most unpleasant – er – affair.' He dabbed at his nose. '*Most* unpleasant!' he repeated with conviction.

CHAPTER EIGHT

AT the Grange a peculiar discomfort reigned. From the moment when it had become known that Scotland Yard was to be called in a constraint descended on the house. Until then every one had been either shocked or ghoulishly excited, according to his or her disposition, but with the mention of Scotland Yard a realization of all the implications arising out of the affair was universally felt. An atmosphere of suspicion crept into the house; the murder was very guardedly discussed, and no one, except Miss de Silva, spoke the thought uppermost in mind without first considering whether it were safe.

It struck Dinah, listening to confidences, theories, discussions, that perhaps no one was speaking the whole truth. Every one had something to hide, something to tone down, or to explain away. No one seemed any longer to be quite natural, from Fay, unusually quiet and self-controlled, down to Guest, more taciturn than ever.

The mere mention of Scotland Yard had produced varied emotions. It was easy to see that Fay was dreading what lay before them all, but she would not say so even to Dinah. Geoffrey was easier still to read. He could not leave the subject alone, but harped continually on it, alternately demonstrating the folly of having detectives down, and off-handedly wondering what the detectives would want to know.

Camilla became a little shrill when she heard the news. She said it was ridiculous for anyone to ask her anything because she knew nothing; she could not see why she and Basil could not go home. Suddenly it had become very inconvenient for her to stay at the Grange; she did not think it fair to expect her to put herself out like this, and at once worked herself into an abortive hatred of the Police Force. Panic evidently possessed her shallow brain, and she displayed quite extraordinary vulgarity in the way she gave way to it. Probably, Dinah thought, she was the type of woman who shrieked wildly in moments of emergency.

Basil Halliday occasionally begged her irritably for God's sake to be quiet, but he seemed to have not the smallest influence over her. He himself asserted that he thought it clearly a case for Scotland Yard. It was absurd to make a fuss about it. Why should one mind having to answer a few questions? Yet Dinah felt, watching his twitching brows, that he did mind, perhaps more than his wife.

There was no saying what Stephen Guest thought about it. No hint of emotion disturbed the inscrutability of his countenance when he heard of the Chief Constable's decision. He folded the evening paper open at the middle page with his capable, deliberate fingers, and said: 'I thought they'd call in the Yard.' That was the only comment he made; he did not seem to be much interested.

Lola was also uninterested. She said that Policemen did not matter to her, and it was incredible that only a reporter on the local paper had as yet called at the house seeking a story. With him she would have nothing to do; it would perhaps be better if nothing was told to the newspapers until she had seen her press agent. 'For it occurs to me,' she said seriously, 'that it may not be a good thing to put this in the papers. In France it would be a success of the most enormous, but England I do not know so well, and one must ask oneself whether it will make good publicity for me, or, on the contrary, not good at all, but very bad.'

Lola, unlike Camilla, evinced not the slightest desire to leave the Grange. She even forbore to complain any more of the matutinal habits of cocks, though she did once announce that when she was married to Geoffrey the matter would have to be arranged.

The murder of her host was from her point of view a good thing. Geoffrey would have a great deal of money, which would enable him to marry her, and there need no longer be an inexplicable dearth of absinthe in the house. These conclusions she expressed freely, for, as she very sensibly pointed out, it was good for every one to look on the bright side.

The absinthe was procured for her by Finch, who informed Dinah apologetically that he had taken it upon himself to ring up the wine-merchant. 'For, if I may say so, miss, it will be one worry the less,' he said.

The other matter could not be so easily settled. Geoffrey, Lola discovered, was behaving quite absurdly, and instead of adoring her openly, showed a marked disinclination to be anywhere near her. If she caught his eye he would hurriedly avert his own glance; if she addressed him he answered her in a constrained way, and would immediately begin to talk to someone else. Even the seduction of her beauty failed to rekindle his passion, and when she tried the effect of stealing her arms about his neck at the foot of the staircase on Monday night, and whispering: 'Kiss me. But kiss me, my Geoffrey!' the result had been anything but happy. He had almost violently disengaged himself, saying: 'Don't! Can't you leave me alone? I don't want to touch you!' And then, when she had opened her eyes at such odd behaviour, he had said, in a high-pitched, excited voice: 'Don't keep on talking about marriage! We're not going to be married. You threw me over when you thought I hadn't any money, and I saw what a fool I'd been about you. And it absolutely *killed* my love for you!'

This was very shocking, quite rude of Geoffrey, and extremely annoying besides, since he spoke in such a loud voice that every one must have been able to hear him. For a moment Lola wavered on the brink of a truly magnificent scene. It would be a splendid end to the day, and she would enjoy a quarrel where one screamed abuse, and hurled vases to the ground. But Geoffrey, though excitable, was, after all, English, and probably he would not enter into the spirit of the thing, but instead of shouting too would just walk away, quite disgusted. She curbed herself therefore, and said reproachfully: 'But I find you entirely cruel, my dear Geoffrey. You hurt me very much, I assure you, but I forgive you, because it is seen that you are not at all yourself.'

After that she had gone upstairs to bed and, meeting Dinah on the landing, had asked her when it would be made known how much money Geoffrey would have.

Dinah was unable to enlighten her. Geoffrey had rung up the offices of Tremlowe, Tremlowe, Hanson and Tremlowe as soon as the Chief Constable had departed but Mr. Horace Tremlowe had not returned from a long week-end, and Mr. Gerald Tremlowe hardly expected to see him before eleven o'clock on Tuesday. Geoffrey had somewhat incoherently explained his need of Mr. Horace Tremlowe, and Mr. Gerald, very much shocked, had said Tut-tut-tut, in a perturbed voice, and promised that Mr. Horace Tremlowe, who was both the General's solicitor and executor, would come down to the Grange by the first available train on Wednesday.

During the course of Tuesday morning Finch was kept busy answering the front door. A great many people drove up, and handed in flowers, or a note for Fay. Nearly all these sympathetic callers told Finch how deeply shocked they were; nearly all supposed that Lady Billington-Smith was not yet receiving visitors, and upon having this guess politely confirmed, drove regretfully away.

Mrs. Chudleigh did not call, or leave flowers. She rang up instead, and she was not to be put off by a butler. She said that she would like to speak to Miss Fawcett, please, on an important matter. When Dinah went reluctantly to the telephone the important matter was disclosed. The Vicar, said Mrs. Chudleigh, had made her ring up, since he hesitated to intrude at such a moment, and yet wished to come to see Fay. Spiritual consolation, said Mrs. Chudleigh. Dinah declined it for her sister.

'No doubt you know Lady Billington-Smith's wishes, Miss Fawcett,' said the sharp voice at the other end of the wire. 'Though I must say I should have thought that at such a time— However, I assure you neither my husband nor myself would dream of coming to see your sister unless she expressed a wish to see either of us. No doubt you have been besieged by callers? I know how vulgarly inquisitive people are, and that is why I rang up instead of leaving a note. Of course, I suppose there will have to be an *inquest*?'

'Yes, I'm afraid so,' said Dinah patiently.

'So painful for the family!' said Mrs. Chudleigh. 'I do hope there is no truth in the story that is going about that the police consider it necessary to call in Scotland Yard? I paid not the slightest attention to it when it was repeated to me, but of course you know that Constable Hammond is engaged to Mrs. Darcy's under-housemaid?'

'I didn't know it,' said Dinah, 'But—'

'Well, that is undoubtedly how it leaked out. Naturally I told Mrs. Darcy that I was surprised at her listening to mere gossip like that. I suppose it is quite untrue?'

'No,' replied Dinah. 'It is perfectly true. I'm sure you'll forgive me, Mrs. Chudleigh, but I'm very busy at the moment, and—'

'I *quite* understand!' Mrs. Chudleigh assured her. 'Everything must be at sixes and sevens, I am sure. And so objectionable for you to have detectives in the house. Reporters too!'

'Yes,' said Dinah. 'Foul. I'll tell Fay you rang up, Mrs. Chudleigh. So kind of you! Good-bye!'

Later still Mrs. Twining rang up. She wanted merely to know how Fay was, and Geoffrey, and whether her presence had been needed.

'No, not yet,' Dinah replied. 'The detective hasn't turned up so far. It'll be quite a relief when he does come if you ask me. This waiting about is getting on everybody's nerves. Are you coming over today, Mrs. Twining?'

'I think perhaps I had better,' said Mrs. Twining in her calm way. 'I understood from Fay that I was to hold myself in readiness to answer questions the detective may want to put to me. I am really not very well versed in the etiquette of these affairs. Does a detective come to me, or do I go to him?'

'I don't know,' said Dinah. 'But I wish you would come. We – we rather badly want a normal person here.'

'Then I will drive over this afternoon,' said Mrs. Twining.

At luncheon Camilla announced that she had a splitting head, and was going to lie down all the afternoon, and if the detective did actually come at last it was no use expecting her to see him, because she was feeling far too ill to talk to anybody.

Upon which Lola turned her candid gaze upon her, and said: 'I do not find that there is any reason for a detective to see you. You are not at all important, let me tell you, so its quite foolish for you to create for us any scenes.'

Camilla, pale with anger, said in a trembling voice that she wasn't going to sit there to be insulted, and flounced from the room. After a moment's uncertainty Halliday got up abruptly, and followed her.

'I am quite pleased that they have gone,' said Lola composedly. 'They are not at all sympathetic, and besides I am nearly sure that her hair has been dyed.'

That seemed to dispose of Camilla. No one found strength to make any comment on this speech, and the meal was resumed in depressed silence.

When it was over Dinah took Fay firmly by the hand and led her upstairs to her room. 'You're going to lie down till tea-time, my girl,' she said. 'How much sleep did you get last night?'

'Not very much,' Fay said, with a forced smile. She let Dinah help her to slip off her frock, and huddled herself into a dressing-gown with a little shiver.

Dinah banked up the pillows on the bed, and patted it invitingly. 'Come along, ducky. You'll feel better if you can manage to put in a little sleep.'

Fay came docilely, and lay down. Her wide eyes stole to Dinah's face for a moment, and then sank. 'Yes, I expect I shall. Dinah—'

Dinah took one of her cold hands. 'What, darling?'

'When the detective comes,' Fay said carefully, 'do you think I need be there? Of course he will want to see me; I quite realize that. But do you think I need receive him? Could you be there instead? Geoffrey isn't much good, and – and I expect he'll want someone, won't he?'

'I haven't the foggiest notion,' said Dinah, 'but I'll be there all right. Don't you worry about it!'

'Thank you,' Fay said.

Miss Fawcett withdrew, and went downstairs to the telephone. She had remembered that no one had as yet broken the news to her mother.

Mrs. Fawcett received the tidings characteristically. After her first exclamations of horror and incredulity she said in a faint, injured voice that Dinah should not have told her over the telephone; the shock was too terrible. So Dinah knew then that her parent was enjoying a spell of shattered health, and there would not be the least necessity to dissuade her from instantly coming to Fay's side. Mrs. Fawcett had made attention to her own comfort her primary consideration for so many years that it was extremely doubtful whether anything could break a habit thus firmly embedded. In a plaintive voice that would have led any stranger to suppose her to be on the point of collapse she said that she only wished she could come down at once to be with dearest Fay. Only what, she asked sadly, was the use of her dragging herself on the long, tiring journey when she would have to go to bed the instant she arrived? It would be the sheerest folly, for she was already far from well, and Dinah must surely know how the slightest exertion prostrated her.

Dinah grinned as she put the receiver down at last. Mother will have a glorious time now, she reflected, picturing Mrs. Fawcett already tottering to the nearest sofa. She'll tell all her friends, and say how terrible it is for her to be tied to her couch, when she would give anything to be here with Fay. And she'll do it awfully well, too, thought Miss Fawcett appreciatively, and went to sit on the terrace till the detective should arrive.

It was a long time before he came, and she was once more reminded of the dentist's waiting-room. It seemed very improbable that the murder could be brought home to her, but she had all a female's unreasonable mistrust of policemen, and what she had seen of the Superintendent did not lead her to view the advent of another of his tribe with anything but the most profound foreboding. However, on one point she had quite made up her mind: if this person from Scotland Yard thought he was going to ask her questions in a rude, bullying tone he would find that he had made a great mistake.

By half-past three the feeling of the dentist's waiting-room had grown considerably, and when, at a quarter to four, Finch came to inform Geoffrey, who had joined her on the terrace not long before, that Sergeant Nethersole and the Inspector from Scotland Yard had arrived, Miss Fawcett was aware of a most curious and disagreeable sensation in the pit of her stomach.

'I suppose I'd better see the fellow, hadn't I?' said Geoffrey. 'Not that I can be of any use to him as far as I can see. What's he like Finch?'

'We shall soon see what he's like for ourselves,' said Dinah bracingly. 'Come on, I'll go with you.' She gave Geoffrey's arm a friendly squeeze. 'Don't let yourself get agitated, my child. He can't eat you.'

'Oh, I'm not agitated!' said Geoffrey with a laugh. 'Only I do hope they haven't sent some frightful bounder down. Where have you put him, Finch?'

'I showed him into the morning-room, sir. He seems, if I may say so, a very quiet gentleman.'

'Well, thank God for that!' said Geoffrey, putting up a nervous hand to his tie. 'Come on, Dinah – if you *are* coming!'

There were two men in the morning-room, one dressed in a sergeant's uniform, and the other in a lounge suit that bore the indefinable stamp of a good tailor.

'Inspector Harding, sir,' said Finch, evidently feeling that an introduction was called for.

'Oh – er – good – afternoon, Inspector!' said Geoffrey.

'Good afternoon,' said Harding pleasantly. He glanced towards Dinah, and found that damsel surveying him with patent surprise.

Good lord, he *is* a gentleman! thought Geoffrey. Well, that's something, anyway. He doesn't look such a bad chap, either.

Miss Fawcett, realizing that her frank stare was being returned with a rather amused twinkle, had the grace to blush. She stepped forward, and held out her hand. 'How do you do?' she said politely.

'How do you do, Miss Fawcett,' said Harding, shaking hands with her.

'How on earth did you know I was Miss Fawcett?' asked Dinah, visibly impressed.

'The butler told me that he would fetch Miss Fawcett,' explained Harding gravely.

'Oh!' said Dinah, disappointed. 'I thought you were being hideously clever.'

'No, I'm afraid I wasn't,' said Harding apologetically.

This man, decided Miss Fawcett, is definitely going to be nice.

CHAPTER NINE

INSPECTOR HARDING was listening to Geoffrey, voluble and slightly injured. 'Of course I know you've got to make inquiries,' Geoffrey said, 'but I do hope you'll be as quick as you can, because it's frightfully rotten for my stepmother – I mean, she's had a simply ghastly shock, you know – we both have, if it comes to that – and having the house crammed full of visitors makes it all absolutely foul for us. And naturally they don't want to hang about here either. Personally, I can't see—'

'I shall be as quick as I can be, Mr. Billington-Smith,' said Harding, evidently feeling that this rambling harangue might go on indefinitely. 'I should like first to inspect the study, please, and then perhaps you will let your butler show me the other rooms on this floor.'

'What on earth do you want to see the other rooms for?' asked Geoffrey. 'Of course, you can if you like, but I must say I don't quite see—'

'Thank you,' said Harding. 'I won't keep you any longer now, Mr. Billington-Smith.' He turned to Finch, still standing by the door. 'Will you take me to the study, please?'

'Yes, show the Inspector the way, will you, Finch?' said Geoffrey, 'If you want me just tell Finch, Inspector – not that I can be much use to you, because I didn't happen to be here when my father was murdered, but if you *do* want me—'

'I'll ask Finch to fetch you if I do,' said Harding, and followed the butler out into the hall.

The constable on duty in the study rose from a chair against the wall when the door was opened, and brightened perceptibly when he saw the Sergeant. It was a dull job, keeping guard on an empty room.

The Sergeant told him he could go and wait outside, and then fixed his gaze on the Inspector, standing still by the desk, looking about him.

'Nothing has been moved, Sergeant, I take it?'

'Nothing but what the Superintendent showed you down at the station,' said the Sergeant.

'I see.' Harding turned. 'Just a minute before you go, Finch.

When you entered this room with Mr. Guest and Mr. Halliday, were these windows shut, or open?'

'The front windows were open, sir. Sir Arthur never had the side window open when he sat here. I thought it best to shut them when we locked the room up, in case of anyone trying to come in for any purpose.'

'Had you any reason to think that someone might wish to come into the room?'

The butler hesitated. 'Not then, sir – in a manner of speaking.'

'But later you had?'

'I don't know that I would go so far as to say that, sir, but it did seem to me that Mr. Halliday was not best pleased.'

'What made you think that?' asked Harding.

'Well, sir, I don't know that I could give any definite reason. Mr. Halliday seemed anxious to get the key into his own hands, to my way of thinking.'

Harding looked consideringly at him for a moment. 'Mr. Guest, however, agreed with you that the room should be shut up?'

'Oh yes, sir. It was Mr. Guest who suggested the key should be put into Dr. Raymond's charge.'

'And eventually you all left the room together?'

'Yes, sir.'

'Who did actually lock the door?'

'Mr. Guest, sir. He gave the key to Dr. Raymond at once.'

'Did he or you ascertain that the door was locked?'

'Yes, sir, I did,' replied Finch instantly.

'And there was no possibility that anyone could have unlocked it with any other key than the one belonging to it?'

'No, sir, none. Sir Arthur had all the locks made different when he built the house.'

'I see.' Harding made a note in his pocket-book. 'Will you now arrange the room exactly as you found it when you first came in after the murder, please?'

'You mean the windows, sir? Everything else is just as it was.'

'Yes, the windows.'

The butler moved over to the front windows, pulled back the curtains and drew the bolts, fixing the windows wide. Then he walked over to the other one, and parted the net curtains a little way. 'They were like that, sir.'

'Thank you. Before you go, I should like you to answer one or two questions. First, where did Sir Arthur keep the dagger he used as a paper-knife?'

'Always on the desk, sir.'

'There should be a sheath, I think, matching the handle. I don't see it here?'

'No, sir, the sheath was lost some years ago, when Sir Arthur had the knife abroad with him.'

'Ah! I wondered about that.' Harding drew a sheaf of papers from his breast-pocket, and ran through them till he found the one he wanted. 'You have said that at five minutes past twelve on Monday you overheard voices in this room, one of which you identified as Mr. Halliday's.'

'Yes, sir.'

'You had no doubt that it was Mr. Halliday's voice?'

'No, sir, none. Mr. Halliday has what I might call a very distinctive voice.'

'Did you overhear anything of what was said?'

'No, sir. The doors are very thick in this house, as you can see, and Sir Arthur was speaking at the same time.'

'Angrily?'

'More what one would call blustering, sir. It was Mr. Halliday who was picking the quarrel.'

Harding looked up from his notes. 'You could not distinguish what was said, and yet you can positively assert that it was Mr. Halliday who picked the quarrel. Isn't that rather curious?'

'Perhaps I should not have said quite that, sir. I assumed it was Mr. Halliday who was angry, on account of Sir Arthur's partiality for Mrs. Halliday.'

'Oh. Was this partiality very marked?'

'Very marked, sir. If I may say so, I had expected something in the nature of a quarrel to occur, Mr. Halliday not relishing Sir Arthur's attentions to Mrs. Halliday.'

'You formed the impression that Mr. Halliday was jealous?'

'Oh yes, sir, very much so. Mr. Halliday was always watching Mrs. Halliday and Sir Arthur. It is not my place to say so, but Mrs. Halliday was what I should call flirtatious, leading Sir Arthur on. It was easy to see that Mr. Halliday did not like it.'

Harding nodded, and resumed his perusal of the butler's original statement. 'You did not see Mr. Halliday leave the study. Where did you go when you left the hall?'

'I went to my pantry, sir, till Mrs. Twining came.'

'How long would that be?'

The butler reflected. 'Well, sir, not more than five minutes, I should say, before the front door bell rang.'

'When you went to admit Mrs. Twining did you still hear voices in the study?'

'No, sir, not a sound.'

'And when you had shown Mrs. Twining on to the terrace — where did you go then?'

'Pardon me, sir, but I did not show Mrs. Twining on to the terrace,' said Finch. 'Mrs. Twining said that she would announce herself.'

'Was that usual?'

'In Mrs. Twining's case, quite usual, sir. Mrs. Twining was a very old friend of Sir Arthur's. She had been motoring in an open car, and she wished to tidy her hair before going on to the terrace. There is a mirror in the hall, as you will notice, sir. Mrs. Twining went to look at herself in it, and told me I need not wait.'

'So that you did not see her go out on to the terrace?'

'No, sir, I went straight back to my pantry to mix the cocktails.'

'Was anyone else in the pantry?'

The butler considered for a moment. 'I rather fancy that Charles — the footman, sir — was, as one might put it, between the pantry and the dining-room, laying the table for lunch. But I could not be sure on that point. When the front door bell rang again — it would be only a few minutes later, for I was in the act of cutting the orange for the cocktails — I went back to the hall.'

'Again you heard no sound from the study?'

'No, sir, it was quite quiet.'

'Who had rung the front door bell?'

'Mrs. Chudleigh, sir — the Vicar's wife. I showed her on to the terrace, and then went back to my pantry.'

'Did you go into the hall again after that?'

'Not until I took the cocktail tray out, sir. That would be just after half past twelve, on account of my being interrupted while mixing the cocktails, and so being a few minutes later than I should otherwise have been.'

'And you did not pass through the hall again until one o'clock, when you met Mr. Guest and Mr. Halliday on their way to the study?'

'No, sir. I was busy preparing for luncheon.'

'In the dining-room?'

'Between the dining-room and the pantry, sir. I should tell you that there is a door leading from the dining-room to the passage outside the pantry.'

'You did not show Mrs. Chudleigh out?'

'No, sir. I understand that Mrs. Chudleigh left by way of the garden.'

'Oh? Which way is that?'

The butler moved towards the west window. 'You may see for yourself, sir. This opens on to the path leading from the drive to the lawn at the back of the house.'

Harding followed him, and looked out. 'I see.' He consulted the paper in his hand again. 'One more question. At what hour did Mr. Billington-Smith leave the house on Monday morning?'

'I really couldn't say, sir,' replied Finch, after a moment's consideration.

The grey eyes lifted to his face. 'Try to remember, will you?' said Harding gently.

'I'm afraid I didn't notice the time, sir. It was before Sir Arthur came in, I know.'

'Would you agree that it was half past eleven?'

'Somewhere about there, sir, I should say.'

'Did it strike you that Mr. Billington-Smith was at all upset when he went out?'

'I did not notice anything unusual, sir.'

'You did not consider it unusual for him to go out without his hat on a hot day?'

'Oh dear me, no, sir! Mr. Billington-Smith very rarely wore a hat in the country.'

'Did he appear to be in a hurry?'

'It did not strike me in that way, sir.'

'He did not, in your opinion, rush out of the house as though he were quite beside himself?'

'No, sir, certainly not. But then I know Mr. Geoffrey very well, and I should not set any store by him moving quickly, as one might say. Mr. Geoffrey has an impetuous way of going about his business, if you understand me.'

'So that you did not think it odd that he should leave the front door open behind him?'

'Oh no, not at all, sir. Mr. Geoffrey is very forgetful in those ways.'

Once more Harding favoured him with a long, appraising look. 'Thank you,' he said. 'I don't think there is anything more I want to ask you at present.'

The butler bowed. 'No, sir. Perhaps you would touch the bell when you wish me to conduct you over the house?'

The Sergeant watched him go out of the room, carefully closing the door behind him, and transferred his gaze to Inspector Harding's face. 'You got more out of him than what the Superintendent did, sir,' he remarked in his deep, slow voice. 'A sight more.'

'A very precise witness – until we got to Mr. Billington-Smith, where I think he swerved a little from the truth,' commented Harding.

'I was watching him close all the time,' said the Sergeant unnecessarily. 'It struck me he was being careful – I won't say more than that. Careful.'

'Sergeant, will you sit down at the desk?' said Harding, going to the west window again. 'I think it might help us to know whether a man seated in that chair would be visible to anyone walking down the path to the drive.' He unbolted the window as he spoke, and stepped out into the garden, drawing the window to behind him. As at the front of the house, a broad grass border ran from the window to the gravel path. Harding crossed this, went a little way up the path, and then turned, and walked down it, past the window. Then he re-entered the room, and bolted the window once more. 'Yes, I think perhaps Mrs. Chudleigh may be able to help us fix the time of the murder more exactly,' he said. He came up to the desk. 'Now, Sergeant, let us look through these papers,' he said, taking the swivel-chair which the Sergeant had just vacated. 'I don't think there's anything else likely to interest us, with the possible exception of the safe. I shall want that opened, of course. Do you know if the Chief Constable warned Mr. Billington-Smith to have his father's lawyer down?'

'Yes, sir, that I do know he did, for I was in the hall at the time. But we found it just like you see, not tampered with at all.'

'Any finger-prints?' inquired Harding, his eyes on the pencil that lay on the desk.

'No, nothing of that kind. Quite clean it was.' He looked rather dubiously at Harding. 'Were you thinking there might have been robbery, sir?'

'No, I should say most unlikely.'

'That's what I thought,' said the Sergeant, glad to find himself in agreement.

Harding had picked up a slip of paper on the top of the sheaf on the desk. Some memoranda had been jotted down on it in pencil. Harding considered the pencil again for a moment.

'Looks like the General was making a list of what he had to do,' suggested the Sergeant helpfully.

'It looks as though he were interrupted while he was doing so,' said Harding. 'He did not finish the last note he made.'

'No more he did!' said the Sergeant, stooping to read the pencilled scrawl more nearly. ' "Speak to Lester," (that's the gardener) and then "See Barker about—" Well, that isn't sense, is it? The General wouldn't write a thing like that. He was a very methodical man. No, you're right, sir. Someone interrupted him before he had time to put down what he wanted to see Mr. Barker about, and what's more he didn't finish that memo. afterwards, because he was dead.'

'Well, perhaps that's leaping to conclusions a bit,' said Harding. 'At the same time it is just possible that he was jotting down that note when his murderer entered the room, and equally possible that at the moment when the blow was struck he was still holding the pencil in his hand.'

The Sergeant turned this over in his mind. 'You're thinking of that bit of writing the Superintendent showed you,' he pronounced.

'I am, yes.' Harding laid the slip of paper aside, and began to go through the others littered over the desk. There was nothing amongst them of any interest, and when he had glanced through them he turned to the waste-paper basket beside the chair. It was half-full of torn and crumpled letters which a cursory inspection informed Harding were either circulars or begging appeals. Under these were the scattered fragments of a cheque, torn into four pieces. Harding lifted these out and laid them on the desk, piecing them together.

The Sergeant drew nearer, watching this process. When it was finished he was silent for a moment. Then he said: 'That's black, sir.'

'At any rate,' said Harding, 'it would seem to explain Mr. Halliday's quarrel with the General.'

The cheque had not been passed through a bank. It was dated July 1st, and was drawn for fifty pounds, made payable to Mrs. Camilla Halliday. The General's signature was written at the bottom of it.

There was nothing else in the waste-paper basket of importance, and after a quick glance at two circulars and the notice of a meeting of the Silsbury branch of the British Fascisti, Harding gathered together the torn cheque and rose to his feet. 'I'll take a look at the position of the other rooms on this floor now, Sergeant. Keep a man on duty here till the safe's been opened, will you?'

'Yes, sir. Do you make anything of it?' inquired the Sergeant diffidently.

'Not very much yet. There are one or two points.' He went to the fireplace, and pressed the bell that flanked it.

The butler came presently in answer to the bell's summons, and escorted the Inspector over the ground floor of the house rather in the manner of a guide in a historic mansion. Leading him through the dining-room to the service door outside the pantry, he brought him back again by way of the swing door shutting off the servant's wing from the hall. He then led the way to the garden-hall, like the kitchens, on the east side of the house, pointed out the back stairs, returned to the hall, and entered the billiard-room. From the windows Harding obtained a view of the terrace, where the house-party was gathered for tea. He declined going into the drawing-room. 'Thanks, I think I have a pretty good idea of the house now,' he said. 'I want to see the various people who are staying here next. Can you show me a room where I shan't be disturbed, or in the way?'

'I think the morning-room would be the most suitable, sir,' said Finch, standing aside to allow him to pass out into the hall again. 'This way, if you please.'

Harding nodded to the Sergeant, waiting for him at the foot of the stairs. 'Will you come along too, Sergeant?' He consulted a list from his pocket-book, and glanced up at the butler. 'Is Mrs. Twining by any chance in the house?' he asked.

'Yes, sir. Mrs. Twining is on the terrace now.'

'Then will you ask her, please, if she will come here?' said Harding.

There was a square table in the middle of the room. When the butler had gone Harding pulled a chair out from it, and sat down with his back to the light. The westering sun was streaming into the room, and the windows stood open to admit as much air as could be obtained on this hot, windless afternoon.

Harding spread his papers out on the table, and chose from amongst them Mrs. Twining's original statement. He was running his eye over this when Finch opened the door, and announced Mrs. Twining. She came in, looking slightly bored. She was wearing a lavender frock that subtly conveyed the impression of half-mourning; and a large black straw hat with a high crown was set at an angle on her well-coiffed head. 'Good afternoon, Inspector,' she said, surveying him in her cool, ironic way.

Harding rose, and came round the table to pull up a chair for her. 'Good afternoon,' he said. 'Won't you sit down? I want you, if you will, to answer one or two questions.'

She took the chair he had placed for her, and moved it a little out of the direct sunlight. 'Certainly,' she said. 'But at my age, Inspector, one does not sit in the full glare of the sun. It is not fair to oneself.' She sat down, leaning one elbow on the wooden chair-arm, and with the other hand holding her bag lightly in her lap. She became aware of the Sergeant standing by the fireplace and fixedly regarding her. Her brows rose a little, and her lips parted in a faint smile. 'Ah, good afternoon, Sergeant!' she said.

'Mrs. Twining, can you remember the precise time of your arrival here yesterday morning?' asked Harding.

'Perfectly,' she replied. 'I arrived at ten minutes past twelve.'

'Thank you.' Harding made a brief note. 'The butler, I think admitted you. Will you describe to me just what you did after entering the house?'

'I'll try to,' said Mrs. Twining. 'But I trust you won't use it in evidence against me.'

He smiled. 'We only do that when we make arrests, Mrs. Twining. If you can carry your mind back successfully – I know it is difficult to remember exactly – it would help me to check up on the various statements.'

'Well, I think I laid down my sunshade first,' said Mrs. Twining reflectively. 'Ah, that doesn't interest you. I told Finch that I wanted to tidy my hair (a euphemism for "powder my nose", of course), and would show myself out on to the terrace.'

'And you did in fact powder your nose, Mrs. Twining, at the mirror over the fireplace?'

'Most thoroughly,' she agreed.

'How long did that take you?'

She looked rather amused. 'When a woman powders her nose, Inspector, she loses count of time. My own estimate would be a moment or two; almost any man, I feel, would probably say, ages.'

'Were you as long, perhaps, as five minutes?'

'I hope not. Let us say three – without prejudice.'

'And during that time, did you hear voices in the study?'

'No,' said Mrs. Twining. 'I heard no sound at all in the study.'

'And when you left the hall, you went straight out on to the terrace? Can you remember who was there?'

She thought for a moment. 'Certainly Miss Fawcett,' she said. 'Ah yes! Mrs. Halliday also, and Mr. Guest.'

'You are sure that there was no one else, Mrs. Twining?'

'Not when I first arrived,' she answered. 'Miss Fawcett and I strolled to the rose-garden to find Lady Billington-Smith, who, however, was in the vegetable-garden. She joined us on the lawn as we were returning to the terrace.'

'Had anyone else come on to the terrace by that time?'

'No. I remember thinking how bored Mrs. Halliday appeared to be with Mr. Guest's sole company.'

Harding made another note. 'Now, Mrs. Twining, can you recall just when the other members of the party joined you? It is rather important, so please take your time.'

She sat for a minute in silence, absently regarding the Sergeant. 'Mrs. Chudleigh,' she said presently. 'She arrived almost immediately after we – Miss Fawcett, Lady Billington-Smith, and myself – had come back to the terrace. She wanted a subscription for some charity. Mr. Halliday was the last to put in an appearance. He came out of the billiard-room a few minutes later.'

'When you say a few minutes, Mrs. Twining, does that mean five? – ten? – fifteen?'

'It is difficult for me to say. We were all talking, you see. I don't think it can have been as much as fifteen. Somewhere between five and ten minutes. But I am merely guessing.'

'Miss de Silva, then, didn't join you at all?'

'Not until very much later – some little time after one o'clock.'

'I see. And before one o'clock, did anyone leave the terrace?'

'I believe Mr. Guest went upstairs for his tobacco,' she replied.

'At about what time, Mrs. Twining?'

'Very soon after Mr. Halliday joined us.'

'Before half past twelve, do you think or after?'

She reflected. 'Before,' she said. 'At half past twelve Mrs. Chudleigh called our attention to the time, and said she must go, or she would be late for lunch.'

'Had Mr. Guest returned by then?'

She frowned slightly. 'I'm not entirely sure. I fancy not.'

'Had he returned, can you remember, by the time Finch brought out the tray of cocktails?'

She made a little gesture with her hand. 'Again, I am uncertain. I don't think I noticed his return. He was certainly on the terrace just before one. That is all I can say.'

Harding looked up. 'He might have been absent for half an hour, in fact?'

'Oh no!' she said. 'I should certainly have noticed that.'

'And no one else left the terrace until you yourself went to fetch Sir Arthur?'

'No,' she answered. 'No one.'

'Thank you, Mrs. Twining. Now as to your own movements: you went to fetch Sir Arthur on to the terrace. Had you any particular reason for wanting to see him?'

She raised her brows a trifle haughtily. 'Particular reason?' she repeated. 'I don't think I quite understand you, Inspector. What precisely do you mean?'

'Nothing very much,' said Harding, with his rather charming smile. 'It merely strikes me, a stranger, as a little odd, if the only reason for fetching Sir Arthur was – as you informed the Superintendent yesterday – that he should not miss his cocktail, that it was not Lady Billington-Smith who went to him, or even Miss Fawcett.'

Mrs. Twining unfastened the catch of her bag, and closed it again. 'It was not really so very odd, Inspector – if you knew the circumstances.'

'But, you see, I don't know the circumstances,' said Harding. 'That is what I want you to explain to me, please.'

Mrs. Twining looked up from her bag. 'It would take rather too long, Inspector, I am afraid. I was a very old friend of Sir Arthur's. There was nothing at all unusual in my going to have a little talk with him.'

'Then you did, in fact, want to see him alone?' said Harding.

She hesitated. 'Yes,' she said at last. 'There was something I wanted to discuss with him.' She met Harding's steady regard. 'His son's marriage,' she said deliberately. 'Sir Arthur was considerably upset by Geoffrey's engagement to Miss de Silva, and I wanted to talk it over with him.'

'When you say upset, Mrs. Twining, do you mean distressed, or enraged?'

'I imagine, both, Inspector. It was, not unnaturally, a blow to Sir Arthur.' She moved slightly in her chair, putting a hand up to shield her eyes from the sun.

'Am I right in assuming, Mrs. Twining, that there had been a serious quarrel between Sir Arthur and his son which you wished if possible to smooth over?'

She smiled. 'Serious, Inspector? Oh no! Noisy, perhaps, but hardly serious to anyone acquainted with Sir Arthur. Sir Arthur had had far too many quarrels with his son – and, in fact, with everybody with whom he came in contact – for his outbreaks to be taken seriously. But while his bad temper lasted he could make himself extremely disagreeable. I am afraid my mission was only to talk him into a good humour so that he shouldn't ruin his wife's luncheon-party – as he was somewhat apt to do when at all put out.'

'You didn't consider the quarrel with his son to be of much moment?'

'You see,' said Mrs. Twining apologetically, 'I knew Sir Arthur too well to set much store by his threats.'

'And you didn't think that his threats might provoke his son to some extreme course of action?'

She gave a faint laugh. 'No, Inspector, I certainly did not. I am also well acquainted with Geoffrey – too well acquainted to expect him to do more than precisely what he did do – fling himself out of the house in a temper, walk it off, and return – a trifle sheepishly.'

'I see,' said Harding. 'And now will you try to tell me, Mrs. Twining, exactly how you found Sir Arthur, when you went into the study, and what you did?'

'I found him dead, Inspector,' she replied calmly. 'He had fallen forward across his desk.'

'You didn't raise any outcry?' inquired Harding.

'If you mean, did I scream, certainly not. I am not a flapper,' said Mrs. Twining with a touch of asperity. 'Nor did I immediately realize that Sir Arthur was dead. If I remember rightly, I spoke his name first. Then I went up to him, and laid my hand on his shoulder.' Involuntarily she glanced down at her hand. 'I didn't see the blood till I had actually touched him,' she said in a level controlled voice. 'I don't think I grasped what had happened even then. I believe I must have stayed quite still for some moments. I felt – a little stunned. When I pulled myself together I tried to rouse him; I think I felt for his pulse.' She stopped, and pressed her handkerchief to her lips.

'And then?' prompted Harding.

She looked at him. 'I felt extremely sick,' she said. 'I sat down on the arm of the chair by the fire – or perhaps I should say, more correctly, that I collapsed on to it. I think if I had not I should have fainted outright. When the – nausea – passed, I left the room, shutting the door behind me, so that no one should see in, and went back to the terrace, and told the others.'

'So that it was at least five minutes, possibly even longer, after you discovered Sir Arthur before you went back to the terrace?'

'I have no idea,' she replied. 'I should think it quite probable.'

Harding got up. 'Thank you, Mrs. Twining. I won't ask you any more just at present.'

She rose, and went towards the door. He held it open for her, and as she passed out, said: 'I wonder if you would be kind enough to ask Lady Billington-Smith if she will come here?'

She bowed. 'Certainly, Inspector,' she said, and went out.

CHAPTER TEN

HARDING shut the door behind Mrs. Twining, and walked slowly back to the table. 'Well, Sergeant?'

The Sergeant pursed his lips. 'You want to know how it struck me, sir?'

'Very much.'

'Well, I'd say she behaved very cool,' said the Sergeant, thinking it over. 'Very cool indeed. I don't say it didn't happen just as she said, but it would have seemed to me more natural-like if she'd run out of the room just as soon as she saw the General was dead.'

'I agree with you. At the same time she gives me the impression of being a woman of considerable strength of character.' He hunted through his papers for Fay's statement. 'She was keeping something back, of course. From what I can gather, Sir Arthur's temper was not quite so evanescent as she would have had us believe.'

'No, sir,' said the Sergeant doubtfully.

'So quickly over,' Harding said.

'Quickly over? That I will say it was not, sir! I wouldn't like to speak ill of the dead, but Sir Arthur was a fair terror. Quite a byword, you might say.'

The door opened; Fay came in, and stood for a moment looking across the room at Harding. In her black dress she had a pathetically frail appearance. Her eyes were deeply shadowed, her lips rather bloodless.

'Lady Billington-Smith?' Harding said. 'Will you come and sit down?' He spoke in a reassuring way, quite unexpected by one who had had experience so far only of Superintendent Lupton's methods.

'Thank you,' Fay said in a low voice, and took the chair Mrs. Twining had occupied. 'I understand – you want to ask me some questions. I – made a statement to the Superintendent yesterday. I don't know – if there is anything more you want to ask me.'

'I'm sorry, Lady Billington-Smith, but I'm afraid I must ask you certain questions – some of them perhaps rather distressing to you,' Harding said. 'Will you try and answer them quite frankly – and believe I wouldn't put them to you unless I considered it necessary?'

Her eyes fluttered to his face again, surprised and grateful. 'Yes, of course. I quite understand.'

He sat down. 'I want to know first, Lady Billington-Smith: were you upon good terms with your husband at the time of his death?'

The suddenness of the question startled her. 'What do you mean?' she faltered.

'I am not insinuating anything,' he said. 'I only want you to tell me the truth.'

'My husband – my husband was not an easy man to deal with,' Fay said with difficulty. 'We had our disagreements sometimes, but we were not on bad terms.'

'Your husband was, I understand, a very hot-tempered man? You had quarrels fairly frequently?'

'I – I am not a quarrelsome person, Inspector. My husband had a way of – blustering, when he was annoyed. We did not quarrel.'

'You mean that your husband was inclined to – may I say – scold you, when anything happened to annoy him?'

'Yes. But it was nothing. He didn't mean it.'

'On the morning of July first – yesterday, in fact – did some such scene occur between you?'

'My husband was very angry with Geoffrey – with his son. Not with me.'

'Sometimes, Lady Billington-Smith, a man who has been very much angered is apt to vent his feelings on a perfectly innocent person. Is that what happened?'

She hesitated. 'He was very angry,' she repeated.

'So angry that he upset you?'

'It wasn't that – only partly! It is true I was a little upset yesterday morning. I have not been very well, and I had had a trying week-end. My husband – had a violent way of – of expressing himself. He shouted when he was at all irritated, and – it made my head ache. That is all.'

'The cause of this violent irritation was, I think, his son's engagement to Miss de Silva?'

'Yes,' Fay replied. 'He was dreadfully angry with Geoffrey, and I – rather foolishly – tried to reason with him.'

'I quite understand. You were afraid that a really serious quarrel might spring up between your stepson and his father?'

'Oh no, no!' Fay said quickly. 'I knew that Geoffrey would never quarrel with his father. He was too much in awe of him. I was afraid that Arthur – that my husband might turn him out of the house. He was – in some ways – a very hard man.'

Harding picked up his pencil, and regarded the point of it. 'Lady Billington-Smith, you must forgive me if I distress you, but was this the only cause of the scene which took place between you and Sir Arthur? There was not, on your side, any feeling of jealousy?'

'Jealousy?' she repeated blankly.

He raised his eyes. 'You were not yourself angry – or perhaps hurt – at any undue attention Sir Arthur may have paid to one of your guests?'

She flushed. 'No. I was not – angry, or hurt. Certainly not jealous. My husband had a – a playful, gallant way of – of treating women, but it didn't mean anything. Such an idea never entered my head. It was purely on Geoffrey's account, the – the scene.'

'Then that is all I wish to know about that, Lady Billington-Smith. At what time did you eventually come downstairs yesterday morning?'

'I didn't come down till my husband called to me, but I was out of my room before that, speaking to the head housemaid upstairs.'

'So that you don't know what happened between Sir Arthur and his son?'

'No.'

'When he called to you, what time was that?'

'It must have been just before twelve. He had just come in with – with Mrs. Halliday, and he wanted me to see that she had some roses to take away with her when she left.'

'Mrs. Halliday was with him at the time?'

'Yes, but she went upstairs to her room to take her hat off. Then my husband went into his study. He said he did not want to be disturbed. It was the first of the month, you see, and he always made up his accounts, and paid the staff on that day. I remember now, it was ten minutes to twelve, because he – he called my attention to the time, saying he had wasted so much of the morning already. Then I went—'

'One moment,' interposed Harding. 'Was Sir Arthur still angry with you at this time?'

'He was – a little testy. Nothing, really.'

Harding picked up a typewritten-sheet, headed: *Statement of Charles Thomson, footman.* 'I will put it to you quite frankly. Lady Billington-Smith: did Sir Arthur, when Mrs. Halliday had gone upstairs, speak to you very roughly, finding fault with the way you behaved towards your guests, and accusing you of lying in bed "till all hours"?'

'I believe he did say something like that,' Fay replied in a suffocating voice.

'And did you answer that you couldn't bear it, that he was driving you out of your mind?'

Her eyes were fixed on his face with an expression of wondering dread in them. 'I don't remember. If I did, I didn't mean it. Perhaps I said it. I was – momentarily annoyed with my husband for speaking to me rather rudely. One – one does say silly, theatrical things sometimes, when one is at all on edge.'

'Yes, very often,' Harding agreed, laying the footman's statement down again. 'Your husband entered his study, then, at ten minutes to twelve. What did you do?'

'I went into the garden, and through the garden-hall, to find Lester, the head gardener.'

'Had you any idea where he was to be found?'

'No, I asked the under-gardener. He was just taking vegetables to the kitchen.'

'And he was able to tell you?'

'Yes, he said that Lester was in the kitchen-garden.'

'Is that any distance from the house, Lady Billington-Smith?'

She looked at him, a worried frown in her eyes. 'No. It's at the side of the house, about two minutes' walk from the garden-hall.'

'How long did it take you to deliver Sir Arthur's message to Lester?'

'Well, I don't— A minute, I suppose.'

'Did you say anything else to him?'

'I told him that Sir Arthur wanted him to mow the front lawn.'

'Nothing else?'

'No. No, I'm sure that was all.'

'And when you had delivered both these messages, what did you do next?'

'I went through the kitchen-garden to the back of the house. Mrs. Twining and my sister were crossing the lawn, and they called to me.'

'Lady Billington-Smith, you left the house by way of the garden-hall just after ten minutes to twelve. Mrs. Twining did not arrive until ten minutes past twelve, and it cannot have been less than twenty-five, or at the minimum twenty minutes past twelve when you joined her on the lawn. What were you doing during that half hour?'

Fay's hands crept along the arms of her chair, and gripped them nervously. 'I'm sorry. I didn't mean to mislead you, Inspector. I didn't go to look for Lester at once. I went into the orchard.'

'Why?' said that calm voice.

She moistened her lips. 'I didn't feel I could face anybody just then. I – I was rather upset.'

'By what Sir Arthur had just said to you?'

'I – yes, a little. I wasn't feeling at all well. Perhaps I am rather easily upset. I went into the orchard because I wanted to be alone, and – and I knew I should be bound to meet someone in the house, or – or in the gardens.'

'Did anyone see you go into the orchard?'

'I – I don't know. I don't think so. I didn't notice anyone.' She stared at him. 'You don't think – you don't think—'

'I don't think anything yet, Lady Billington-Smith. When you met Mrs. Twining and Miss Fawcett, what did you do?'

'We all went up on to the terrace. Mrs. Halliday was there with Mrs. Guest. Mr. Guest is a connection of my husband's. Then Mrs. Chudleigh arrived, to speak to me about the Children's Holiday Fund. Oh, and I think Mrs. Halliday must have come on to the terrace just about then. I'm not quite sure. I had a very bad headache.'

'Did anyone leave the terrace between then and one o'clock?'

'Mrs. Chudleigh went away. Oh, and Mr. Guest went indoors for a few minutes to fetch his tobacco.'

'Would you say that was before Mrs. Chudleigh left, or after?'

'I don't know. I can't quite remember. Before, I think – but I'm not sure.'

'Was Mr. Guest gone long?'

'Oh no, not more than a minute or two. He just went up to his room to get his pouch, that was all.'

'Had he returned when Mrs. Chudleigh got up to go?'

'I really can't remember, Inspector. I'm not even sure that she didn't go first. I wasn't paying much attention,' Fay said, a little breathlessly.

'Try and remember, Lady Billington-Smith, whether Mr. Guest was on the terrace when the butler came out with the cocktails.'

'Oh, I think he must have been! I don't exactly remember, but I know he was only away a very little while,' Fay said. 'I'm sorry to be so vague. You must forgive me, but – this has been a dreadful shock to me, and I find it very hard to – to think back over what happened yesterday.'

'I know, and I'm not going to worry you any more now, Lady Billington-Smith,' Harding said, rising, and going towards the door. 'I should like to see your stepson next.'

'I'll tell him,' she said. In the doorway she hesitated. 'I – perhaps I ought to warn you that Geoffrey is rather excitable. He was terribly shocked by the news of his father's death. I hope you won't— I hope you need not—'

'I'll be as considerate as I can,' Harding promised.

'Thank you,' she said, and went out.

When she had gone there was a moment's silence; Harding came back to the table, frowning slightly. The Sergeant scratched his cheek, and presently said: 'I never heard anyone say anything against her ladyship, sir. Very well spoken of, she is, and always has been. At the same time, I wouldn't say that the General didn't try her pretty far, because by all one hears that wouldn't be the truth. Very far he tried her.'

'You know her better than I do, Sergeant.'

'Well, sir, that's a fact, and if you was to ask me, I should say her ladyship wouldn't hurt a flea.'

'At the same time,' Harding said, 'she is in an extremely over-wrought condition. If half of what the servants deposed in the statements the Superintendent took is true it wouldn't be very difficult to believe that she was goaded to the pitch of murder.'

The Sergeant thought it over. 'To my mind, sir, it wasn't her. More likely to be that foreign hussy, or this Mr. Halliday.'

At this moment the door opened to admit Geoffrey, who came in with an air of nonchalance only too palpably assumed, and broke straightway into speech. 'Oh, I understand you want to see me! The trouble is I can't really be of much use to you, Inspector – I say, I absolutely can't go on calling you Inspector, Mr. Harding. It sounds so utterly wrong – I mean—' He glanced towards the Sergeant, and ended lamely: 'Oh well, you know!'

'I think, if you don't mind, we'll stick to Inspector, Mr. Billington-Smith,' said Harding unresponsively. 'Will you sit down, please?'

'Oh, just as you like!' Geoffrey said, a trifle sulkily. He cast himself into the chair, and began to play with his tie again. 'I'm quite ready to answer anything I can – er – Inspector. I expect you've seen my original statement, haven't you?'

'I have it here,' replied Harding. 'There are one or two things in it that I want you to explain.'

'Well, I've nothing to add to it, really, but I'll explain anything you like,' said Geoffrey handsomely. 'Only, as a matter of fact, I don't see myself what more you can possibly want to know. I mean, considering I wasn't here when my father was killed—'

'Will you tell me, Mr. Billington-Smith, what sort of terms you were on with your father?' said Harding, interrupting this speech without ceremony.

'Look here, what on earth has that got to do with it?' expostulated Geoffrey. 'I keep on telling you I wasn't here when Father was murdered!'

A certain sternness made Harding's voice less pleasant all at once.

'Mr. Billington-Smith, my time is limited. Will you have the goodness to answer the question?'

Geoffrey swallowed. 'All right, but I still don't—' He saw the Inspector's face harden, and broke off. 'Well, I suppose we didn't hit it off frightfully well. My father was absolutely hide-bound, you know. One just had to make allowances for him.'

'When you say that you didn't hit it off, do you mean that you quarrelled?'

'Oh no, we didn't exactly quarrel. My father used to rave a bit at me, but I didn't quarrel with him, because as it happens I'm not the quarrelsome sort, and besides, it wasn't worth while.'

'Why did your father rave at you?'

'Good God, *I* don't know! It was just his way. Well, as a matter of fact, he wanted me to go to Sandhurst, only I wasn't strong enough – not that I would have if I had been, because I should have loathed the Army – and he was frightfully fed-up when I took to writing. Of course, as far as he was concerned, there simply wasn't any other profession but the Army. I've had Army dinned into my ears till I'm sick to death of the sound of it. I've got a cousin who's a cavalryman – well, he was here this week-end, he left soon after breakfast yesterday morning – and all I can say is if he's a fair specimen I'm glad I didn't go to Sandhurst. Only of course, the mere fact of Francis – my cousin – being in the Army was quite enough to make Father think him the devil of a fine fellow. Of course Francis always took jolly good care to keep on the right side of Father. Though as a matter of fact I happen to know that for once in a way he failed to touch Father yesterday. However, that was probably only because Father was in such a filthy mood. I've no doubt he'd have stumped up in the end. But because I happened to be a bit delicate, and – well, literary – Father never had the slightest use for me. I may say that the only books he ever read in all his life were Dickens and Scott, so that just shows you the sort of man he was. I mean, he simply knew *nothing* about art or literature, and he hadn't the slightest sympathy for anyone who was different from himself.'

'You must have had a very hard time of it,' prompted Harding kindly.

'Well, I did, to be quite honest. Not that it made any odds, really, and I don't want to give you the impression that we were always at loggerheads, because we weren't. Naturally, when I was a kid it was pretty rotten for me, but since I grew up I simply went my way and he went his.'

'In fact, there was never much love lost between you?'

'Good lord, no! Father had no time for me at all. Personally, I've always believed it was because of my mother. She ran away with another man when I was a kid – not that I blame her for that, because I'll bet he was a swine to her – but anyway I'm pretty sure that was why he didn't like me.'

'Would you describe him as having been "an absolute beast" to you ever since you could remember?'

'Oh, I shouldn't put it as strongly as that!' Geoffrey said. 'To me he was more of a joke than anything, though of course he was often frightfully annoying.'

At this point the Sergeant's gaze transferred itself to Harding's profile, dwelt there a moment, and fixed itself finally on a blank space on the opposite wall.

'You don't live here, do you, Mr. Billington-Smith?' inquired Harding.

'No, I share a flat with a man I know in town. But that isn't because I don't get on with my father!'

'I wasn't suggesting that,' replied Harding equably. 'You have recently become engaged to be married, have you not, to a Miss Lola de Silva?'

Geoffrey stirred restlessly. 'That's all off now, I can assure you.'

Harding looked up from a note he was making. 'Indeed? But it was not all off, was it, when you brought Miss de Silva here on Saturday?'

Geoffrey gave a short laugh. 'No, it wasn't. But since then— However, that's a subject I prefer not to discuss.'

'That's a pity,' said Harding, 'for it is a subject which I'm afraid I must ask you to tell me about. When was this engagement broken off?'

'If you must know, yesterday,' said Geoffrey.

'Did you break it off, or did Miss de Silva?'

Geoffrey got up quickly. 'Look here, I've already said I don't want to discuss it! It can't have anything to do with you, and I may as well tell you that I very much object to having my private affairs pried into.'

'Sit down, Mr. Billington-Smith,' said Harding. Geoffrey hesitated, and obeyed. 'There are two ways of giving evidence to the police,' continued Harding in his even voice. 'One is to answer the questions that are put to you, and the other is to have the truth pumped out of you. I recommend the first of these. You will find it less unpleasant.'

Geoffrey looked rather frightened. 'I didn't mean – of course, if you assure me it's necessary, that's another matter. Only I don't mind telling you that I've been utterly disillusioned about Lola – Miss de Silva, you know, and I simply don't want to hear her name mentioned again.'

'Did she, or did you break off the engagement?' repeated Harding.

Geoffrey ran his hand along the arm of the chair. 'Well, it's all rather difficult to explain. In a way, she did.'

'What do you mean by "in a way"?'

'Well – I found she was completely mercenary. Of course, I'd been living in a fool's paradise. I see that now.'

'You are wandering from the point, Mr. Billington-Smith.'

'Oh, I don't know that I meant anything in particular!' said Geoffrey irritably. 'She said she wasn't going to marry me, and that opened my eyes, and I can assure you nothing would induce me to marry her now, however much she may think I'm going to.'

'Does she think you are going to?'

'God knows what she thinks. She's one of these beautiful, utterly soulless fiends. I was blinded by her—'

'Why has she changed her mind?' asked Harding.

'Because all she cares for is money. Money! Now Father's dead she thinks I shall be frightfully wealthy – though he may have left all his money to Francis for all I know. It wouldn't surprise me in the least; it's just the sort of thing he would do.'

'Did Miss de Silva, then, break the engagement for pecuniary reasons?'

'Yes,' Geoffrey admitted reluctantly.

Harding put down his pencil. 'I see. Now, I am not going to ask you whether your father disliked this engagement, because I know that he did. Also—'

'You seem to know the hell of a lot,' muttered Geoffrey.

'I'm glad you are beginning to realize that,' replied Harding calmly. 'It is no use trying to put me off with these half-truths and evasions, you see. You are only giving me an impression I am perfectly sure you don't want me to have. On Monday morning you had an interview with your father, who was very angry with you. That is so, isn't it?'

'Yes,' Geoffrey answered, somewhat subdued. 'At least, he was angry about Lola.'

'What was the result of that interview, Mr. Billington-Smith?'

'Well, we had a bit of a row – more than that, really, because he was absolutely livid with rage – and in the end he said I could get to hell out of his sight, and he was going to cut off my allowance, and he never wanted to set eyes on me again. Not that that was likely to worry me, any of it, because as I said, we didn't hit it off, and as for starving in a ditch, which was the way he put it, money simply means nothing to me, and in any case I can support myself with my pen. I can tell you, it was a very jolly interview.'

'It seems to have been,' agreed Harding. 'When it was over, what did you do?'

'Naturally I went up to tell Lola what had happened. It simply didn't occur to me that it would make any difference as far as she was concerned. Of course, being practically disowned was a bit of a bore, but I really wasn't worrying much *then*.'

'You say you went up – I take it Miss de Silva had breakfasted in her room?'

'Oh yes, she never gets up before eleven. In fact she wouldn't let me see her till then, and I had to kick my heels on the landing for ages. And when she did let me into her room, and I told her – well, it was an absolute knock-out. I thought she was joking at first, when she said she wouldn't marry me if I hadn't got a lot of money. Then I saw she wasn't, and I suppose I had a sort of utter revulsion of feeling, because all I could think of was to get out of the house, and away from Lola. I felt I should be sick if I stayed another moment. So that's exactly what I did do.'

'What?' said Harding.

'Got out of the house,' Geoffrey said impatiently.

'Have you any idea what the time was when you left the house?'

'No, of course I haven't,' replied Geoffrey. 'When a man's stood up to a blow like that, had his faith in women completely destroyed – well, what I mean is, you don't suppose I stopped to look at the time, do you? All I know is it was some while after eleven, and before Father came in.'

'And when you left the house, Mr. Billington-Smith, where did you go?'

'Oh, I don't know! Miles away. I simply walked and walked.'

'I quite appreciate the fact that you were extremely upset,' said Harding, 'but surely you must have some idea where you went?'

'Yes, well, I went through the woods first, and over Longshaw Hill, and I suppose I sort of circled round, more or less by instinct, because I found myself on old Carnaby's land – he owns the place on the main road, between us and the village – and I came home by way of the footpath through his park. As a matter of fact, I didn't come out on the main road at all, because you can get from Moorsale Park on to our land without touching a road. There's just a farm-track you have to cross, and then you come to the spinney at the bottom of this garden. That's how I came.'

'I see. Did you meet anyone while you were out?'

'To meet anyone was the last thing I wanted!' said Geoffrey bitterly.

'Try to remember, Mr. Billington-Smith. I don't know this countryside, but you have described what sounds to me a very lonely walk.'

'Of course it was! I didn't want to run into people. I wanted to be alone!'

'Are you well known here?' Harding asked. 'If someone did happen to see you during the course of your walk, would they be likely to recognize you?'

'I don't know. I dare say. It depends.' Geoffrey looked defiantly across the table. 'I see what you're driving at, but if you think—'

'I am not driving at anything,' Harding said gravely, 'but I want you, in your own interests, to try and remember whether you did not meet someone.'

'I tell you I don't know! My mind was in an absolute turmoil. I'm pretty sure I didn't actually meet anyone, but how on earth can I know whether anybody saw me or not?'

'Very well, Mr. Billington-Smith,' Harding answered. 'That is all I want to ask you at present. Will you ask Mr. Halliday to come here, please?'

Geoffrey got up jerkily. 'Look here, Inspector!' he burst out. 'This is all jolly fine, but if you've marked me down as a suspect simply because I can't bring a lot of witnesses forward to prove I'm speaking the truth – well, I call it a bit thick! There are heaps of people with just as much reason for wanting to kill Father as I had

– and if you want to know there's one person in particular with a damned sight more reason – and to single me out—'

Harding glanced up from his notebook. 'Mr. Billington-Smith: really, this is not leading us anywhere. Will you send Mr. Halliday in to me, please?'

Geoffrey hesitated, and then flung round on his heel and strode to the door. As he opened it Harding spoke again. 'Oh, just one moment! Did the Chief Constable warn you that it would be necessary for the safe in your father's study to be opened in my presence?'

'Yes, he did, and Father's lawyer is coming down tomorrow,' snapped Geoffrey, and walked out, banging the door behind him.

Inspector Harding gazed meditatively after him. He said, without turning his head: 'You looked at me once, I think, Sergeant. What was it?'

'Well, sir, I couldn't help thinking that for Mr. Billington-Smith to say the General was a joke to him was a very different tale from any I ever heard. It didn't seem to me that you could very well rely on anything he said. What I should call a mighty bad witness, sir.'

'Atrocious,' said Harding.

The Sergeant coughed behind his hand. 'Begging your pardon, sir, I thought you was a bit high-handed with him – if I might pass the remark. If he *had* happened to object to the question he took exception to I couldn't help wondering where we'd have been then.'

'We should have apologized gracefully, Sergeant. But if I hadn't bullied him a little I should have got nothing out of him at all. A tiresome young gentleman.'

'Yes, sir. And it's a weak story he told you.'

'A very weak story,' said Harding.

'He's what you might call hasty-tempered too,' pondered the Sergeant. 'Very excitable, he seemed.'

'Excitable, and badly frightened,' said Harding, and turned his head as the door opened to admit Basil Halliday.

CHAPTER ELEVEN

HALLIDAY walked forward, glancing from Harding to the Sergeant, and back again. 'Good afternoon,' he said. 'You want to ask me some questions, I think.'

'Yes,' Harding answered. 'Sit down, will you, Mr. Halliday? You and your wife are guests in the house, I believe?'

'We came down for the week-end,' replied Halliday, crossing one leg over the other. 'In the ordinary course of events we should have gone back to town yesterday, but naturally that was impossible until this business had been cleared up. My home address is—'

'I have it here, Mr. Halliday,' said Harding. 'Had you known Sir Arthur for long?'

'No, we were quite recent acquaintances. We met at Nice, last winter. I had a temporary job that took me out to the South of France, and the Billington-Smiths were staying there during January and February. Lady Billington-Smith and my wife struck up a bit of a friendship. Then after we came home we rather lost sight of them, until my wife happened to run across Sir Arthur in town one day, and the acquaintance was picked up again.' As he spoke he looked once or twice, as though compelled, at the Sergeant, and his brows twitched a little; he shifted his chair slightly to get out of the direct line of that paralysing stare.

Harding asked in his impersonal way: 'When did you last see Sir Arthur alive, Mr. Halliday?'

'On Monday morning,' replied Halliday promptly. 'I saw him in his study about twelve o'clock. I'm not sure of the exact time, but it must have been about then. It's best that I should be quite frank with you, Inspector, so I'll tell you at once that Sir Arthur and I had – most unfortunately, as it turns out – a disagreement.'

'A quarrel, Mr. Halliday?'

'No, not a quarrel. I don't say there might not have been a quarrel had the circumstances been rather different, for I had cause to feel considerable annoyance with Sir Arthur. But my being a guest in his house put me into an awkward position. One doesn't quarrel with a man under his own roof.'

'Was your disagreement of a serious nature, Mr. Halliday?'

Halliday gave a quick, mirthless smile. 'Well, that is rather difficult to answer, Inspector. The contretemps concerns my private affairs, and I should prefer not to take you into them. I can only say that it made me determine not to accept another invitation to stay with Sir Arthur.'

'Did the interview become heated?' inquired Harding.

'Not on my side, I hope. Ah, you are thinking of Finch's somewhat exaggerated statement! He, I believe, told the Superintendent that he had overheard me having a violent row with Sir Arthur. I'm afraid that was a highly coloured version of what actually occurred – though I must admit that I had to raise my voice to make myself heard. Sir Arthur had a habit of shouting when he was at all put out, as I dare say you've been told.'

'What you had to say to Sir Arthur, then, had the effect of angering him?'

'Oh, very much!' replied Halliday with a short laugh. 'Sir Arthur did not like finding himself in the wrong any more than most people do.'

Harding drew his pocket-book out and opened it. Halliday shot one quick glance at it, and fixed his eyes on Harding's face again. 'Do you know anything about this, Mr. Halliday?' asked Harding, arranging the four torn quarters of the General's cheque.

Halliday's right hand clenched on the chair-arm, and relaxed again. It was a moment before he answered, and then he said carefully: 'I do, Inspector. I am sorry you found that cheque. You'll understand why I didn't wish to tell you what I went to see Sir Arthur about.'

'Perfectly,' said Harding, and waited.

'I suppose I had better tell you exactly what happened,' Halliday said. 'My quarrel with Sir Arthur was purely on account of that cheque. Sir Arthur had been paying my wife a great many unwelcome attentions during our stay. I can best describe his attitude as pseudo-fatherly. You probably know what I mean. It made it very difficult for my wife to choke him off. Yesterday morning he pressed that cheque on her with a lot of talk about wanting to make her a little present. She tried, of course, to make him understand that it was quite impossible for her to accept such a thing, but he made it extremely awkward for her, and in the end she gave it up, and instead came at once to consult me. Naturally, I—'

'One moment, Mr. Halliday. At what time during the morning did Sir Arthur give this cheque to your wife?'

'That I can't tell you. It was when he and she were over at his keeper's cottage, inspecting a litter of puppies. Somewhere between eleven and twelve.'

'They returned to the house shortly before ten to twelve, I understand. At what time did your wife confide what had happened to you?'

'Immediately, of course. She thought it was the best thing she could do – quite rightly.'

'Where were you when this confidence took place, Mr. Halliday?'

'Upstairs. My wife came up to take her hat off.'

'You were in the bedroom, in fact?'

'Well, no, not when she first came in. I joined her there – oh, a couple of minutes later!'

'How long did you remain there with your wife?'

'Well, I don't really know. Not more than a few minutes. I realized that the only thing for me to do was to see Sir Arthur myself, and I went down at once, to get it over.'

'Where did your wife go?'

'Out on to the terrace, I think. She was there when I joined them later.'

'And how long were you in the study with Sir Arthur?'

Halliday considered. 'It can't have been much more than ten minutes, if as much. I tried to be as civil about the thing as I could, but naturally I was very much annoyed, and I had to make it quite clear to the General that he was making a bad mistake. He tried to bluster it out, and I saw if I argued it would only lead to a lot of unpleasantness, so I tore up the cheque, as you see, dropped it into the waste-paper basket, and left the room.'

'And then, Mr. Halliday?'

'Let me see, what did I do then? Did I – no, I went upstairs just to see that all my stuff had been packed, washed my hands and came down again on to the terrace.'

'Did you go straight out on to the terrace, Mr. Halliday?'

'Yes, straight – oh no, I was forgetting! I went into the billiard-room first, where I remembered leaving my pipe. Then I went out on to the terrace through the billiard-room windows.'

'Have you any idea what time it was then?'

'No, I'm sorry, but I don't think I noticed.'

'Do you think it was before half past twelve, or after?'

'I really couldn't – oh, wait a minute, though! Mrs. Chudleigh got up to go quite soon after I joined the party and I think she said it was then half past twelve, so I must have come out on to the terrace at about twenty-five minutes past, more or less.'

'You did not leave the terrace again, until one o'clock?'

'No, not until Guest and I went to the study.'

'Did anyone else leave the terrace?'

'Yes, Guest did.'

'Do you remember when that was?'

'It was just about the same time that Mrs. Chudleigh left, a moment or two before, I think. I'd only just sat down when he began to feel in his pockets for his pouch. I offered him mine, but he said he preferred to go and get his own tobacco.'

'How long, in your opinion, was he away?'

'Oh, some little time. Quite a quarter of an hour, I should say.'

Harding wrote something down in his notebook. 'Thank you. Sergeant, will you ring the bell, please?'

Halliday sat watching him in a fidgety silence. After a moment he said with forced lightness: 'If there's anything else I can tell you, Inspector, naturally I should be only too glad to.'

'I don't think there's anything else just now, Mr. Halliday.' Harding looked up as the butler came in. 'Would you be good enough to ask Mrs. Halliday to come here?' he said.

'You'll find her in the drawing-room, Finch,' interpolated Halliday. He turned back to Harding. 'She's a bit upset about the whole business, you know. I must say, it came as a bad shock to me too. I was absolutely thunderstruck. I suppose there's no chance it could have been done by an outsider? That's what Lady Billington-Smith thinks, you know. Someone who must have entered by the window.'

'Until I have a little more data, Mr. Halliday, I'm afraid I can't venture any opinion,' replied Harding expressionlessly.

'Of course the unfortunate part of it is that there are so many of us who might have done it,' said Halliday ruefully. 'Myself, and Guest, and young Billington-Smith, and I suppose Miss de Silva as well. I don't mind telling you that I shall be rather glad when it's been cleared up. I'm not a fool, and I can't but see that so far everything points either to me or to Billington-Smith.' He looked round quickly as his wife came in. 'Ah, there you are, Camilla! Come along, dear: the Inspector just wants to ask you one or two questions.'

Harding had risen. 'Will you sit down, Mrs. Halliday? Yes, in that chair, please.' He turned to Halliday. 'I won't keep you any longer Mr. Halliday,' he said pleasantly.

'Oh, that's all right, Inspector!' Halliday replied. 'I'll stay till you've finished with my wife.'

'I would rather see your wife alone, if you don't mind,' said Harding, still pleasantly, but with a note of purpose in his voice.

Halliday frowned. 'Is that entirely necessary? My wife would much prefer me to stay with her – she's feeling very nervy still, aren't you, Camilla?'

Harding smiled down at Camilla. 'There's no need for you to be at all nervous, Mrs. Halliday. Sergeant, will you open the door for Mr. Halliday?' He sat down again at the table, and pushed the papers on it a little way away from him. His attitude was rather that of one settling down to a comfortable talk; he did not look towards Halliday again, and after a moment's indecision Halliday left the room.

The Sergeant, having shut the door, went back to take up his dogged stand again before the fireplace, but was foiled.

'Sit down, Sergeant,' said Harding, nodding to a chair behind Camilla's. 'Now, Mrs. Halliday, I'm sure this has all been a great shock to you, and you would much rather not talk about it. But I'm afraid I shall have to ask you one or two rather important questions, over which I think probably you can help me.'

Camilla, who had entered the room with a mixture of fright and defiance on her pretty, weak face, revived somewhat under this gentle handling, and spoke quite cordially. 'Of course, I don't mind a bit, only I simply don't know anything, Inspector.'

'Well,' said Harding, laughing, 'if I ask you anything you don't know you must just say so, and we'll try again.'

Camilla gave a little titter, and patted the set waves of her hair. 'Oh, if you're not going to be cross with me for not knowing things, I'm ready to answer anything. Only I've got awfully highly strung nerves – I've always been like it: most frightfully sensitive – and that ghastly policeman yesterday simply barked at me, and it was too awful for words.'

'I won't bark at you,' promised Harding. Without appearing to look very closely at her he had, nevertheless, kept his eyes on her face from the moment she had entered the room. As a result of this trained observation he said now: 'You will have to forgive me if I ask you something rather personal, Mrs. Halliday. You are, if I may say so, a very attractive woman. I think the General thought so too, didn't he?'

Camilla laughed again, and threw him her coquettish glance. 'Well, I must say I never expected to receive compliments from the police, Inspector! 'Tisn't for me to say whether I'm attractive or not.'

'I should hardly believe that the General did not find you so,' prompted Harding.

'Oh well, perhaps he did, a bit. You know what old men are, and although Lady Billington-Smith's awfully sweet – I'm frightfully fond of her, you know – she always gives me the impression of being rather cold. Poor Sir Arthur wanted to have some fun, I expect, and he happened to like me rather – I don't know why, I'm sure – and that's how it was.' She paused, and added: 'Of course, there was nothing in it! He just liked to flirt a little, and he was ever so much older than me.'

'I quite understand,' nodded Harding. 'And I expect that like a great many men of his type he was inclined to be tactless in his flirtations – forgetting that you had a husband by you.'

A wary look crept into the shallow blue eyes. 'Oh, Basil absolutely trusts me, Inspector!'

'I'm sure he does. But he might still feel a trifle jealous,' suggested Harding.

'You know too much, Inspector. I daresay Basil was a tiny bit jealous, but not seriously – because, I mean, he had no cause.'

Harding raised his brows quizzically. 'No cause at all, Mrs. Halliday? Are you going to tell me you didn't lead Sir Arthur on just a little?'

Again she patted her hair. 'Perhaps I did – a very little,' she said archly. 'However did you guess?'

'Well, there must have been some reason for his extraordinary behaviour in trying to make you accept a cheque for fifty pounds,' Harding replied. 'I imagined that in all probability you did flirt with him just enough to make him leap to quite wrong conclusions.'

At the mention of the cheque she had flushed, and seemed to retire into her shell. She said cautiously: 'I don't know why he gave me that cheque. It was frightful cheek, and of course I ought to have told him so, only it was so awfully awkward.'

'It must have taken you very much by surprise,' said Harding sympathetically.

'Oh, it did, absolutely! I didn't know what to say.'

'Where were you, Mrs. Halliday, when he gave it to you?'

'We were at the keeper's cottage. You see, Sir Arthur had promised to show me a litter of puppies just as soon as he'd been to the bank in Ralton. I simply adore puppies.'

'At what time was this, Mrs. Halliday?'

'Well, I don't think – oh yes, I do! It was eleven o'clock – well, a minute or two later, probably, because he had to put some notes, or something, into his safe first.'

Harding looked up. 'Was Sir Arthur wearing gloves, Mrs. Halliday?'

'Gloves? No, of course not. Why?'

'I merely wanted to know. You were saying that you were in the kennels when the cheque was given you. Was there a pen and ink for him to write with there?'

'Oh, he had his fount—' She broke off, and added a trifle shrilly: 'He didn't write the cheque there, Inspector. He just pulled it out of his pocket and sort of pressed it into my hand. He'd written it before, of course.'

'Ah, I see!' said Harding. 'And – quite honestly, Mrs. Halliday – you hadn't given him any reason to think that you would accept it?'

'Oh no, I was simply astonished at him!' averred Camilla.

Harding moved several of the papers on the table, and chose one from amongst them. With his eyes on it he said: 'You hadn't at any time during the week-end allowed Sir Arthur to kiss you?'

Camilla, her gaze also riveted to the paper, hesitated. The Sergeant, aware that amongst the various statements before Harding there was none in the least relevant to the question, nodded his head slowly in appreciation of this stratagem.

Harding looked up from the document in his hand. 'Come, Mrs. Halliday! Did Sir Arthur kiss you or not?'

'There's no harm in a kiss,' she said defensively. 'What if he did?'

'Once, Mrs. Halliday, or several times?'

'I don't know who it is who's been spying on me,' Camilla said, 'but I think it's the absolute limit!'

Harding did not pursue the question any further. He laid the paper down again, and sat back in his chair. 'Let us go back to where we were,' he said. 'What happened after the General had pressed this cheque on you?'

'We motored back to the house,' answered Camilla sullenly.

'And then?'

'Sir Arthur wanted me to take some of his roses home with me, and he called Lady Billington-Smith down to see about it. I must say, I did think at the time that she was rather fed-up. Sir Arthur was being awfully complimentary to me, and I could see she didn't like it, so I just ran upstairs to take my hat off. Of course I've always had a sort of feeling about Fay, that though she's so quiet, and sweet, if you know what I mean, she's one of those people who get simply frightfully jealous underneath. At least, that's how she struck me, and of course one couldn't help seeing that she didn't get on with Sir Arthur. I was rather sorry for him, in a way. I simply hate saying anything about my friends, and I'm not in the least narrow-minded – in fact, quite the opposite – but I must say I did think the way she and Mr. Guest behaved was a bit thick. I mean it was utterly obvious that she's in love with him, and he with her. And poor Sir Arthur was quite unsuspecting, which did seem to me rather pathetic.'

'When you say that the way Lady Billington-Smith and Mr. Guest behaved was a bit thick, do you mean that there was love-making between them?'

'Oh, not in public!' said Camilla, with a little laugh. 'They were much too clever for that. Only anybody could tell by the way he looked at her that he was absolutely potty about her.'

'But you did not actually see anything more than these looks?' persisted Harding.

'No, but I can put two and two together, Inspector.'

'I see that you can, Mrs. Halliday. But I think we have wandered away from the point. Will you tell me what you did when you went up to take your hat off?'

'Well, I took it off,' said Camilla flippantly. 'And then I powdered my nose, and one thing and another, and then – oh, I forgot to say that Basil, my husband, came in, and I gave him the cheque, and told him what had happened.'

'Was he very much annoyed, Mrs. Halliday?'

'Oh no, not annoyed!' Camilla assured him. 'I mean, it was really quite funny, the General being smitten by me. We made up our minds to treat it as a joke, only of course Basil said the cheque must be given back at once. So he said he'd do that, and I went down on to the terrace.'

'Do you remember what the time was then?'

'No, I can't say I do, but that's the worst of me, I simply never look at the clock.'

'You were on the terrace, I think, when Mrs. Twining arrived?'

'Yes,' admitted Camilla.

'And when did your husband join you?'

'Oh, quite soon afterwards – I don't know exactly. Every one was there, except Geoffrey and that sickening Mexican girl, and where they were I don't know, though I do know that Geoffrey *said* he'd been out walking, which I must say I thought sounded very odd.'

'You remained on the terrace until one o'clock?'

'Yes, *I* did,' said Camilla significantly. 'And so did my husband.'

'Did anyone leave the terrace before one o'clock?'

'Mr. Guest did. He pretended he hadn't got his tobacco pouch on him—'

'Have you any reason for saying "pretended", Mrs. Halliday?'

'I don't know whether he had or not, but I thought at the time that it was only an excuse, because Basil offered to let him have some of his, and he wouldn't take it. He insisted on going indoors for his own, and he was gone for ages.'

'What does "ages" mean, Mrs. Halliday?'

'Oh, I don't know, but ever so long! I couldn't think what he could be doing. In fact, I told him he was nearly too late for a cock-tail when he came back. And I thought then that he seemed funny in his manner – awfully silent, you know. I don't know whether Basil told you, but I do think you ought to know about the blood on Mr. Guest's shirt-cuff.'

'Yes, I think I certainly ought to know about that,' said Harding. 'Perhaps you'll tell me, Mrs. Halliday?'

'Well, I don't like saying anything against anybody, but all I know is that there was blood on his cuff, and Basil called attention to it. And Mr. Guest was obviously annoyed, and he told us some story about cutting his wrist when he was opening his tobacco tin. But all I can say is nothing would induce him to let us see the cut, though both Fay and I wanted to. He got frightfully curt, and pulled his sleeve down. I didn't think anything of it at the time – I mean, one doesn't – but when Mrs. Twining came out with her glove all soaked with blood (it was too frightful: it made me feel absolutely sick!) and told us what had happened I couldn't help wondering. Because I know Mr. Guest is mad about Fay, and of course Sir Arthur had been pretty awful to her, going for her in public, and that sort of thing, and – well, anyway, I do think you ought to know about it, because if anyone had a reason for wanting to kill Sir Arthur it was him, or Geoffrey, and not Basil.' She wrenched at her handkerchief as she spoke, and added: 'Mind, I don't say it was him, because it might just as easily have been

Geoffrey. I shan't forget in a hurry what he did when the doctor told him his father had been murdered. I'm not easily shocked, but that just about finished me. He came in through the drawing-room window looking absolutely wild – his face was simply ghastly: dead white; and his eyes all queer and, sort of burning – and he just burst out laughing! He did honestly! It was perfectly awful; I was quite frightened of him. I said so at the time.' She glanced up at Harding, and made as if to rise. 'Of course, I shouldn't have told you, only that I knew no one else would, and it doesn't seem to me *right* the way they all try to shield one another, when poor Sir Arthur's been killed like that. Do you want to ask me anything else?'

'No, nothing else, thank you,' Harding answered getting up.

'Well, can Basil and I go home? It's frightfully inconvenient for us having to hang about here, and I can't sleep a wink, my nerves are utterly on edge.'

'I shall let you go home just as soon as I can,' said Harding, and went to open the door for her.

When she had gone the Sergeant said severely that she seemed to him to be real spiteful. In his opinion the evidence against Basil Halliday was strong. He wanted to know what the Inspector thought of it.

Harding refused to say. 'The trouble is, they're all lying,' he said. 'Lady Billington-Smith wants to make me believe she was not on such very bad terms with her husband; young Geoffrey wants me to think that his mood of desperation was caused by Miss de Silva, and had nothing to do with his father; Halliday is trying to shield his wife, who undoubtedly angled for that cheque; and Mrs. Halliday is attempting to throw suspicion on anyone who is not Halliday!' He ran through the papers on the table. 'The head housemaid: I think I'll see her next, to check up on Mrs. Halliday's story. Ring, will you?'

It was not many minutes before the starched and rigid Peckham came into the room. She looked prim and uncompromising, and took up a stand before the table. Yes, she perfectly remembered what had happened yesterday morning. She had been packing for Mrs. Halliday when Mrs. Halliday came in to take her hat off.

'What did you do then?' inquired Harding.

A faintly scornful look crossed Peckham's sharp features. 'I hope I know my place, sir. Naturally, I left the room immediately.'

'Did you go downstairs?'

'I did not, sir. I went into the still-room, opposite, to wait for Mrs. Halliday to go down.

'Did anyone go into Mrs. Halliday's room while she was in it?'

'Not to my knowledge they didn't, sir.'

'And when Mrs. Halliday left the room, what did you do?'

'I went back to finish the packing, till Mr. Halliday came in.'

'When was that?'

'I couldn't say for sure, sir. Perhaps five minutes later; perhaps not so long.'

'And when he came in you again left the room?'

'Certainly, sir.'

'How long was he in the room?'

'Not more than a minute or two, the first time.'

'He came back, then?'

'Yes, sir; he came back as I was leaving the room.'

'Did you notice anything unusual about him – any signs of agitation?'

'It is not my place to notice the guests, sir, but I thought Mr. Halliday seemed a little upset. He brushed by me in a rough way, not what I am accustomed to in a gentleman, and went into his bathroom, and slammed the door.'

'Thank you. One more question before you go: I think you told the Superintendent yesterday that Mr. Billington-Smith sat in the upper hall for nearly an hour that morning, waiting to be admitted into Miss de Silva's room. Did it strike you that he was in any way upset?'

'I didn't give any heed to Mr. Geoffrey, sir. I have my work to do, unlike others I could name who waste their time goggling at their betters and making up a pack of theatrical nonsense about them.'

With Dawson's colourful statement under his hand Harding asked: 'When you sent Dawson out of Captain Billington-Smith's room, was Mr. Geoffrey – er – "holding his head in his hands, and looking fit to kill himself"?'

Peckham gave a sniff. 'I'm sure I couldn't say, sir. I didn't notice him particularly.

'Thank you, that's all then. Will you ask the butler to send Mr. Guest to me, please?'

When she had left the room the Sergeant shook his head. 'She's speaking the truth all right, sir. That was a lie what Mr. Halliday told you: he never had that talk with his wife which he said he did. If you was to ask me, I should be bound to say that to my way of thinking he had his suspicions about her little game all along, and he found that cheque when she'd gone out on to the terrace. It looks bad, sir; uncommon bad it looks.'

Harding had picked up Stephen Guest's statement. 'Do you know if there's any truth in what Mrs. Halliday said about Guest and Lady Billington-Smith?'

'I never heard anything about it,' said the Sergeant. 'Of course the General was a lot older than her ladyship, not that that proves anything.'

'Mr. Guest!' announced Finch, from the doorway.

Stephen Guest came in with his slow, deliberate tread.

CHAPTER TWELVE

GUEST'S deep-set eyes considered the Sergeant for one indifferent moment, and then passed on to Harding's face, and remained there. 'Good afternoon, Inspector,' he said, and walked up to the chair by the table and sat down.

'Good afternoon,' Harding returned. 'I have one or two questions I want to ask you concerning your movements yesterday morning, Mr. Guest.'

'Carry on,' said Guest, feeling in one coat-pocket for his pipe and tobacco-pouch. He settled himself at ease in his chair and began in a methodical way to fill his pipe.

'Can you remember just what you were doing up till twelve o'clock?'

Guest smiled slightly. 'Rather a tall order, Inspector. I don't think I did anything in particular. I read the paper, knocked the billiard balls about a bit, and went out to sit on the terrace – round about eleven-thirty, I should say. Halliday was with me: he might know the exact time.'

'Then it was not because you had something particular to do that you told the footman he need not be in a hurry to pack your bag, as you had changed your mind and were not leaving by the early train?'

Guest struck a match, and waited for it to burn a little way up the stick before holding it to his pipe. 'No,' he said.

'What did induce you to change your mind, Mr. Guest?'

Stephen Guest puffed at his pipe, and pressed the tobacco down with one spatulate finger. 'I thought I might as well travel up with the Hallidays on the afternoon train,' he replied.

Harding glanced up from the paper in his hand. 'There had been, before breakfast, some unpleasantness between Sir Arthur and Lady Billington-Smith, I think?'

'So I believe,' replied Guest uncommunicatively.

'Did you hear this quarrel in progress?'

'I did.'

'Did that in any way influence you when you decided to leave by the later train?'

'It did not.'

There did not seem to be anything more to be got out of him on this point. Harding scrutinized him for a moment in silence, and then asked: 'You were, I believe, related to General Billington-Smith?'

'Some kind of cousin,' agreed Guest. 'More like a connection.'

'You visit this house fairly frequently?'

'Now and again,' said Guest, carefully laying the charred match down on the edge of the table.

'You were, then, on good terms with the General?'

'We didn't quarrel,' replied Guest?'

'What does that mean, Mr. Guest?

'Well—' Guest shifted the pipe to the corner of his mouth – 'The General wasn't just the type of man I get on very good terms with.'

'Yet you stay in his house?'

'Oh yes!' said Guest with equanimity.

Harding looked at him for a moment; there was nothing to be learned from that square, contained face. Stephen Guest returned the look, and continued to puff at his pipe. 'Will you now describe to me, as accurately as you can, what your movements were after twelve o'clock yesterday morning?'

Stephen Guest reflected. 'That would be about the time the General came in with Mrs. Halliday, wouldn't it? I was on the terrace.'

'Was anyone with you?'

'Yes, Miss Fawcett joined me there.'

'Mr. Halliday was not on the terrace?'

'Halliday went into the billiard-room shortly before Miss Fawcett turned up.'

'When did you leave the terrace, Mr. Guest?'

'Very hard to say,' Guest answered. 'Somewhere about twelve-thirty, I should put it.'

'Were you on the terrace when Mrs. Chudleigh arrived?'

'I was.'

'And when she left?'

'No, I didn't see her go.'

'And when the butler brought out the cocktails?'

'No.'

'How long would you say that you were absent from the terrace, Mr. Guest?

Guest considered the point. 'Some little while. Ten to fifteen minutes.'

'What were you doing during that time?'

'I went up to my room to get some tobacco.'

'Is that all, Mr. Guest?'

'Substantially,' nodded Guest. 'I opened a new tin, and cut my-self on the jagged edge. It took a few minutes to stop it bleeding.' He pulled up his shirt-cuff in a leisurely way, and showed Harding a long scratch on his wrist. 'Nothing much, but I'm an easy bleeder.'

'Did you see anyone while you were upstairs?'

'No.'

'And when you had stopped the bleeding, did you go straight back to the terrace?'

'Straight back.'

'Mr. Halliday, I think, called attention to the fact that there was blood on your cuff?'

'He did.'

'Did you show him that cut?'

'I should say not.'

'Or anyone else?'

'No.'

'Did anyone ask you to show it?'

'I fancy Mrs. Halliday had a deal to say about it. I didn't show it. It was nothing to make a song about.'

Harding picked up his pencil. 'Thank you, Mr. Guest: that's all at present. Will you please ask Miss de Silva to come here?'

Guest got up. 'I will,' he said tranquilly, and walked out.

Harding lifted an eyebrow in the Sergeant's direction. 'Did you make anything of that, Sergeant?'

'You can't, not when they stick to Yes, and No,' said the Sergeant rather disgustedly. 'Tough-looking customer. Daresay he wouldn't stick at much.'

Harding propped his chin in his hand, and looked thoughtfully before him, at the closed door. 'He's got a very cool head on his shoulders,' he remarked. 'And he doesn't mean to give anything away. I wonder.'

The Sergeant gave a little cough. 'There was one thing as struck me, sir.'

'Let's have it, Sergeant.'

'Well, sir, he wouldn't show that scratch on his wrist to anyone yesterday, but he was what I'd call very prompt in letting you see it today.'

'He was,' agreed Harding.

'Of course, it doesn't *prove* anything,' said the Sergeant.

'That,' replied Harding, 'is just the trouble.'

The door opened, and Miss de Silva sailed into the room.

Harding rose, betraying no visible sign of surprise. 'Miss de Silva?' he asked.

'Yes,' announced the lady. 'I am La Lola.' Her eye alighted on the Sergeant, and kindled. 'Is it you whom I have told that I will not have looking at me as though I am an assassin?' she demanded

'No, miss, that was Constable Fletcher,' replied the Sergeant hastily.

'To me,' said Lola, 'there is not any difference between you. Moreover you too stare at me. Perhaps, it is that you like to look at me a great deal because I am beautiful?'

'I'm sure I never—' began the Sergeant, flustered.

Lola smiled kindly at him. 'If that is it I do not at all mind, for you must understand that I am quite accustomed to be stared at.'

'Miss de Silva, will you sit down?' interposed Harding. 'Yes, in that chair. I want you to try and remember just what happened yesterday morning.'

'That is not at all difficult,' said Miss de Silva composedly. 'I have a very good memory, let me tell you. But I must say that I do not understand why you have not seen me before that stupid woman who I find is not a true blonde in the least, but on the contrary dyes her hair. She is not at all important, and besides she has no sense, for she tells extremely foolish lies. I do not like her, she is to me quite unsympathetic, quite repulsive, but I will tell you that if you think it is she who has stabbed the General you are entirely wrong. For one thing she has not enough courage, and for another she wanted the General to make love to her, and, I think, to give her money. She had not any reason to stab him. It is I to whom he was so cruel who had reason.'

The Sergeant looked helplessly at Harding, who, however, preserved a calm front.

'In what way was the General cruel to you, Miss de Silva?'

'I will tell you,' replied Lola cordially. 'From the moment when I have entered his house he has behaved to me with rudeness and brutality, though partly I blame Geoffrey, who was very foolish not to warn his papa that I do not like gin in my cocktail, but only absinthe. Then at dinner he was quite abominable to me because I would not sit and look at a dead hare with blood on its nose, which I find completely disgusting. And after dinner when I, La Lola, have said that I will dance he was not grateful, not at all, but on the contrary very rude, quite insupportable. I have great patience, so I did not walk straight out of the house, and besides it is not sensible to walk out of the house when it is time to go to bed. So next day I was very nice to him, very kind, and I talked to him for quite an hour, but in spite of that, and because he was entirely disagreeable and of an immense stupidity, he declared that Geoffrey should not have any money at all if he married me. So you see it is I and not in the least Camilla Halliday who had reason to stab the General.'

'I see perfectly,' said Harding. 'Will you tell me just what happened when Mr. Billington-Smith informed you of his father's threat?'

'But certainly I will tell you everything. It was a great shock to Geoffrey; he became quite out of his senses, for he tried to come into my bedroom at ten o'clock when he knows perfectly well that I do not see anybody but my maid until eleven. I forgive him because he was distracted.'

'Was he distracted when he entered your room, Miss de Silva?'

'I will be very truthful,' promised Lola. 'You are a policeman, though I find that quite surprising, and it is not wise to tell lies to policemen. That I leave to Camilla Halliday. At first Geoffrey was angry only a little, but when I have pointed out to him that naturally it is impossible that we should be married when he has no longer any money, he became like a lunatic. That may be understood, for I must tell you that he loves me with desperation. I was sorry for him, most sorry for him, but happily it all arranges itself now that the General is dead.'

'You are going to marry him, in fact?'

'Naturally I shall marry him, though I must tell you that I am very much upset by what Miss Fawcett says, that he will not after all be Sir Geoffrey. It is to me quite incomprehensible.'

'Then it is not true that Mr. Billington-Smith no longer wishes to marry you?' asked Harding bluntly.

Lola's lovely eyes opened to their widest extent. 'But how could it be? He is a little upset now: one must make allowances for him. Presently he will be very glad, quite transported, to find that our marriage is now possible. If he has told you that he does not want to marry me it is a great piece of nonsense.'

She spoke somewhat heatedly, and Harding tactfully introduced a fresh subject. 'Tell me, Miss de Silva,' he said. 'What did you do when Mr. Billington-Smith had left your room?'

'At first I did not do anything, because Geoffrey was very violent, and it was necessary that I should compose myself. Presently Concetta, who is my maid, prepared my bath – and that is another thing that I must tell you: there is not any shower to my bath, and I must share it with Miss Fawcett and Mr. Guest. And after my bath I made my *toilette*, and when I had made my *toilette* it was already past one o'clock, and I came downstairs.'

'Was your maid with you all the time you were dressing?'

'No, for she had not enough spirit for the machine which makes a fire for my waving-irons, and she was forced to go to the kitchen to get some more. So you see when she was not there it was quite easy for me to go down in my *négligée* and stab the General. I did not stab the General, because I did not think of it, and besides, in England I find it does not make one popular to kill people.'

Harding said gravely: 'Thank you for being so frank, Miss de Silva. I won't keep you any longer.'

'Do you not wish to ask me any more questions?' inquired Lola, not best pleased.

'Not just now,' answered Harding.

'It does not seem to me that you are a very good policeman,' said Lola with austerity.

A twinkle lit Harding's eyes. 'Would you like me to put you under arrest, perhaps?'

'As to that,' said Lola candidly, 'I have not made up my mind. It is a very good thing to have publicity, but I must speak first to my agent, whom I have sent for to come immediately and discuss with me this affair.'

'I expect that will be best,' agreed Harding, and firmly ushered her out.

The Sergeant passed his handkerchief across his brow. 'Lor', sir, if she wasn't a foreign lady, which accounts for it, I'd say she was barmy. And what's more, sir, you can't trust these foreigners. Subtle, that's what they are. Supposing she did do it? What I mean to say is, who'd suspect her after the way she goes pointing out that she might have done it?'

'Well, if she did do it, Sergeant, it's for us to find the proof.' Harding tapped his fingers lightly on the table, considering. 'It isn't a nice case,' he said presently. 'I think I'll see Miss Fawcett.'

'Yes, sir. But she's the only person who couldn't have done it,' the Sergeant pointed out respectfully. 'That we *do* know.'

'I wasn't suggesting her as a possible suspect, Sergeant. But she seemed to me, from the glimpse I had of her, to be perhaps the only person in this house who might be trusted to give a plain, unvarnished account of what happened here yesterday. Ask the butler to find her, will you?'

Miss Fawcett did not keep Inspector Harding waiting long. She appeared in about five minutes' time, and said at once in her friendliest way: 'I say, have you had any tea? Do detectives drink tea? Because if so, please shout, and I'll send for some.'

Harding regarded her with amusement. 'Thank you very much, but detectives never have tea when on duty.'

Dinah grinned. 'I thought perhaps they didn't. Do you want me for anything special? I'm stiff with alibis, you know. Which,' she added reflectively, 'is rather a good thing, as a matter of fact, because I didn't hit it off with Arthur at all.'

'Was he very unpleasant, Miss Fawcett?'

'Yes,' said Dinah. 'He was a stinker. To tell you the truth, I rather hope you won't find out who killed him, because it's no use being sentimental and talking a whole lot of *de mortuis* rot – it's a jolly good thing for everybody all round that he is dead.'

'For everybody?' said Harding.

'Well, for most of us, anyway. It's a good thing for Geoffrey because now he'll be free to do as he likes without being roared at; and it's a good thing for Francis (that's Geoffrey's cousin), because

I should think Arthur has left him some money; and it's a good thing for Fay because he was a loathly husband.'

'And a good thing for Mr. Guest?'

Dinah looked at him sharply. 'No, I didn't say it was a good thing for him. I don't suppose he's been left anything.'

Harding sat down on the edge of the table. 'Miss Fawcett, I'm going to be quite frank with you, and I have hopes that you will be frank with me. So far I have interviewed a number of people who all had the motive and the opportunity to commit this murder. Not one of them, with the possible exception of Mrs. Twining and the head-housemaid, told me the whole truth. Now, if I ask you one or two questions, will you try and answer them honestly?'

Dinah considered the matter. 'Well, I can't promise to answer them, but I won't lie, anyway, Ins— Look here, do you mind if I call you Mr. Harding?'

The Sergeant waited confidently for the official snub he knew would be dealt out.

'You can call me anything you like,' said Inspector Harding, smiling down at Miss Fawcett.

The Sergeant regarded him in pained surprise, but concluded that the Inspector probably had his reasons.

'Thanks,' said Dinah. 'What do you want me to tell you?'

Harding folded his arms across his chest, and looked meditatively at her for a few moments. 'I think I'll tell you what I know first,' he said.

'Why?' inquired Dinah, mystified.

'Because I think you'll be much more open with me if you realize that it's no use trying to conceal certain facts. To start with, I know that the General didn't get on with his son, but seemed to prefer his nephew; I know that he disapproved violently of Miss de Silva, and behaved towards her with unparalleled cruelty.'

'How much?' interrupted Dinah.

Harding replied with perfect gravity: 'No absinthe, no shower in her bathroom, dead hares, and—'

'Did she tell you all that?' said Dinah. 'Don't you think she's rather good value?'

'Yes, but she wastes my time. I know that young Billington-Smith sat outside her door holding his head in his hands for an hour after his father had disinherited him; I know he left the house in an extremely overwrought condition, and had hysterics when he

137

returned. I know that Mrs. Halliday was encouraging the General to flirt with her, and that Halliday loathed it. I know that your sister had a quarrel with the General yesterday morning that upset her very much, and I know also – I am being perfectly straightforward, Miss Fawcett – that she and Guest are in love with each other. Does that clear the air at all?'

Dinah grimaced. 'You know too much, Mr. Harding. What on earth is there left for me to tell you?'

'You're going to tell me your version of what happened yesterday – bearing in mind that I've received from one at least of the people I've mentioned a highly coloured account.'

'Yes, but I don't want to say anything that might make you suspect Fay, or Stephen, or even Geoffrey of having done the murder,' objected Dinah frankly.

'Remember, Miss Fawcett, that I've already enough data about all these people to make me suspect them.'

'Well, go ahead,' sighed Dinah, folding her hands in her lap.

'We'll start with a talk you had with Geoffrey Billington-Smith on Saturday, outside Miss de Silva's bedroom door. Is it a fact that he threatened to do something desperate if his father interfered between him and Miss de Silva?'

'That,' commented Dinah, 'sounds to me like that ass of a housemaid, Dawson. I wonder where she was lurking?'

'Never mind about the ass of a housemaid,' said Harding, with the hint of a smile in his eyes. 'Did he say something to that effect?'

'Yes – a lot of dramatic stuff. I've noticed that ineffectual people usually do go in for highfalutin threats.'

'Is he ineffectual?'

'Ghastly. No guts at all,' said Miss Fawcett elegantly.

'So I inferred. At the same time, he's undoubtedly very emotional. Isn't that so?'

'Yes, but it's the sort of emotionalism that raves instead of doing anything. I've no use for Geoffrey, but I honestly don't think he killed Arthur, Mr. Harding.'

'We'll hope not, anyway. Now about this week-end party: was the atmosphere very thunderous?'

'Rather! It always is when Arthur's on the rampage.'

'Did he take it out of your sister?'

'More or less.

'In public?'

'Anywhere.'

'And yesterday morning it culminated in a more than usually serious quarrel with her?'

'You've got that bit wrong,' said Dinah. 'Fay couldn't quarrel with anybody, and certainly not with Arthur. I wasn't present, so I don't know exactly what happened, but from what I can gather she tried to intercede for Geoffrey, and he flew straight away into a rage, and stormed at her about everything and anything. He was like that, you know.'

'It upset your sister?'

'Yes, thoroughly. I put her back to bed, because she was too weepy to come down to breakfast.'

'She didn't seem to be resentful?'

'Lord, no! Just over at the knees.'

'I see. And what about Guest?'

'Well, if you must know,' replied Dinah, 'he's the faithful swain. Inarticulate, and a bit of a goop. He might easily have knocked Arthur's teeth out, but somehow I don't see him stabbing him in the back.'

'Forgive me, Miss Fawcett, but was there never any talk of divorce between your sister and Sir Arthur?'

'On account of Stephen? No, never. There ought to have been, but Fay would never face the scandal. I am absolutely convinced, Mr. Harding, that nothing would induce Fay to take any action that would lead to – well, this sort of unpleasantness.'

He met her look. 'Quite, Miss Fawcett. Tell me, did you see the cut on Guest's wrist yesterday?'

'No, of course I didn't. Camilla and Fay yapped at him to show it them, but naturally he wouldn't do any such thing. He's frightfully he-mannish, is Stephen. Loathes a fuss.'

'And the Hallidays?'

'She's a gold-digger, and he's nervy and a bit jealous. Dotes on her.'

'Mrs. Twining?'

'Mrs. Twining?' repeated Dinah. 'What do you want to know about her?'

'Anything you can tell me,' said Harding.

'I don't think I can. I hardly know her. She's an old friend of Arthur's, and she came to live here about a year after he did. I've always imagined that she could tell some pretty ripe tales about him if she wanted to, because he was much more polite to her than to anyone else.'

'Do you know why it was she who went to fetch the General on to the terrace?'

'Yes, of course I do. She came specially to talk to him about Geoffrey, because she was about the only person he'd listen to. That's what makes me think he was a bit afraid of her.'

'Is there a Mr. Twining?'

'Colonel. He's dead.'

'I see. Tell me what happened when she went to the General's study. How long was she gone?'

Dinah pondered this. 'I'm not sure. We were all talking. I should think, about five minutes, or even a little longer.'

'And when she came back – was she very much upset?'

'Yes, I think she was. In fact, I'm certain she was. She's awfully self-controlled, and doesn't give away much but she looked pretty queer. I'm not surprised: she actually touched Arthur before she realized he was dead, and her glove was all over blood. Luckily she's strong-minded enough not to have fainted on the spot.'

Harding nodded rather absently. He did not say anything for a minute or two, and Miss Fawcett, respecting this mood of abstraction, sat and studied him in silence. Aware presently of her clear gaze, he glanced down at her, and smiled. 'Has Billington-Smith broken off his engagement to Miss de Silva?' he asked.

'He says he's had a revulsion of feeling,' replied Dinah. 'It's all rather trying (though quite humorous), because the mere sight of Lola sends him flying, and she's got a habit of tracking him down and – and wreathing her arms round him, so to speak.'

'His passion for the lady seems to have been somewhat transient,' remarked Harding dryly.

'Well, she turned him down first, you know,' Dinah pointed out.

'So she did,' agreed Harding and stood up.

'Inquisition over?' inquired Miss Fawcett.

'The inquisition is over for today,' said Harding.

'I see!' said Miss Fawcett sapiently. 'Thumbscrews not yet arrived.' She rose, and stood facing him. 'I wish the murderer hadn't got to be discovered, but I quite see that he must be, and I hope you find him quickly. Because the sort of atmosphere of suspicion and suspense we're living in now is utterly unnerving. Moreover, the sooner we get the house cleared of all these ill-assorted visitors, the better it will be for my sister. By the way, am I under lock and key too, or can I leave the place?'

There was a slight pause. 'I've no shadow of right to keep you here, Miss Fawcett,' said Harding. 'At the same time I wish very much that you would stay.'

'Oh, I'm going to! All I meant was, can I go into Ralton to do the shopping, and pay the bills?'

'Of course you can. Go anywhere you like,' said Harding.

'Thanks very much. And one other thing, Mr. Harding: if you want anything at any time – to be shown round, or to ask any question – do you think you could send for me, and not my sister? She's dreadfully shattered by all this, and I want to keep her out of it as much as I can.'

'I will,' promised Harding. 'But I shall want both your sister and her stepson to be present tomorrow when the safe is opened. Do you know what train the General's solicitor is coming by?'

'Do you mean to say Geoffrey didn't tell you that?' demanded Miss Fawcett. 'Really, he is the most unreliable ass I know! The solicitor arrives at ten-fifty at Ralton Station. His name is Tremlowe. I'll see Fay and Geoffrey are on the spot when you're ready for them. Do you want to see anyone else now?'

'No, I'm going to relieve you of my presence for today, Miss Fawcett. I shall be back in the morning.'

'*Au revoir*, then,' said Dinah, holding out her hand.

The Sergeant, a forgotten spectator, watched the handshake with dawning suspicion. Inspector Harding closed the door behind Miss Fawcett, and stood for an instant, a little smile lurking at the back of his eyes. The Sergeant, his suspicion growing, said with some severity: 'A very pleasant-spoken lady, sir. Very helpful.'

Harding looked up quickly, and a tinge of colour stole into his face. 'I thought she might be,' he said, walking back to the table and collecting his papers into a bundle.

'Yes, sir,' said the Sergeant. 'What I should call a nice-looking young lady too.'

'Quite,' said Inspector Harding casually.

CHAPTER THIRTEEN

INSPECTOR HARDING, driving his car back to Ralton, was rather silent, and frowned at the road ahead of him. The Sergeant ventured presently to ask him what he meant to do next. 'Will you be wanting me, sir?'

'No, I don't think so, Sergeant. I want to tabulate all these statements, and think the thing out a bit. And I want also to see Mrs. Chudleigh. But you needn't come with me there if you'll explain just where the Vicarage is.'

'You want to see Mrs. Chudleigh, sir?'

'Of course I want to see her. Where does she live?'

'At Lyndhurst,' replied the Sergeant. A slow grin spread over his solemn countenance. 'I'm bound to say, sir, I hadn't thought of her, but I wouldn't put it above her – and no more would most of them who knows her. She's a tartar, that's what she is.'

'What I want to see Mrs. Chudleigh about,' explained Harding patiently, 'is to find out from her whether she heard or saw anyone in the study yesterday when she passed that side window.'

'Yes, sir. It was only my little joke,' said the Sergeant, abashed.

When Harding arrived at the Crown, having dropped the Sergeant at the police station, it was close on seven o'clock. He went straight into the dining-room, and had dinner. With the exception of one old gentleman seated at the far end of the room, he was the only diner at this early hour, and was able in the vault-like silence to study his notes while he ate. The knowledge of his identity had reached every one in the hotel by this time, in the mysterious manner peculiar to small country towns, and the waiter hovered about him with respectful assiduity, while various other members of the staff, including two awe-struck chambermaids, peeped at him through the service-door. As he remained quite unconscious of the interest he was creating, this did not discompose him in the least. He continued to study his notes, and ordered black coffee, and an old brandy. Shortly after this the Chief Constable looked into the dining-room, and seeing Harding, came over, and sat down at his table. This was very thrilling, and the chef, who had till then taken very little interest in the Inspector, was moved to peep into the dining-room also.

Major Grierson, who was wearing evening-dress under a light overcoat, explained that he was on his way to a dinner-party in the immediate vicinity, and had just dropped in to have a word with Harding.

'Delighted, sir,' said Harding, and beckoned to the waiter, who came up with great alacrity.

The conversation between the detective from London and the Chief Constable was, however, somewhat disappointing.

'What will you have, sir? Martini? Sherry?'

'Thank you, thank you, I think a sherry – a dry sherry. Dear me, Harding, how it – er – takes one back! Fancy running across you again like this! Most – er – extraordinary!'

When the waiter returned with a glass of sherry for the Chief Constable the conversation was still more dispiriting. All he had to report to the chambermaids, the house porter, and the chef, was that the detective and the Major seemed to know one another very well, and were swopping yarns about the war.

But when he was out of earshot the conversation took a swift turn. The Chief Constable, having enjoyed a reminiscent chuckle over what had happened in a certain billet behind the lines, stopped laughing, and said in a low voice: 'Well, well, you must – er – come and dine with me, Harding. But about this business: you've been up to the Grange?'

'Yes, I've been there, but I haven't reached any conclusions yet,' said Harding.

'Naturally not. Quite. I didn't expect it, my dear fellow. You consider it – er – a difficult case?'

'I do indeed, sir. There are too many people mixed up in it.'

'My view – er – exactly! You haven't – er – discussed it yet with the Superintendent?'

'Not yet, but I will tomorrow morning,' promised Harding.

'Yes, yes, I was sure I could – er – rely on you,' said the Major, swallowing the last of his sherry. 'Must try not to tread on – er – corns!' With which he took his leave, and bustled out to join his wife in the car outside.

Inspector Harding drove up to Lyndhurst Vicarage at half past eight, and sent in his card. The parlour-maid, reading it, stepped back from him as from a coiled cobra and, leaving him standing in the hall, disappeared into a room at the back of the house. She came back in a few minutes, and intimated that he was to step this way, if you please.

He passed unannounced into the room she had come from, and found himself in a fair-sized apartment crowded with china cabinets, incidental chairs, small tables, knick-knacks, and hassocks. The walls were papered in a design of white and silver stripes, and hung with a heterogeneous collection of paintings, photographs, and

Crown-Derby plates. A tapestry fire-screen was set before the empty grate, and the long windows were obscured by very stiffly starched white muslin curtains, and flanked on either side by faded blue brocade ones, looped back with thick silken cords. The room was lit by a central light in an alabaster bowl, and had besides a standard lamp with a pink silk shade behind the sofa.

Mrs. Chudleigh, in a nondescript garment known to her as 'semi-evening dress', was seated bolt upright on the sofa with her work-basket beside her, and a piece of embroidery in her hand. The Vicar, as Harding entered the room, got up from a deep arm-chair on the opposite side of the fireplace. He held Harding's card between his fingers, and said in a vague way: 'Er – good evening, Inspector. Pray come in. You find us all unprepared for visitors, I fear.' With a slight gesture and an apologetic smile he indicated his carpet slippers, and his wife's needlework.

Harding came forward. 'I hope I haven't come at an inconvenient hour, sir? My time is rather limited, you know, and I wanted to be sure of finding Mrs. Chudleigh at home.'

Mrs. Chudleigh removed the steel-rimmed spectacles she wore for working or reading, and replaced them by her pince-nez. 'I must say, it is a very odd hour to come,' she said. 'However, please don't apologize! I am quite at liberty, though what you can have to say to me I am entirely at a loss to discover.' She broke off to admonish her husband, who had placed one of the incidental chairs for Harding. '*Not* that one, Hilary: you know one of the legs is broken.'

'Ah, tut, tut! My memory again!' said the Vicar ruefully. He returned the chair to its place, and pulled forward another. 'I trust we have no broken legs here. Sit down, Inspector. It was my wife, I think, you wanted to see?'

'Thank you. Yes, I have something I want to ask Mrs. Chudleigh,' said Harding, seating himself. 'I'm working, as I expect you've guessed, on the case up at the Grange.'

The Vicar shook his head. 'Shocking, shocking! A terrible affair! What a judgment! Dreadful, dreadful!'

Mrs. Chudleigh stuck her needle into her work, drew off her thimble, and executed a profound shudder. 'I'm sure I have no desire to speak of it,' she said. 'Either my husband or I would have been willing and glad to have visited Lady Billington-Smith in her hour of trouble, but since she apparently feels no need of spiritual consolation I have nothing further to say. I have no doubt that a great many vulgarly inquisitive people will flock to the inquest, which I suppose will be held any day now, but I for one should not dream of forcing my way in.'

'Quite, Emmy, my dear, quite! Naturally you would not wish to be present,' said the Vicar gently. 'That goes without saying. But I think the Inspector wants to ask you some questions.'

Mrs. Chudleigh regarded Harding with unveiled hostility. 'I do not know how *I* can be expected to help you,' she said. 'No one has told me anything about it, I can assure you. The only person I have been permitted to speak to is Miss Fawcett. I'm sure I don't wish to call her secretive, but really I must confess I found her reticence most overdone and foolish.'

'Emmy, dear!' said the Vicar again, still more gently.

She bridled a little, but subsided. Harding took swift advantage of the lull. 'I only want to ask you a few questions about your own movements yesterday morning, Mrs. Chudleigh. Can you remember just when you arrived at the Grange?'

'Oh, if *that* is all—! I rang the front-door bell at twenty minutes past twelve precisely, for I looked at my watch, fearing it might be later. I may say I had ample opportunity for doing so since the butler kept me waiting on the doorstep longer than I should permit any servant of mine to do.'

'And when he admitted you, did he take you straight out on to the terrace?'

'Certainly. Since Lady Billington-Smith was there, I do not know where else he would have taken me.'

'How long did you remain on the terrace, Mrs. Chudleigh?'

'I remained until half past twelve.'

'And you left by way of the path leading round the side of the house to the drive?'

'Yes. I told Lady Billington-Smith there was no need for her to disturb herself on my account. She seemed to me to be far from well, which I am sure was not to be wondered at. Though I shall always consider that she brought it all on herself, marrying that man.'

'Emmy, we must not speak ill of the dead,' said the Vicar.

'No, Hilary, but truth is truth, and it would be clear hypocrisy to pretend that the General was anything but a rude, overbearing, and ill-natured person. No doubt he had his good qualities; I can only say that they were hidden from *me*. He treated Lady Billington-Smith abominably – not that I have any sympathy to waste on her, for I have always considered such a marriage, between a man of his age and a girl of hers, as little short of disgusting – and his behaviour to his son – such a *delicate* boy, too! – was positively brutal!'

'He seems to have been a very unpleasant man,' interposed Harding tactfully. 'What I want to know, Mrs. Chudleigh, is this: when you walked down that garden path, you must have passed the study window. Did you notice whether anyone but Sir Arthur was in the study?'

Mrs. Chudleigh sat up straighter than ever. 'In my young days, Inspector, we were taught that to look in at other people's windows was the height of ill-breeding!' she pronounced.

'I wasn't suggesting that you – shall we say, peered in? But it would have been a perfectly natural thing for you to have glanced that way. Are you sure that you did not do so?'

'It would have been a very unnatural thing for me to have done,' replied Mrs. Chudleigh with asperity, 'particularly since I knew that the General was in his study. Really, I don't know what the world is coming to if I am to be suspected of staring in at windows!'

'Had anyone been talking in the study do you think you would have heard voices?' asked the unwearied Inspector.

The Vicar leaned forward to pat his wife's hand. 'Come, my dear, the Inspector is not accusing you of peering in at the window,' he said soothingly. 'You must see that if you did hear or see anyone it may have an important bearing on the case.'

'If I had seen or heard anyone in the study when I passed I should have communicated with the police the instant the news of Sir Arthur's murder came to my ears,' said Mrs. Chudleigh. She met her husband's mild gaze, and relented a little. 'So far as I am aware there were no voices raised when I passed the window. I daresay my attention would have been attracted had there been any sounds, though I trust I should not have given way to idle curiosity.'

'Equally, Mrs. Chudleigh, any movement in the study would have caught your eyes – er – irresistibly?'

She thought it over. 'It might have. I should not care to say definitely. My impression is that there was no movement.'

Harding got up. 'Thank you, Mrs. Chudleigh; that was all I wanted to ask you.'

He drove back to the Crown at Ralton, and almost immediately retired to his room. It was not until midnight, however, that he at last put his papers away, and went to bed, and by that time he had done much writing, much thinking, and had smoked several pipes.

He visited the police station at nine o'clock next morning, and found the Superintendent in a slightly peevish mood.

'I *was* expecting you to give me a look up last night,' said that worthy austerely.

'Were you?' said Harding. 'I hope you didn't wait about for me. Good morning, Sergeant: have you had any bright ideas?'

'No, sir, I can't say that I have,' replied the Sergeant. 'The more I think of it the more I see that it might have been anybody.'

'Well, let's try and work it out a bit,' said Harding, drawing up a chair to the table, and opening his dispatch-case. 'I'll give you back the statements you took, Superintendent. I think I've tabulated the important points.'

The Superintendent took the sheaf of papers, and put them in a drawer. 'Of course if you don't *want* them—' he began in an aggrieved voice.

'They were most valuable. When I got in last night I thought it might help us if I drew up a time-table. Here it is.' He laid a neat sheet before the Superintendent and nodded to Sergeant Nethersole. 'Come and have a look at it, Sergeant.'

'I take it,' said the Superintendent ponderously, 'that this refers to the morning of the first of July?'

Having received confirmation on this point, he bent his gaze on the time-table, and carefully read it through.

11.30 Geoffrey Billington-Smith left the house.

11.45 The General and Mrs. Halliday returned to the house. Lady Billington-Smith called downstairs; Mrs. Halliday upstairs to her room.

11.50 Lady Billington-Smith into the garden-hall; the General into his study.

?11.55 Mrs. Halliday on to terrace. Halliday upstairs to their room.

12.5 Halliday's voice heard in study.

12.10 Arrival of Mrs. Twining. No sound from study.

?12.10–12.15 Mrs. Twining in hall.

?12.15 Mrs. Twining on to terrace.

12.20 Lady Billington-Smith on to terrace from kitchen-garden.
Mrs. Chudleigh on to terrace from house.

12.25 Halliday on to terrace from billiard-room.

?12.27 Guest left terrace.

12.30 Departure of Mrs. Chudleigh by way of garden path.

12.35 Butler on to terrace with cocktails.

?12.40 Guest back on to terrace.

?12.55 Mrs. Twining to the study.

?1.0 Mrs. Twining back on to terrace.

'You've got a lot of queries,' said the Superintendent, having mastered the time-table.

'They occur where I've had to guess at the exact time. My figures ought not to be more than a minute or two out either way.'

'Well, I daresay it's all very nice,' said the Superintendent disparagingly. 'Not that it leads us anywhere.'

'I think it may,' replied Harding. 'Let us take Lady Billington-Smith first. If you glance at the time-table you'll see that from eleven-fifty till a few minutes before twelve-twenty when she interviewed the gardener, her movements are not accounted for. But at twelve-five Halliday admits to having been in the study, and from twelve-ten to about twelve-fifteen Mrs. Twining was in the hall, and heard no one in the study. That leaves only five minutes for Lady Billington-Smith to murder Sir Arthur, and reach the kitchen-garden at the other side of the house.'

'That's as may be,' said the Superintendent. 'But supposing she did it *before* twelve-five? What about that?'

Harding looked up. 'You are forgetting that Halliday saw the General at twelve-five alive.'

The Superintendent, who never felt at his best so early in the day, glared at the Sergeant, and said: 'You've only got his word for that, Mr. Rarding.'

Evidently Harding did not consider it worth while to argue this point, for he passed on to his next suspect. 'Now we come to Halliday,' he said. 'Somewhere round about twelve he entered the study, to give back the cheque presented to his wife. Has the Sergeant told you of that?'

'Yes, Mr. Rarding, he has, and to my way of thinking that's our man. If you remember, I said so right from the start.'

'I agree with you that a great deal of the evidence points to him. Yet I'm not entirely satisfied. The motive is there, and so is the opportunity. I should say that he is very hot-tempered. I could easily believe in a violent quarrel between him and Sir Arthur, culminating in that blow with the nearest weapon to hand, if it were not for just one thing. On top of the fragments of the cheque in the waste-paper basket were quite a number of other papers. If Halliday committed the murder you would expect to find the cheque uppermost.'

Some shadow of emotion crossed the Sergeant's face. 'I ought to have thought of that,' he said sorrowfully. He stroked his moustache, pondering the question. 'You could account for it, sir,' he pronounced at length. 'Supposing it was Mr. Halliday himself who threw them other papers into the basket?'

'I have considered that point,' admitted Harding. 'It seems to me possible but unlikely. One can argue, of course, that if Halliday had the presence of mind to wipe any finger-prints off the hilt of the dagger he would also have had enough presence of mind to throw papers into the basket on top of the torn cheque. Yet wouldn't it have been a simple matter to have gathered up the pieces of the cheque, and taken them away with him?'

'There is that, of course,' conceded the Sergeant, and stroked his moustache anew.

'Similarly, it is possible that during the quarrel with Halliday, Sir Arthur continued to tear up letters and throw them into the basket.'

'Yes, that's so,' reflected the Sergeant. 'What's more, he might easily have done so, wanting to get rid of Mr. Halliday.'

'To my mind,' struck in the Superintendent, 'we've got a case against 'Alliday.'

'I should hate to arrest him on this evidence,' said Harding. 'Admitted that there are strong grounds for suspicion, let us take a look at Stephen Guest. On his own showing he left the terrace somewhere between twelve-twenty-five when Halliday appeared, and twelve-thirty when Mrs. Chudleigh departed. He says that he was in the house for ten minutes, and possibly longer. When he returned to the terrace attention was called to a blood-stain on his shirt-cuff, for which he accounted by saying that he had cut his hand opening a tin of tobacco.'

'I must say, sir, when I heard him give his evidence I suspicioned him strongly,' said the Sergeant. 'But, come to think of it, that was the effect they all of 'em had on me. It's a nasty-looking case against Mr. Guest, though – seeing as he's in love with her ladyship.'

'It is a nasty-looking case,' agreed Harding. 'And, as I think you said at the time, he's a tough customer. Given two important facts: one, that he loves Lady Billington-Smith; and two, that she wouldn't consent to divorce, things begin to point to him. We have to consider the man himself too. I don't know what impression he made on you, Sergeant – or on you, Superintendent – but he seemed to me a man who knows what he wants, and gets it. He's a strong man, possibly a ruthless one, and certainly – which make it difficult for us – a very deliberate one. If he committed the murder I am convinced that it was not done in the heat of the moment, but was carefully planned – and we're going to have the hell of a job – lacking further evidence – to bring it home to him.'

'Personally,' said the Superintendent, 'I hold to that 'Alliday.'

'You may be right. There are points against it being Guest. To murder a woman's husband (and, incidentally, your host) with the object of marrying her yourself argues an abnormal degree of cold-bloodedness. To stab him in the back isn't a thing you'd expect a man of Guest's type to do. Further, if he committed the murder he did it between twelve-twenty-seven and twelve-forty. Now I have been to see Mrs. Chudleigh, and although she is most annoyed at the suggestion that she would have looked at the study window I am fairly certain that there can have been no one in the room with the General when she passed. Had there been she must have noticed. And, more significant still, the weapon used was the General's own paper-knife, which was always kept in his study, on the desk. That circumstance leads one to suppose that the murder was quite unpremeditated, the knife being snatched up through impulse. At the same time we've got to remember that Guest, who was a connection of Sir Arthur's, frequently stayed in the house, and may easily have known that the dagger was always to be found on the General's desk, and used it deliberately.'

'Look here, Mr. Rarding,' said the Superintendent, affronted. 'Seems to me you're arguing away every bit of evidence you find! How are we going to get on if that's what you do?'

'I see you've reached the same conclusion I have,' said Harding with not the veriest flicker of a smile. 'Following up these suspects is leading us precisely nowhere.'

'Eh?' ejaculated the Superintendent, considerably startled.

'What about Mr. Geoffrey, sir?' asked the Sergeant.

'Still more hopeless. We know he left the house at eleven-thirty and returned considerably after one. According to his tale, he went for a long walk. He may have done so, or he may have slipped back to the house, and murdered Sir Arthur. With a youth of his type it's almost impossible to say what he might or might not do. In a rage he might be capable of anything. I would suggest, Superintendent, that you have a few inquiries made. I want to know whether anyone saw Mr. Billington-Smith between eleven-thirty and one on Monday, and if so where, and at what time. I jotted down the route he said he took.' He hunted in his dispatch-case, and handed over a slip of paper. 'And at the same time, I should very much like to find out whether Captain Billington-Smith was seen in the neighbourhood at any time that morning.'

'Captain Billington-Smith?' repeated the Superintendent. 'You're on the wrong scent there, Mr. Harding. The Captain left the house at ten-forty-five, as you might see by my notes.'

'Yes, I did see it,' said Harding. 'But I should like those inquiries to be set on foot all the same, please.'

'What about the foreign young lady, sir?' asked the Sergeant.

'Somehow I don't think so, Sergeant. We shall have to bear her in mind as a possible suspect, of course, but she doesn't interest me much so far.'

'The butler, sir?'

'Extremely unlikely. We have discovered no motive.'

'This is all very well,' interrupted the Superintendent, 'but what are you driving at, that's what I'd like to know?'

'This,' said Harding. 'That, at present, investigation into the motives and movements of the various suspects is not getting us any forrarder, because though anyone might have done it, there is no proof that any one of them did. Therefore we must change our plan of attack. Now there are just two pieces of evidence which seem to be totally unrelated to any of the people I've mentioned. One is the slip of paper with the word *There* scrawled on it, which was found under the General's hand; the other is the fact that there were no finger-prints on the handle of the safe.'

The Superintendent looked him over with tolerant amusement. 'I thought you'd come to the conclusion, Mr. Rarding, that this wasn't a murder with robbery thrown in?'

'I had. But I am no longer so sure of that.'

'Well, if there weren't any finger-prints on the safe-handle – which there weren't, because I was there when our man took them – I don't see what you want to start thinking about robbery for, and that's a fact.'

'But there should have been finger-prints,' said Harding quietly.

'How do you mean, *should* have been?' demanded the Superintendent. 'Whose finger-prints?

'The General's,' replied Harding. 'At eleven o'clock he opened that safe to put something in it, and according to Mrs. Halliday he was not wearing gloves.'

'You mean,' said the Sergeant slowly, 'you mean that someone had hold of that handle after the General touched it? And, what's more, wiped it carefully afterwards?'

'Of course,' said Harding.

CHAPTER FOURTEEN

AT half past ten Inspector Harding got his car out of the garage at the Crown and started to drive to the police station, where he was to pick up the Sergeant. As he emerged from the inn-yard, sounding his horn, a damsel in a severe linen coat and skirt, and a shirt-blouse with a tie, drew hastily back on to the kerb-stone. Inspector Harding recognized Miss Fawcett, and promptly put on his brakes.

'Hullo!' said Dinah. 'It's you!'

'Hullo!' returned Harding. 'Are you escaping from the clutches of the Inquisition, or just shopping?'

'Shopping. If it weren't for a little matter concerning a licence for my wireless I could face you with a limpid conscience.'

He laughed. 'Wireless licences don't come under my jurisdiction, you'll be relieved to hear.'

'I didn't think they would. I expect you're too big a pot,' said Miss Fawcett naïvely.

'How nice of you!' he said, with a twinkle. 'I'm glad you're not escaping.'

'Couldn't if I wanted to. The dam' car's just died on me,' said Dinah gloomily. 'She was giving trouble all the way here – its a rotten little runabout Arthur used to let Fay drive – and she finally conked out in the middle of the High Street. Like a fool, I let the engine stop when I was in a shop, and of course, she wouldn't start again. So there she is, complete Wreck of the Hesperus, waiting for the garage people to take her away and – burn her, for all I care. Look here, I mustn't stop: I've got to catch a bus to the station.'

'Wait a minute, I'll take you to the station, if you promise not to vanish on the first train.'

'Thanks awfully,' said Dinah. 'I call that handsome. I'm not doing a bunk, I swear. All I want to do is to catch Peacock with the big car, so that I can get home. He's gone to meet Mr. Tremlowe on the ten-fifty, you know.'

Harding leaned across to open the car door for her. 'If that's your reason for going to the station, why bother?' he said. 'Won't you let me drive you back to the Grange?'

'Would you mind?' asked Dinah doubtfully.

'No,' replied Inspector Harding. 'I shouldn't mind at all.'

'Well, it's frightfully decent of you, but I ought to warn you that I've got one or two parcels to pick up. I don't want to waste your time.'

'Where are these parcels?' inquired Harding, letting the clutch out.

'Waiting for me at Dove's, the big linen-draper's in the High Street. Fay feels she must wear mourning, and as she's only got one black day frock, I've had to get her some on approval. I call it rather rot, myself, but she's hot on the conventions.'

'All right, we'll go and collect them, and they can share the dickey with Sergeant Nethersole. We've got to collect him too. Will you direct me to this shop you want?'

'Straight down the High Street. I'll tell you when to stop.' Miss Fawcett settled herself at her ease beside the Inspector, and added chattily: 'Do you mind if I ask you something?'

'Not at all. What is it?'

'Well, do you really wear a god-forsaken badge under the lapel of your coat, and show it to anybody who wants to know who you are?'

'No, of course I don't. I'm not an American!' protested Harding.

'Oh, is it only American detectives who do? I didn't know, but in films they always have hidden badges, and I was wondering whether it was correct. Whoa, that's the shop, just over there.'

Ten minutes later, outside the police station, Harding was resolutely avoiding the Sergeant's eye. The Sergeant surveyed him with mingled pain and disapproval, and clambered in amongst the dress-boxes in the dickey. There was no doubt about it, the Inspector was taking a lot of interest in that Miss Fawcett. It wasn't what the Sergeant had expected of an inspector from Scotland Yard, and while he hadn't got anything against the young lady, at the same time it didn't seem to him the right thing at all.

Such considerations did not appear to weigh with Inspector Harding, and the Sergeant, as he carefully balanced one of the boxes on his knees, was grieved to hear him assure Miss Fawcett that it did not matter if Mr. Tremlowe arrived at the Grange before he did.

Then Harding started the car again, and the Sergeant heard no more. He was able, however, to study Miss Fawcett's charming profile, every time she turned her head to speak to Harding, and from time to time he had a fleeting glimpse of Harding's face as well, as the Inspector glanced down at his lively companion. It seemed to the Sergeant that they were hitting it off a fair treat.

He was quite right. Miss Fawcett, never one to be afflicted by shyness, was talking to the Inspector about himself.

'If it weren't for the general grisliness of the whole business,' she remarked confidentially, 'I think I should rather enjoy seeing a real sleuth at work. It's quite an eye-opener, because till yesterday I'd only met one detective in all my life. He was a man they sent up from the police station when a burglar broke into our flat in town, and pinched a brooch of my mother's, and a couple of plated entrée-dishes. He was definitely sub-human. The detective, I mean. I don't mind telling you that I was rather hostile about you before you arrived.'

'You didn't show it,' said Harding. 'I thought you were very charming, and most efficient.'

'Well, of course I saw you weren't in the least noisome as soon as I set eyes on you,' replied Dinah candidly. 'As a matter of fact, I never should have guessed you were a detective if I hadn't been told.'

'I wasn't always,' explained Harding.

'I thought perhaps you weren't. If it isn't a rude question – snub me, if it is – why are you now?'

'Partly because of the war, and partly because I've always had rather a liking for criminology.'

'How ghoulish!' remarked Miss Fawcett. 'What were you going to be?'

'A barrister. I was reading for the Bar up at Oxford when the war broke out.'

'Couldn't you have gone on with it afterwards?'

'Not very well. My father died the year the war ended, and there wasn't any too much money. So I thought I'd better be self-supporting as soon as I could.'

'Mouldy for you,' said Miss Fawcett with real sympathy.

'Oh no!' said Harding cheerfully. 'I didn't mind.'

'Well, I suppose it's fairly interesting work in a way, and you'll end up by being the head of Scotland Yard or something.'

'I can't imagine anything more improbable. In any case I'm thinking of retiring and rearing chickens or pigs instead.'

'There's absolutely no money in chicken-farming unless you do it on a colossal scale,' said the wordly-wise Miss Fawcett. 'I know several people who tried it, and they all went bust.'

'Then it'll have to be pigs,' said Harding philosophically.

'Awfully mucky,' objected Dinah.

'Chickens on a colossal scale then.'

She shook her head. 'You'd have to sink a frightful lot of capital in it,' she said seriously.

'Never mind, I've come into quite a pleasant legacy, most unexpectedly.'

'Well, I shouldn't blue it on fowls,' said Dinah.

They were still discussing the disposal of Inspector Harding's legacy when the car swept up the Grange drive, and might, Dinah reflected, as she alighted at the front door, have known one another for years. 'Now I suppose you want to get on with this impressive ceremony of opening the safe,' she remarked. 'I don't know if Mr. Tremlowe knows the combination, but if he doesn't he's about the only person in the house who doesn't.'

Harding looked quickly down at her. 'Is that really so?'

'Yes, of course. It's only a potty affair,' Dinah answered. 'I've seen Arthur work it myself.'

'Have you indeed?' murmured Harding, and followed her into the house.

Mr. Tremlowe had already arrived, and was standing in the hall, talking in shocked and lowered tones to Fay, who had evidently come out of the drawing-room to meet him. Dinah at once introduced Harding to him.

'I have just been telling Lady Billington-Smith how more than distressed I am that I should have been out of town on Monday,' said the lawyer in a precise voice. 'I trust my unavoidable delay in coming down has not in any way hindered you, Inspector?'

'Not at all,' replied Harding. He bowed slightly to Geoffrey, who just then came out of the billiard-room.

'Oh – er – good morning!' said Geoffrey. 'Hullo, Mr. Tremlowe! The Inspector wants you to open Father's safe. I suppose Fay and I ought to be there, oughtn't we?'

'Undoubtedly,' said Tremlowe. 'I have also your father's Will with me, which presently I will read to you. I should tell you, Lady Billington-Smith, that I thought it proper to advise Captain Billington-Smith of what has occurred, in case you had omitted, in the very natural flurry of the moment, to do so. As no doubt you are aware, Captain Billington-Smith is one of the principal legatees. I am expecting him to join me here for the reading of the Will.'

'Oh, my God!' exclaimed Geoffrey. 'You don't mean to say Francis is coming back?'

'Certainly,' said Mr. Tremlowe coldly. 'It is very right that he should be here. Now, Lady Billington-Smith, if you are ready I am sure the Inspector would like to see the safe opened without further delay.'

'Yes, of course,' Fay answered, looking nervously towards Harding, and slipping her hand in Dinah's arm. 'Come along, Geoffrey.'

There was a constable on duty in the study. Harding dismissed him, and shut the door. Fay clung tightly to Dinah's arm, shivering a little, her eyes on the empty chair by the desk. Dinah pressed her hand reassuringly, and adjured her in a whisper to buck up.

'Do you know the combination, Mr. Tremlowe?' asked Geoffrey. 'Because if not I can open it for you.'

'Thank you, the General deposited the key with me some time ago,' replied Mr. Tremlowe, putting on a pair of horn-rimmed spectacles. He produced a piece of paper from his pocket-book, and advanced towards the safe.

He was checked by Harding's voice. 'Just one moment, please. Lady Billington-Smith, before Mr. Tremlowe opens the safe, can you tell us what we may expect to find in it?'

Fay withdrew her gaze from the swivel-chair with an effort. 'I'm sorry,' she said shakily. 'What did you say?'

Harding repeated his question. She put up her hand to push the hair off her brow. 'I – I don't think I know,' she said. 'My – my husband never actually showed me. I have an idea he kept certain documents in it, but I'm not really sure.'

'Is it likely that there is any money in it, do you think?'

'Yes, quite a wog,' replied Miss Fawcett, seeing her sister quite vague on the subject. 'Arthur told us he was going to the bank at breakfast on Monday.'

'Yes, yes, of course!' Fay said. 'It was the first of July, wasn't it? I'm sorry to be so stupid, I don't seem to be able to think. My husband invariably paid all the staff, and the household books, and any other bills there might be on the first of each month. And there would be money for current expenses too.'

'About how much, Lady Billington-Smith? Can you give me any idea?'

She frowned over it, trying to collect her thoughts. 'I don't know exactly. About two hundred and fifty pounds. It was usually something like that. Sometimes rather more, sometimes less.'

'Thank you. Yes, please open it, Mr. Tremlowe.'

The lawyer bent over the lock of the safe; after a few moments the heavy door swung open, revealing a quantity of legal-looking documents, tied up with pink tape, some other papers, and, just inside the safe, a bundle of new bank-notes, and some bags of silver. Mr. Tremlowe lifted these up, glancing at the Inspector. 'I take it that you would like me to count these before I inspect the rest of the contents of the safe?' he asked.

'I should, please,' Harding answered.

'Then I will do so,' said Mr. Tremlowe, and walked over to the desk, and sat down in the swivel-chair.

Fay gave a tiny shudder. Geoffrey said in an undertone to Dinah: 'This room feels absolutely ghastly. I wish he wouldn't be so beastly slow; I shall be damned glad to get out of here.'

It seemed a long while before Mr. Tremlowe looked up from his task. 'There are one hundred and ten pounds here, in notes of varying denominations, and ten pounds' worth of silver,' he announced, and methodically slipped the rubber band round the bundle again.

Harding looked at Fay, who was frowning. 'One hundred and twenty pounds?' she said. 'Are you sure, Mr. Tremlowe?'

'Perfectly,' said the lawyer placidly.

'There must be more than that,' she said. 'I mean, there ought to be more. One hundred and twenty pounds couldn't possibly cover all the expenses.'

'Your husband paid no bills by cheque?' suggested Harding.

'No, not local ones. He always used to say it was wasting twopence to do that. I can't understand it.'

Geoffrey said, stammering slightly: 'D-do you mean someone's robbed the safe, Inspector?'

'I have no idea,' replied Harding. 'But a visit to your father's bank will tell us what was the exact sum he drew on Monday morning.'

'If anyone robbed the safe, why not have taken the lot?' said Dinah practically. 'He must have paid bills in Ralton before he came home.'

'That we can easily find out,' said Harding, and glanced at his wrist-watch. 'I'll go along to the bank now, if you will tell me which one it is, Lady Billington-Smith, and if you, Mr. Tremlowe, will let me have the numbers of those notes.'

Five minutes later his car swept past the window. Fay, who had been staring unseeingly at the safe, raised her eyes and said breathlessly: 'If someone did steal the money it means – don't you see, Dinah – it means I was right, and it must have been someone from outside who killed Arthur!'

'Well, we shall see,' said Dinah. 'Meanwhile, let's go and sit somewhere else.'

Mr. Tremlowe rose from his chair. 'With your permission, Lady Billington-Smith, I will take charge of these notes. And' – he looked over the top of his spectacles at the Sergeant – 'if you care to remain with me, Sergeant, I will go through the papers in the safe while we are waiting for the Inspector to return.'

The other three went out into the hall again, and after a moment's indecision Fay said that she supposed they had better join the rest of the party.

Miss de Silva had not, of course, come downstairs yet, but Guest and the Hallidays were on the terrace. Camilla, who was one of those people who never seemed to get any time for reading, had now ample leisure to indulge her declared passion for literature and, in proof of her sincerity, was flicking over the pages of a novel selected at random from Fay's book-shelves. Stephen Guest, whom she had attempted, quite unavailingly, to engage in conversation, was hidden behind *The Times*, and Halliday was sitting in a deep chair with a pipe clenched between his teeth, and his moody gaze fixed on nothing in particular.

When the others came out on to the terrace, Camilla closed her book immediately, and sat up. 'Well, have you opened the safe, and was everything all right?' she inquired.

'We don't know until we find out just how much money my husband drew on Monday,' answered Fay, apparently feeling that there was no need to admit Camilla further into her confidence. 'Geoffrey, did Mr. Tremlowe mention what time we were to expect Francis? I wonder if I had better warn Finch that he may be here for lunch?'

'Oh, is Captain Billington-Smith coming back?' said Camilla, brightening visibly. 'He'll cheer us up!'

'Cheer who up?' snapped Geoffrey disagreeably.

'Well, all of us! I mean, somebody from outside will make a sort of break, in a way, don't you think?'

'No, I don't,' said Geoffrey.

Camilla bridled, and gave vent to a somewhat metallic laugh. 'Well, all I can say is that *some* of us seem to be in need of cheering up – not to mention any names!'

'Oh, do be quiet, Camilla!' said Basil wearily.

Guest, who had risen when Fay came on to the terrace, drew her a little apart, and was talking to her in a low voice. Camilla said meaningly: 'Or perhaps some of us don't happen to need any cheering up. One never knows!'

'Well, I don't,' said Dinah. 'I think the whole situation's rather funny.

'Well!' gasped Camilla, quite diverted by this skilful red herring. 'What a thing to say! *Funny*, when Sir Arthur's been murdered, and one of us is the person who did it!'

Halliday got up, rasping his chair across the paved floor of the terrace. 'For God's sake shut up!' he said roughly. 'Do you think we want that thrown at us? Aren't things bad enough as it is? Oh, lord, can't we *do* something instead of sitting about and looking sideways at each other?'

'That's just it,' said Geoffrey gloomily. 'What *can* we do? Personally, I'm ready to do what anyone wants to, but we can't play tennis, which is the obvious thing – at least, Fay thinks it would look rather bad, and I suppose she's right, really. I don't know about billiards: it's rather different – I mean, it's a quiet game, and indoors. I don't think we ought to play snooker, but a hundred up at billiards surely can't offend anybody.'

'Thanks very much,' said Camilla. 'And I suppose I can mark for you? That *will* be nice!'

'Why don't you play Bridge?' suggested Dinah. 'You can play on the terrace, and Stephen can make a fourth.'

'Oh, do you think we ought?' said Camilla. 'Wouldn't it be rather heartless? I'd give anything for something to do, but I couldn't bear to show disrespect to poor Sir Arthur's memory.'

'Well, I don't know about cards,' said Geoffrey doubtfully. 'Of course, we wouldn't play for money – or at any rate, only for something very small. What do you think, Halliday?'

'I don't see why we shouldn't. It's not as though we were proposing to play poker. Lady Billington-Smith, have you any objection to us having a rubber of Bridge?'

'Bridge?' said Fay vaguely. 'Do you think you ought to? It isn't that I mind, only— Geoffrey, what do you feel about it?'

'Well, I can't see why we shouldn't, if we only play for threepence a hundred,' declared Geoffrey. 'Stephen, will you come and make a fourth?'

'Yes, sure,' said Guest amiably.

'That's settled them anyway,' remarked Dinah, leading her sister into the house. 'Come on, ducky, you've got to try on the raiment I've brought home on approval.'

Twenty minutes later, Francis Billington-Smith walked through the drawing-room and stood for a moment framed by the window, somewhat cynically observing the card-players. 'What a touching sight!' he drawled. 'The bereaved household! Little Geoffrey, too – just bearing up, I see.'

Camilla jumped, and looked over her shoulder. 'Oh, Captain Billington-Smith, how you startled me!'

'Oh, so you've arrived, have you?' said Geoffrey. 'I suppose I can play Bridge if I want to without asking your permission? Two down, vulnerable. That's two hundred and fifty to them above. What on earth you put me up for, Stephen, I can't imagine. Cut, please, Camilla.'

Camilla's attention, however, was all for Francis, to whom she was already pouring out a garbled version of Sir Arthur's murder and a description of her own psychological reactions to it.

Francis broke in on this. 'So interesting!' he said politely. 'But as

I don't know yet when my uncle was murdered or where, or by whom, these observations are somewhat lost on me. Would somebody – not Geoffrey, I think – be kind enough to enlighten me?'

'Your uncle was stabbed in his study between twelve and one o'clock on Monday morning,' stated Guest. 'We don't know by whom.'

'Stabbed?' Francis repeated.

'Yes, with the Chinese dagger he used as a paper-knife,' said Guest unemotionally.

Francis looked rather white. 'My God!' he said. He put his hand into his pocket and mechanically drew out his thin gold cigarette-case and opened it. The fingers that groped for a cigarette were just a trifle unsteady. 'What an appalling thing!' he said.

Geoffrey eyed him with resentment. 'Yes, and it's a damned sight more appalling for us than for you, let me tell you. You weren't here. We were.'

Francis shut his case and tapped his cigarette on it. 'Rather appalling for Uncle too – if you should happen to be looking at it in that light,' he remarked. 'Poor old chap!'

'Naturally we all feel that,' said Halliday, shuffling and reshuffling the cards. 'It's a terrible tragedy. We're all most upset, and shocked.'

Francis's faintly mocking glance lingered for a moment on the Bridge-table. 'I'm sure you must be, he said. 'Quite shattered!'

'Hang it all, you needn't be so pious!' said Geoffrey, firing up. 'You weren't so damned fond of Father yourself!'

Francis raised his brows. 'On the contrary,' he said, 'I was probably fonder of him than any of you. You would hardly believe it, but I'm almost distressed to think he's dead.'

'Let's hope you won't be more distressed when the Will's read,' replied Geoffrey.

'Oh, I hardly think so,' said Francis. He struck a match, and lit his cigarette. 'Does anybody know who murdered him, by the way?'

'No!' said Halliday, pushing the pack of cards away.

'It might,' said Guest, 'have been any one of us.'

'You, for instance?'

'Me, for instance.'

'But how extremely piquant! remarked Francis. 'Let us all put the name of the person each of us thinks did it into a hat, and see who gets the most votes.'

'How can you be so awful?' shuddered Camilla. 'How you can joke about it—! When one thinks of poor Sir Arthur, and all these ghastly policemen spying on us, and everything, it's enough to make one go quite *mad*!'

'You should think of others, Mrs. Halliday. It is very nice for the local police to have something else to do besides having me up for what they call dangerous driving.'

'The locals!' ejaculated Geoffrey. 'I could put up with them, but when it comes to having a damned nosey inspector down from Scotland Yard, behaving as though the place belonged to him, it's a bit thick!'

Francis regarded the tip of his cigarette. 'Dear me!' he said. 'So Scotland Yard has been called in has it? How unnerving for you! And where, by the way, is Fay? Prostrate, I suppose. It is too much to hope that Dinah is still here? Perhaps Dinah committed the murder: she is so strong-minded.'

'Dinah is in the fortunate position of being perhaps the one person who couldn't possibly have done it,' said Guest.

'Oh no, she is not!' said Camilla hotly. 'I daresay you'd all of you like to put it on to me or Basil, and you needn't think I haven't eyes, because I have! Your precious Dinah hasn't got any better alibi than I have. And why anyone should *want* her to be here still is more than I can imagine. Bossing everybody, and trying to monopolize the Inspector, and going on as though she was the only person capable of doing anything!'

'From what I know of Dinah, and from what I can see of the rest of you – always excepting Stephen, of course – I should imagine that she is,' replied Francis. 'Perhaps she will be able to tell me whether I condole with Fay or just tactfully say nothing. It is so awkward, isn't it? I will go and find her.' With which affable speech he walked into the house leaving Camilla to exclaim that she thought his manner quite odd, and Geoffrey to break forth into a bitterly expressed opinion of his personality, impudence, and conceit.

Miss Fawcett was not far to seek. As Francis strolled into the hall she was standing at the foot of the staircase, conferring with Finch.

'Well, beloved?' said Francis. 'I hear you have a perfect alibi. I should have guessed it anyway, from your face of conscious rectitude.'

'Hullo, Francis!' said Dinah casually. 'But, Finch, what sort of a person?'

'A Hebrew person, miss, to my way of thinking. He states that Miss de Silva asked him to call.'

'It sounds to me like a reporter,' said Dinah. 'Where have you put him?'

'In the morning-room, miss. Shall I take his card up to Miss de Silva's room, or would you wish to see him yourself?'

'I don't know. What do you think, Francis? Finch says a man has turned up asking for Lola. Only we're having such a god-forsaken time keeping the press out that I feel a bit suspicious.'

'Who is he?' asked Francis, picking the visiting-card up from the tray Finch held. 'Mr. Samuel Lewis. Unknown to me, I fear.'

'Permit me to introduce myself!' said a rich and cheerful voice. 'Samuel Lewis, always at your service!'

They looked quickly round. A stout gentleman in a navy blue suit and a satin tie had come out of the morning-room, and was advancing upon them. He had a somewhat Jewish cast of countenance, several gold stoppings in his teeth, which made his wide smile quite dazzling, a handsome ring on his finger, and a pearl pin in his tie. He held out his hand to Dinah, and clasped hers with reverent fervour. 'Lady Billington-Smith, I presume. Allow a stranger to offer you his deepest sympathy, madam! And Mr. Billington-Smith! A sad loss, sir: believe me, I feel for you.'

'Thank you so much,' said Francis. 'But I'm not the man you think me. Nor, to be strictly accurate, is this Lady Billington-Smith. We are, alas, quite insignificant persons.'

'I'm happy to meet you, sir,' said Mr. Lewis. 'This is a terrible business. When I got Lola's letter I said to myself at once: This won't do. Definitely No. That is my view, and I don't fancy I shall change it. So you need have no fear of me at all. You'll set your minds at rest right now. Your interests are mine.' He turned, and laid a hand on the outraged Finch's shoulder. 'Now, you'll trot straight up to Miss de Silva's room, my man, and you'll say to her that Sam Lewis is right here.'

'I think perhaps you'd better, Finch,' said Dinah chokingly.

Mr. Lewis regarded her with sympathy. 'On your nerves a little? I understand. A loving husband and a fond father done to death under his own roof while at hand the light-hearted guests, all unthinking of the grim tragedy being enacted, pursue their innocent amusements. What a story! Double columns, I give you my word, and pictures on the front page. But it must not be. That is my verdict. Now I'll tell you something, and believe me what Sam Lewis doesn't know about the publicity racket you can put into a match-box and throw into the incinerator.' He drew closer to Francis, and tapped him on the chest with one stubby forefinger. 'Get a hold on this,' he said impressively. 'What will make you a top-liner in France, with your name in electric signs six foot high, may land you into the first turn in a third-rate music-hall show in England, with people getting into their seats, and fumbling for sixpence for the programme while you're doing your stuff. Take it from me, sir, that's the solid truth. I know what you're going to say. And I tell you, me, Sam Lewis, that you're wrong. Definitely wrong. Glamour's O.K. I'm not saying it isn't. But the public's a ticklish thing. You want to get your fingers on its pulse. That's where mine is, and that's where I'm keeping it. Right on the Public Pulse. And this is what I'm telling you: what the English Public wants is Sentiment. It sees La Lola in her Apache Dance with Greg Lamley. It's a riot. But God bless you, do you suppose the Public wants to think of Lola as the Girl in the last Murder Case? No, sir! Wash that right out. You've got the Public wrong. It wants to think of Lola being a Wife and Mother off the stage, just the same as you or I might be.'

'Hardly, I feel,' murmured Francis.

'And that,' said Mr. Lewis, paying no heed to this interruption, 'is why I say we've got to hush this up. If it had happened in any other country I could have used it. But it's gone and happened in England, and it's no use crying over spilt milk: we can't use it.'

At this moment Finch came downstairs, and said frigidly: 'Miss de Silva desires you to go up to her room, sir. This way, if you please.'

'I'll be right with you,' said Mr. Lewis. He beamed upon Dinah, besought her to rely on him, and followed Finch up the stairs.

Inspector Harding, entering the house three minutes later, found Miss Fawcett clinging to the banisters in a hopeless fit of giggles, while a slim and handsome young man, who was propping his shoulders against the wall, regarded her with a world-weary but tolerant eye.

'You've g-got the Public wrong, F-Francis!' gasped Miss Fawcett.

'Possibly, but I have hidden potentialities of a domestic nature, may I remind you?' He became aware of Inspector Harding, and turned his head. 'How do you do? I regret that I don't know who you are, but pray come in.'

Dinah looked up. 'Oh, hullo!' she said. 'I'm not having hysterics: it's only Lola's manager, or whatever he is. He says we've got to hush it up.'

'I should think you'll have some difficulty in doing that,' replied Harding. 'If someone has arrived to see Miss de Silva, he's her press-agent, I imagine. She told me she had sent for him.' He looked in his grave, considering way at Francis. 'Captain Billington-Smith?'

'The correct answer is, I believe, that you have the advantage of me,' said Francis.

Dinah pulled herself together. 'This is Mr. Harding, Francis.'

'How nice!' said Francis, shaking hands. 'Ought that to en-lighten me?'

'Inspector Harding of Scotland Yard,' explained Dinah.

'Really?' Francis's brows rose in surprise. 'That certainly didn't occur to me.'

There was a light footfall on the stairs; Fay came round the bend, and stood looking down into the hall. For the first time since the discovery of her husband's murder there was a tinge of colour in her face, some shadow of eagerness in her wide eyes. 'Is that the Inspector? You've been to the bank? I – I was right wasn't I? Please tell me what they said!'

'Of course I'll tell you, Lady Billington-Smith,' Harding replied gently. 'Will you come into the study for a moment?'

She came down at once, and passed without hesitation into the study, where Mr. Tremlowe was packing the contents of the safe into a leather satchel. She hardly seemed to notice Francis; her attention was all for Harding. Almost before he had shut the door she repeated: 'Wasn't I right?'

'You were exactly right,' answered Harding. 'Your husband drew two hundred and fifty pounds out of the bank on Monday morning.'

Mr. Tremlowe removed his spectacles, and carefully wiped them. 'That is very interesting, Inspector,' he said. 'Two hundred and fifty pounds, you say. H'm!'

Fay said quickly: 'It proves it was robbery, doesn't it – if my husband didn't pay any bills that morning? Don't you think it does, Inspector?

'Not quite, I'm afraid. I am having the numbers of the missing notes circulated, but until they are traced—'

'Forgive me,' said Francis, 'but do you think I might be told what has happened?'

'Arthur drew two hundred and fifty pounds out on Monday, and there was only one hundred and twenty pounds found in the safe when Mr. Tremlowe opened it today,' explained Dinah tersely.

'Arithmetic is not my strongest point,' said Francis. 'Would somebody work it out for me?'

'The difference,' said Harding, 'is one hundred and thirty pounds.'

'I thought it was.' Francis strolled over to the desk, and stubbed out the end of his cigarette in the brass ash-tray there. 'I don't think you need bother to circulate the numbers, Inspector. I rather imagine I have the missing notes.'

CHAPTER FIFTEEN

AN astonished silence greeted this casual announcement. Only the Inspector continued steadily to watch Francis, without betraying either surprise or suspicion.

'Or, rather,' added Francis, still in a conversational voice of unconcern, 'I had them yesterday. Since then they have, to my regret, changed hands.'

'This is very extraordinary,' pronounced Mr. Tremlowe.

'Yes, that was what I thought,' agreed Francis.

'I must ask you to explain a little more fully, please, Captain Billington-Smith,' said Harding.

'Certainly,' said Francis. 'One hundred and thirty pounds was the precise sum I asked my uncle for on Monday morning.' His glance flickered to Dinah's face. 'No, my sweet, he did not give it to me. He was not in the mood. Geoffrey had been so tactless, hadn't he?'

'Was your need of that exact sum urgent, Captain Billington-Smith?' interposed Harding.

'Decidedly. A debt of honour. Isn't that delightfully old-world? But my cousin Geoffrey had been inconsiderate enough to enrage his father. It was stupid of me to approach him at that moment, of course. I quite thought that between us my cousin and I had queered the financial pitch for some little time to come. However, my uncle apparently relented sooner than I had expected. I received notes to the value of one hundred and thirty pounds yesterday morning.'

'How did you receive them, Captain Billington-Smith?'

'Oh, most thankfully!' replied Francis.

'I am afraid you don't understand me,' said Harding, a hint of steel in his pleasant voice. 'I will put it quite plainly. Through what medium did you receive the notes?'

'The medium of the post,' answered Francis.

'Registered post?'

'No, in a plain envelope.'

'Did it not strike you as strange that your uncle should send such a considerable sum to you in that manner?'

'To tell you the truth, Inspector, I was too much taken up with the contents to think about the envelope.'

Fay spoke, in a queer, harsh voice. 'Arthur would never have done such a thing! I know he wouldn't. I am positive that he wouldn't.'

'My very dear Fay,' said Francis silkily, 'you mustn't think I don't appreciate your motive, but in your anxiety to lead suspicion away from Stephen you mustn't overdo it, you know. You will only defeat your own ends.'

'I have no ends,' Fay said breathlessly. 'If Arthur had sent you the money you wanted it would have been by cheque. He would not have taken it out of the household expenses.'

Francis looked her over with bland contempt. 'Don't let's beat about the bush, darling,' he said. 'And don't worry about my feelings either. Are you suggesting that I murdered Uncle for the sake of one hundred and thirty pounds?'

'I didn't say that! But I know he wouldn't have sent the money like that.'

Harding moved over to the door, and opened it. 'I think, Lady Billington-Smith, that it will be best if I talk to your nephew alone,' he said.

Mr. Tremlowe picked up his satchel, and once more removed his spectacles. 'Come, my dear lady,' he said. 'The Inspector will do better without us.'

Fay lingered for a moment, her eyes on Francis. 'I'm sorry, Francis, I didn't mean that. But it wasn't Arthur who sent you those notes.'

'Come on!' said Dinah briefly, and took her out.

Francis lit another cigarette, and flicked the dead match into the grate. He gave a slight laugh. 'Poor little Fay!' he remarked.

Harding paid no heed to this, but said abruptly: 'This plain envelope that you say the notes were sent in, Captain Billington-Smith: was it addressed to you in your uncle's handwriting?'

'It was,' said Francis.

'Did it contain anything but the notes? Any letter that you can produce?'

Francis inhaled a long breath of smoke before he answered. 'Just a slip of paper telling me he had paid my debts for the last time. What an insight you must be getting into our family!'

'Did you keep this note?'

'I'm afraid I didn't. Thoughtless of me, but then I hadn't visualized the possibility of someone murdering the old man.'

'By what post did you receive the notes?'

'By the first post. I imagine my uncle must have sent them off from Ralton when he went in to cash his cheque.'

'In which case,' said Harding, 'it is rather surprising that the letter didn't reach you by the last post on Monday, isn't it?'

'Oh, is it?' replied Francis, mildly interested. 'I expect you're right, but I've always found the post from Ralton wonderfully irregular.'

'You are probably more familiar with it than I am,' said Harding. 'When were you first aware of your uncle's death?'

'Last night, when Tremlowe rang me up.'

'At what hour was that?'

'I've no doubt he could tell you, if you really want to know. I should say it was at about half past ten but I may easily be wrong. Is it so important?'

'It is not very important,' explained Harding 'but I am wondering why you did not acknowledge receipt of the money?'

Francis stretched out his hand towards the ash-tray and tapped his cigarette over it. 'I said you were getting an insight into the family peculiarities,' he said. 'An inability to answer letters by return of post is one of them. Is there anything else I can tell you?'

'Several things, Captain Billington-Smith. At what time did you leave this house on Monday morning?'

'I'm led to wonder,' said Francis reflectively, 'whether you of the Police Force invariably time all your actions? I don't.'

'In fact, you don't know when you left the house?

'I haven't an idea. Somewhere round about eleven, I should imagine.'

Harding stepped back to the the wall, and pressed the electric bell. Francis watched him with cynical amusement. 'I admire your painstaking attention to detail, Inspector.'

'Yes,' said Harding. 'We have to be painstaking in my profession.' He sat down in the swivel-chair, and drew out his pocketbook, and made a note in it. When the butler came in answer to the bell, he looked up. 'Finch, do you know at what time Captain Billington-Smith left this house on Monday morning?'

Finch thought it over. 'I sent Charles up to fetch down the Captain's suitcase,' he mused. 'That would have been at about half past ten. Now I come to think of it, it was half past ten, sir, for Charles was, as you might say, hanging around, waiting for the Captain, and he happened to pass the remark to me—' He stopped, and gave a deprecatory cough. 'Well, sir, he drew my attention to the time, him having his regular work to get on with.'

Harding looked at Francis. 'Do you agree with that estimate of the time, Captain Billington-Smith?'

'I always agree on trivial points,' replied Francis. 'It saves trouble.'

'That's all, then, thank you,' said Harding, nodding dismissal to Finch. 'Now that we have succeeded in establishing that fact, I want to know when you arrived in London, please.'

'Hope seems to spring eternal in your breast, Inspector. I'm tempted to give you a probably erroneous but definite answer – just to please you.'

'I shouldn't,' said Harding. 'Was it before lunch or after?'

'After. Early afternoon.' He met the Sergeant's intent gaze, and raised one slender hand. 'I know exactly what you are thinking, my very dear friend. We have met before, have we not? You are quite right: it would have been much more like me to have made London in time for lunch. Such was the general intention. Fate, however, one puncture, and one clogged jet decreed otherwise. The memory of that drive is still rather painful.

'Did you stop for lunch on the road?' asked Harding.

'I ate an extremely disgusting meal at the Stag, at Bramhurst.'

'Bramhurst!' ejaculated the Sergeant. 'Bramhurst's no more than a matter of forty miles from here, sir!'

'I am quite aware of that, thank you. You will probably cover the distance much quicker than I did. The garage that had my distinguished patronage, by the way, is the big one on the right as you drive down the main street. Not the one on the left, remember; they won't know anything about me there.'

'How long did it take you to cover those forty miles?' inquired Harding.

'Do I subtract the time spent changing a flat tyre, and tinkering with the plugs?'

'From door to door, please.'

'Two hours,' said Francis, putting out the stub of his cigarette.

'Do you say that from conviction, Captain Billington-Smith, or to gratify me?'

'My felicitations, Inspector: you are becoming quite human. From conviction. I had the curiosity to look at my watch. I arrived at Bramhurst at half past twelve. I can even tell you what I had for lunch.'

'I don't think I'll trouble you to do that, thank you. Are you staying here for the inquest, may I ask?'

'Oh, I think so, certainly. I shouldn't like to miss anything,' said Francis.

'Then I won't keep you any longer now,' said Harding, rising to his feet.

The Sergeant opened the door for Francis to pass out, and shut it carefully behind him. He waited for several seconds before he spoke, as though to be sure that Francis was out of earshot, and then he said emphatically: 'That's the queerest story we've heard yet, sir – and we haven't half heard some fishy ones. Him take two hours to cover forty miles? Yes, I wish I may live to see it. That's all I say, sir: I wish I may live to see it!'

'All right, Sergeant. We'll talk it over while we have lunch.'

'Yes, sir,' said the Sergeant, still brooding. 'What's more, I don't believe he had a puncture nor a dirty jet either.'

'Well, you'll be able to verify that,' said Harding. 'I'm going to send you off to Bramhurst this afternoon. Now let's go back to Ralton and have lunch.'

Lunch at the Grange was a somewhat constrained meal. The presence of Mr. Lewis, whom Lola had commanded to remain, made it impossible for Geoffrey to tell his cousin that he believed not one word of his story, and even prevented Camilla from indulging in her usual free-spoken recapitulation of all that she had felt since she had heard of poor Sir Arthur's murder. Fay did not appear in the dining-room at all; Dinah was wrestling with inward giggles; Mr. Tremlowe ate and drank in almost complete silence, occasionally casting a cold and disapproving glance at the voluble Mr.

Lewis; Halliday confined his conversation to an exchange of views on Disarmament with Stephen Guest; and Francis laid himself out to annoy every one by being extremely agreeable to Mr. Lewis.

Lola, who was still wearing the trailing black frock, and had brushed her hair in two sleek wings framing her face, seemed to be satisfied with the result of Mr. Lewis's visit. 'It is seen that my picture must not go into the papers,' she announced. 'I am very reasonable, and I do not make further objection.'

Mr. Lewis patted her hand. 'That's a good girl,' he approved. 'You trust Sam's judgment, and you'll never go wrong.'

'If I did not trust you, I should not any longer permit you to arrange my affairs,' said Lola. 'And that reminds me that after lunch you must tell this Inspector, who is, I think, not altogether a fool, that I will not be arrested for murdering Sir Arthur, since it is not after all good publicity, but on the contrary, very bad. Besides,' she added thoughtfully, 'you would not like me to be arrested, would you, Geoffrey?'

'I don't mind what you do,' said Geoffrey. 'I mean, no, of course I don't want you to be arrested, but it's your own affair, not mine.'

'But certainly it is your affair, my dear Geoffrey,' said Lola. 'And you must let me tell you that I have been very patient, because I have much sympathy, but it becomes absurd, the way you are behaving.'

Francis surveyed his cousin benignly. 'How is love's young dream? You must tell me, Lola, what you would like me to give you for a wedding-present.'

Mr. Lewis wagged his finger admonishingly. 'Now, now, now!' he begged. 'I've been talking to Lola about this marriage racket, and believe me I haven't finished yet. Don't get me wrong: I'm not against marriage. I'm a believer in it. It's a good thing – in its place.' He nodded affably at Geoffrey. 'I know just how you feel, Mr. Billington-Smith, but you've got to look at it from Lola's angle. You want to call her yours, but you've got to remember—'

'No, I don't,' interrupted Geoffrey, choking over a piece of salad.

'Well, well, that's what you say,' said Mr. Lewis tolerantly, 'but I guess we all know what a young husband gets like when he's won a peach like Lola here for his bride. Don't we, sir?' he added, taking Mr. Tremlowe suddenly into his confidence.

'I fear I cannot give an opinion,' replied Mr. Tremlowe icily.

Geoffrey had swallowed the salad by this time. 'I may as well tell you, Mr. – er – Lewis, that my faith in women is absolutely shattered.'

'Now, you don't want to take it like that,' said Mr. Lewis kindly. 'Lola's got a duty to herself and the public. She's young. She's a top-liner. Supposing she was to marry you, right now, at the height of her career? Do you know what it would be? It would be a downright sin!'

'Yes, I quite agree, and I've already told her I don't want to marry her.'

Francis turned his head. 'But how clever of you, Geoffrey!' he said. 'All broken off, is it?'

'It is not in the least broken off!' said Lola firmly. 'Naturally I could not marry him when he had not any money, for that would have been a great piece of folly, but now he will have a fortune, and we can be married at once. Let me remind you, my dear Geoffrey, that on Monday you wanted so much to marry me that you became like a madman.'

'Don't distress yourself, dear Lola,' said Francis. 'I feel quite sure that if you wait – till all these tiresome policemen have gone away, you know – he will once more wish to marry you.'

Geoffrey started up. 'What the devil do you mean?' he shouted.

Dinah said fiercely: 'Shut up, Francis! Can't you stop trying to make mischief, just for half an hour? Sit down, Geoffrey: don't be drawn, you ass!'

Geoffrey banged his fist on the table. 'I insist on your telling me what you mean! If you're insinuating that I've broken it off with Lola simply to put the police off the scent – not that there is a scent, because there isn't—'

'Of course I shouldn't have said it,' apologized Francis. 'So thoughtless of me! I'm so sorry.'

'I'm telling you it isn't so!' said Geoffrey, his voice rising.

'No, no, of course,' replied Francis soothingly.

Camilla, who had been staring at Geoffrey as she slowly assimilated the significance of this interchange, said: 'Well, I must say I hadn't thought of that, though I did think it funny that the engagement was off so suddenly. You needn't try and shut me up, Basil. It seems to me anyone can say what they like about anybody in this house except me, but nobody need think I'm going to sit by while the murder's being pushed on to my husband, because I'm not! I haven't said a word till now, but I've seen the way you all look at me and Basil, just because we don't belong to your precious family.'

There was a note of hysteria in her voice. Halliday tried to frown her down. It was Mr. Lewis who dealt with the situation. 'What we need is a little glass of something to steady our nerves,' he said, and picked up the port decanter, and poured some into her glass. 'A charming lady like you doesn't want to let herself get worked up. Look at you, do they? Well, if you take a peep in the mirror maybe you'll guess why. "My face is my fortune, sir, she said," and a fortune it would make you if ever you were to think of going on the stage.'

Camilla was momentarily appeased by this fulsome flattery, and at once started to tell Mr. Lewis of all the people who, having seen her act in amateur theatricals, had not been able to imagine why she did not take it up professionally.

Lola, who had been sitting in frowning silence, suddenly smiled. 'I see!' she said. 'Certainly it is a very good thing that we should pretend we do not at all want to be married. But why did you not explain it to me, my dear Geoffrey? It is quite ridiculous, quite unreasonable, for you to imagine that I must think of everything for myself, though naturally now it is shown to me I see that if we pretend that we do not any longer love each other the police will not think that it is you who have stabbed the General because he would not permit that we should be married.'

'Oh, my God!' cried Geoffrey, and rushed from the room.

Guest folded up his napkin and put it into its ring. 'I rather think we've sat over this meal long enough,' he remarked, and got up. 'Anyway, I'm through.'

'Well, tell Fay I hope her headache's better,' said Francis, selecting a nectarine from the dish in front of him.

Guest had reached the door, but he stopped and took a half-step back into the room. For one moment a very ugly light indeed shone in his eyes. Then he turned, and walked calmly out of the room.

'A strong man roused,' commented Francis, peeling the nectarine. 'Whatever can I have said to annoy him?'

At half past two Mr. Lewis took his departure, and both Lola and Camilla went upstairs to rest until tea-time. Stephen Guest was nowhere to be seen, and Halliday, realizing that Mr. Tremlowe was waiting to read the General's Will, tactfully withdrew into the billiard-room.

The Will had been drawn up five years previously, and contained no surprises. Fay received an annuity on the condition that she did not marry again; Francis received £20,000; and with the exception of a number of small legacies to servants and pensioners, the rest of the General's property was left to his son Geoffrey.

Geoffrey was so much relieved to find that he had not been disinherited in favour of Francis that he became quite friendly towards his cousin, and having told him that he was sorry Sir Arthur had not left him a larger sum, he took him into the garden, and tried to impress upon him the true nature of his feelings towards Lola.

Dinah, gathering flowers on the other side of a clipped yew-hedge, heard him say earnestly: 'Of course I realize you were only joking, but you know it might be frightfully serious for me if a story like that got about.'

Gosh, what a fool he is! thought Miss Fawcett scornfully, and withdrew to the garden-hall with her basket.

Twenty minutes later she walked into the morning-room, carrying a bowl of sweet-peas, and found Inspector Harding standing in front of the bookcase with a volume open in his hand. 'Oh, I'm so sorry!' she said. 'I didn't know you were here. May I just put these on the table?'

'You can do anything you like,' said Harding, with a smile. 'It isn't my house, you know!'

'Well, it isn't mine either, if it comes to that. I thought I might be disturbing you.' She glanced at the book in his hand. 'Hullo, doing a crossword puzzle?' she inquired.

Harding returned *Chambers's Twentieth Century Dictionary* to its place on the shelf. 'No,' he replied. 'Not a crossword puzzle. Another sort of puzzle. What has been happening to annoy you?'

Dinah looked sharply up at him. 'You don't miss much, do you, Mr. Harding?' she said.

'I only thought you looked a trifle cross,' explained Harding.

She grinned. 'Well, as a matter of fact I'm fed to the back teeth,' she announced. 'At any moment now I should think we shall all turn into a set of lunatics, and start gibbering at you.'

'Oh no, don't!' begged Harding. 'Tell me what's fed you up instead.'

Dinah sat down on the arm of a chair. 'I'm not at all sure that you aren't being serpent-like,' she said. 'However, I'm past caring, and the sooner you arrest somebody for this murder – preferably Francis – the better.'

'What has he been doing?' inquired Harding.

'Making mischief,' said Dinah viciously. 'I say, did he pinch that money, do you think, or did Arthur really have remorse, and send it to him?'

Harding said, watching her: 'I don't know. Are you anxious about it?'

'Anxious?' said Dinah.

'I thought,' Harding said diffidently, 'that you seemed to be on terms of great friendship with Captain Billington-Smith.'

'Then I don't think much of you as a detective,' said Dinah. 'I can't stand Francis. How on earth did you come to make such a mistake?'

Inspector Harding apologized. 'I don't think my judgment was likely to be entirely impartial on that point,' he said in extenuation.

Since this was spoken almost inaudibly Miss Fawcett did not quite gather its import, and continued briskly: 'In fact, if someone's got to be arrested for having killed Arthur I'd rather it was Francis than anyone, except perhaps Camilla, and I suppose you can't manage to shove it on to her?'

Inspector Harding allowed this aspersion on his integrity to pass without demur, and merely remarked that he thought it would be difficult.

'A pity,' said Miss Fawcett regretfully. 'She's a frightful cad. And if she comes oiling up to you, as I rather think she may, with a whole lot of tales about anybody else, don't encourage her! You can't place the slightest reliance on anything she says, and she'll only lead you off on quite the wrong track.'

'Thank you very much for warning me,' said Harding meekly.

Miss Fawcett blushed. 'You're laughing at me.'

'I shouldn't dream of laughing at you,' he said.

Miss Fawcett became aware suddenly that Inspector Harding was regarding her with a light in his grey eyes that was far from professional. She felt her cheeks grow rather warmer. 'Well, I must go and do the rest of the flowers,' she said, with great presence of mind, and got up. 'I suppose there's nothing you want? You'll ring if there is, won't you?'

'No, I don't think I shall ring for it,' said Harding, with a faint smile. He held open the door, and Miss Fawcett retired in good order.

CHAPTER SIXTEEN

THE police car which had conveyed the Sergeant to Bramhurst did not return to Ralton until quite a late hour. The Sergeant found Inspector Harding at the police station, and at once proceeded to give him a faithful account of his investigations. These had been most thorough, for, acting on the Inspector's instructions, he had made inquiries at numerous points along the road, and although in most instances he had drawn blank, he had traced an A.A. official to his home, and ascertained from him that Captain Billington-Smith's car had passed the big cross-roads a few miles south of Bramhurst shortly after one o'clock. The A.A. man remembered the car, for he had held it up to allow a lorry to pass first, but he had not noticed whether it was running badly. This, coupled with a positive statement from the mechanic at the garage in Bramhurst that Captain Billington-Smith had driven his car into the yard at one-thirty precisely, seemed to prove that either Captain Billington-Smith's watch had been an hour slow when he looked at it, or that he had his own reasons for wanting to make the police believe that it was twelve-thirty when he arrived at Bramhurst. As to the choked jet, it had certainly been cleaned, but whether it had been in a bad enough condition seriously to impede the running of the car was a point on which the Sergeant could not induce the garage hands to put forward an opinion. The spare tyre had certainly been flat, and they had mended this while Captain Billington-Smith was having lunch. The waiter at the Stag corroborated the evidence inasmuch as he was able to state that the Captain had not entered the dining-room until a quarter to two, which circumstance he remembered perfectly, the Captain having been the last person to order lunch that day.

Inspector Harding had also been making investigations, and the results of one of these came to hand at ten o'clock that evening, when he received a note from the Superintendent summoning him back to the police station. Here there awaited him a spare and weather-beaten man in a plain suit who had certain information to give him. He was the postman who served the Lyndhurst district, and he was able to state definitely that on Monday morning at eleven-thirty when he was on his way up to Dean Farm by the cart-

176

track that ran between Moorsale Park and the Grange, he had passed Captain Billington-Smith's car, parked a little way up the track hard against the spinney at the bottom of the Grange garden. The track was scarcely ever used, the main approach to Dean Farm being from the main road on the other side, but he himself always used this back entrance, to save a long detour.

The Sergeant had gone home some time before the postman's visit, but the Superintendent was still in the police station, and found this new disclosure so conclusive that he would have liked to go at once to the nearest magistrate to procure a warrant for Captain Billington-Smith's arrest.

Inspector Harding was not so enthusiastic. When the postman had left them, he said (most unreasonably, the Superintendent thought) that the case seemed to be getting in a worse tangle than ever, and picked up his hat. 'It's all wrong, Superintendent,' he complained. 'I'm going to bed, to sleep on it.'

The Superintendent watched him walk over to the door, and made up his mind to tell the Chief Constable that they'd have done better without calling in Scotland Yard, just as he'd always prophesied. Here was a piece of news come to hand that solved the whole case, and all this precious Inspector did about it was to go off home to bed. 'What about the inquest tomorrow morning?' he asked.

'I think an adjournment, don't you?' Harding suggested.

'The way things are shaping that's what I shall *have* to ask for,' said the Superintendent crushingly.

As might have been expected, the court-room at Silsbury was crowded next morning, but those who had come in the hope of hearing thrilling disclosures were disappointed. Of the Grange party, only Geoffrey and Francis, the Hallidays, and Stephen Guest were present. The police evidence was followed by the evidence of both doctors, and there was nothing in what they had to say to interest an audience who already had all the facts of the case in mind. Dr. Raymond gave it as his opinion that death had occurred some time between twelve and one o'clock, but admitted, upon pressure, that it was difficult to reach any degree of certainty on this point. Death had been caused by a blow from a sharp instrument driven into the deceased's neck below the right ear, and severing the carotid artery. He agreed with the Divisional Surgeon that the blow was struck by someone standing slightly behind the General.

Here a slight quickening of interest was caused by Inspector

Harding, who rose to his feet to put a question to the doctor. He wanted to know whether, in Dr. Raymond's opinion, death would have been instantaneous.

'Practically instantaneous,' replied the doctor.

'What in your opinion, doctor, would have been the maximum time to elapse between the actual striking of the blow and death?'

The doctor hesitated. 'I should not like to give any very definite opinion on that point. In my view, death must have taken place within a minute, or even less.'

'Thank you,' said the Inspector, and sat down again.

After Dr. Raymond, Mrs. Twining was called, and recounted in a composed manner the circumstances under which she had discovered the General's body. She was followed by Guest, Halliday, and Finch, who in turn described briefly how they had found the General's body, and what measures they took to ensure that nothing should be disturbed until the police came. After that, the Superintendent arose, and asked for an adjournment.

This being granted there was nothing left for the disappointed audience to do but to go discontentedly home.

In spite of her declared intention not to be present at the inquest Mrs. Chudleigh was foremost amongst those who filed out of the court-room. By the time she got outside, however, Geoffrey, Francis, and Mr. Tremlowe had all embarked in Francis's car, so that she was unable to get a word with any of them. The Hallidays, with Stephen Guest and Finch, had come in the Daimler, and would return in it as soon as Guest had bought some tobacco, and Camilla a new lipstick. Mrs. Chudleigh saw Camilla just leaving the building, and caught up with her, explanations for her presence at the inquest hurrying off her tongue.

'Oh, good morning, Mrs. Halliday! Such a lovely day, I thought I would come into Silsbury to do a little shopping. I always take the bus in at least once a month: it is really most convenient. And since I happened to be in town I thought I would just pop in at the inquest to try and get a word with Lady Billington-Smith. But I see she is not here.'

'No, she stayed at home,' said Camilla. 'It wasn't as though anything was *done* at the inquest. I must say, I can't see the sense of it because we all knew everything that was said. It wasn't my idea of an inquest at all, and what on earth the police want an adjournment for when they've had all this time to find out who did the murder

I can't imagine. Especially as it's absolutely under their noses. It's perfectly obvious who did it, and I don't mind telling you that I suspected it from the start. I mean, the way he behaved!'

'Really?' said Mrs. Chudleigh, keeping step with her along the street. 'I hope I'm not inquisitive, but it is rather absurd that there should be so much mystery about it.'

Camilla gave her empty laugh. 'Yes, it makes me pretty wild, the way they all stick together, just because it's in the family. Well, I spoke my mind about it. Of course they didn't like it, but what I say is, why should everything be shifted on to my husband when someone else had far more reason to want to get rid of poor Sir Arthur? It's absolutely unfair, and so I told them!'

'Oh, but surely no one suspects Mr. Halliday?' said Mrs. Chudleigh.

'Oh, don't they?' snapped Camilla. 'I've got eyes, and I'm not quite a fool, Mrs. Chudleigh!'

'But who do you think did it?' asked Mrs. Chudleigh, hurrying to keep up with her.

'Well, I won't mention any names,' said Camilla darkly, 'but we all know who had a simply frightful row with poor Sir Arthur the very day he was murdered, and was going to be thrown out of the house. Yes, and *then*, if you please, we are told that he'd broken off his engagement! Of course every one could guess that's simply a blind to lead the police off the scent, but if you ask me Inspector Harding's on to him already, and if there's any more talk of asking Basil a whole lot of insulting questions, I shall say right out that they'd better ask why that engagement was broken off so suddenly, that's all!'

'Good gracious, you don't think *Geoffrey* did it?' gasped the Vicar's wife. 'Oh, but that *can't* be so! Such a nice boy, and so delicate! And besides he couldn't have done it, for I saw him myself that morning, quite a long way from the Grange.'

'You saw him?' said Camilla, stopping in front of a draper's window.

'Yes, I saw him on my way home. I wonder if I ought to tell the Inspector? I think it is my clear duty to find him, and tell him. I suppose he will be at the Grange, won't he?'

'You could just as easily tell them at the police station,' said Camilla maliciously.

'No, Mrs. Halliday, I shall do no such thing. I hope I should never shirk what I know to be my duty, and I am quite aware that it is the Inspector who is in charge of the case. It's most inconvenient, for I have a great deal on my hands, but I always say one can *make* time if one wants to, and I shall call at the Grange on my way home. And at the same time I shall hope to have a little *quiet* talk with Lady Billington-Smith.'

'I expect she'll love that,' said Camilla. 'I don't know when you saw Geoffrey, but I do know it would take a lot to convince me he didn't do it!'

The first person to reach the Grange after the inquest was Inspector Harding. He was admitted by the footman, and had hardly set foot inside the house when Miss Fawcett came running downstairs, and leaned over the banisters. 'Is that you, Geoffrey?' she called. 'What happened?'

'No, it's not Geoffrey,' said Harding, walking forward. 'Nothing much happened. We asked for an adjournment.'

'You don't mean to say we've got to go on as we are?'

'Not for long, I hope.'

'Oh, my giddy aunt!' groaned Miss Fawcett. 'This is ceasing to be funny!'

Harding regarded her in some amusement. 'Do tell me,' he said, 'is that how a murder generally strikes you?'

'Not the murder,' explained Dinah. 'Just the – the general effect. When I joined this little house-party every one seemed more or less human. You ought to see us *en famille* now. More like a zoo than anything – 'specially when Camilla starts screeching.' She looked down at him from her superior elevation, and inquired with friendly interest: 'What are you going to do now? Crawl round looking for footprints?'

'That was all done before I came,' explained Harding gravely.

Miss Fawcett shook her head. 'If you want a thing well done you should do it yourself,' she said.

'I wish you'd come downstairs; I'm getting a crick in the neck,' returned Inspector Harding.

'Surely,' said Miss Fawcett with severity, 'you didn't come here to waste time talking to me, Inspector?'

'Don't call me Inspector. I came to talk to Captain Billington-Smith, but I have an idea he hasn't yet come back from Silsbury.'

'Deduction, I suppose?' said Dinah, cocking her head on one side.

'Pure deduction. I can't find his footprints. I wish you'd come down.'

Dinah obeyed. 'As a matter of fact he isn't back yet. He had to take Mr. Tremlowe to the station. Did you see him wending thitherwards?'

'I didn't, but I saw him drive off with his cousin. So when you called, "Is that you, Geoffrey?" I leaped to the con – that is to say, I deduced that they hadn't yet arrived.'

'What a loss you'll be to Scotland Yard when you start that chicken farm!' remarked Miss Fawcett admiringly.

'I shall, of course, but it can't be helped. I'd very nearly made up my mind this should be my last case when I first came down here. I'm quite decided now that it shall be.'

'You mustn't let yourself get disheartened,' said Miss Fawcett, firmly putting the conversation back on to a flippant basis. 'For all you know you may suddenly hit on a first-class clue, proving that I did it. You should never trust to alibis. I know I've read that somewhere.'

'If I found that you had done it—' said Inspector Harding in much too serious a voice. 'Well, that's too horrible a thought. Let's talk of something else.'

Ten minutes later, when Geoffrey and Francis entered the house, Miss Fawcett and Inspector Harding were seated side by side on a black-oak settle, amicably exchanging views on Life, Tastes, and Ambitions.

'Dear me!' said Francis, at his blandest. 'I'm afraid we have interrupted a *tête-à-tête*. Or is it just police investigation?'

Inspector Harding, betraying no sign of discomfiture, got up. 'Good morning,' he said impersonally. 'I want a word with you, Captain Billington-Smith. Will you come into the morning-room, please?'

'Oh, was I the person you came to see?' said Francis. 'It all goes to show one ought never to judge by appearances, doesn't it?'

Harding vouchsafed no answer to this, but merely held open the door into the morning-room. Francis strolled in, stripping off his wash-leather driving gloves.

Harding shut the door, and walked slowly forward.

Francis tossed his gloves on to the table between them, and drew out his cigarette-case. 'From your expression, Inspector, I'm led to suppose you have something of great importance to disclose.'

'You are perfectly right,' said Harding. 'What I have to say to you is extremely serious, Captain Billington-Smith. Your car was seen, parked on the track leading to Dean Farm, at eleven-thirty on Monday morning.'

For a moment Francis's hand remained poised above his open cigarette-case, while his eyes, suddenly narrowed, looked straight across into Harding's. Then, he drew out a cigarette, and shut his case with a snap. 'Damn!' he said, and returned the case to his pocket. He set the cigarette between his lips, lit it, and blew a cloud of smoke. 'Well?' he said. 'What now?'

'Now,' said Harding quietly, 'I should like you to tell me the true story of what you did on Monday morning. Where were you at eleven-thirty?'

'Robbing the safe in the next room,' replied Francis with something of a snap. 'Who was the meddlesome busybody who nosed out my car?'

'That doesn't concern you, Captain Billington-Smith. Now, you are not bound to make a statement, but in your own interests I advise you to do so.'

'It is quite obvious that I must,' replied Francis. 'Well, my uncle didn't send me the notes. You never really thought he had sent them, did you? It would have been remarkably difficult to have proved that he hadn't, though. I robbed the safe when I knew he would be out of the house. I hope you notice my use of the phrase "robbed the safe". It sounds much better than "stole the money", and comes to the same thing.' He gave a mirthless laugh, and threw his half-smoked cigarette into the grate. 'I wanted it pretty badly. A card debt, as I quite truthfully told you. A cheque on my bank, judging from an engaging chat I had with the manager a week ago, didn't seem to me to stand much chance of being honoured. For which very good reason I came to spend the week-end in this house. My uncle rather liked me, you know. In his saner moments he would have paid much more than one hundred and thirty pounds to keep me – or his name – out of the mud. Unfortunately I didn't strike him in one of these. That was thanks to my cousin's perfectly insane infatuation with the fair Lola. I did what I could, but even my handling of Uncle failed. I tackled him on Monday, immediately after breakfast. He was all tuned up for one final, cataclysmic quarrel with Geoffrey. I might as well have talked to a brick wall. So I left him to have it out with Geoffrey. If Geoffrey had promised to abjure Lola and be a good boy there might have been a chance for me. So I waited till the row was over. The sight of Geoffrey gnawing his fingers and rolling his eyes in the manner of one goaded beyond endurance told me, however, that there was still no hope. I took my departure. The car, by the way, was running badly – dam' badly, but I was really too worried to care. I drove slowly towards London, wondering what the hell I was to do next.' He stopped, and sat down in a chair by the table. 'By the time I'd covered about ten miles I knew what I was going to do. And now I shall have to go back a bit. Do tell me if I'm boring you!'

Harding said only: 'Go on, please.'

'At breakfast my uncle had favoured us with a short dissertation on method, and the way to run a household. He announced that at ten o'clock he was going to Ralton to cash a cheque for the month's expenses, and at the same time he made an assignation with the Halliday woman, to take her to see a litter of pups at his keeper's cottage at eleven o'clock. Wasn't it providential?'

'I take it you knew the workings of the safe?'

'Oh lord, yes! Who didn't? I turned the car and drove back, running it finally up the track where it was found. Criminals always make at least one mistake, don't they? That was mine. I thought the track was disused. I walked up through the spinney, skirted the edge of the drive, keeping to the cover of all those gloomy rhododendrons, and entered the study by the front window, at eleven-thirty. The money was, as I had expected, in the safe. I took the exact sum I wanted, and departed again. Time, probably about eleven-forty-five, when I got back to the car. May have been later, but not much. Then I drove to Bramhurst.

'What I told you yesterday about that run was substantially correct, though I actually fetched up at the garage at one-thirty and not, as I first stated, at twelve-thirty. Ah, you'd found that out already, had you? Stupid of me to have lied on that point, but I thought it more than likely that they wouldn't have any idea at the garage what time I handed the car over to them. They mended my tyre, cleaned the jet, which was badly choked, and I accomplished the rest of the journey in record time. Not really a good story, is it?'

'You must have been very badly in need of the money to take such a risk, Captain Billington-Smith.'

'I was, but not, believe me, badly enough in need of it to murder my uncle. I admit it was an idiotic thing to do. I yielded to impulse.

I usually do. The risk wasn't of exposure, though. But if Uncle succeeded in tracing the notes to me I ran a fair chance of being cut out of his Will. At the time I didn't consider that. One can't think of everything, can one?' He got up, and walked over to the old-fashioned mirror over the mantelpiece, and straightened his tie. In the mirror his eyes met Harding's. 'Well, what is the next move? Are you going to arrest me on suspicion of having murdered my uncle? I don't somehow think you'll get a verdict.'

'No, I haven't applied for a warrant for your arrest yet,' answered Harding. 'But it's not, as you said, a good story. I shall have to ask you to remain on the premises until I've investigated it. Meanwhile, I want you to sit down and put on paper what you have just told me.'

'Certainly,' said Francis. He went over to the desk against one wall, selected several sheets of writing-paper, and dipped a pen in the ink-pot. He wrote unhurriedly, and without any evidence of discomfort in the task. At the end he signed his name with a flourish, and handed the statement over to Harding, who read it through, and put it away in his pocket-book.

'And is that all for the moment?' inquired Francis.

'Yes, that's all,' replied Harding.

'Quite enough too, don't you think?' said Francis, walking over to the door. 'I said you were getting a remarkable insight into the family.' He opened the door, and went out. Then he looked back. 'It seems you're wanted, Inspector,' he said languidly. 'More disclosures, probably.'

Harding turned, but Francis had gone, and it was Geoffrey who stood in the doorway.

Geoffrey said impetuously: 'Can I come in? There's something frightfully important you ought to know! It absolutely clears me!'

'That's good,' said Harding pleasantly. 'Yes, of course come in. What is it I ought to know?'

Geoffrey looked back over his shoulder. 'I say, will you come in, Mrs. Chudleigh? Mrs. Chudleigh saw me on Monday, Inspector. And look here! Do you know that that b— I mean, that cat of a Halliday woman is going about saying that it was I who murdered Father? She told Mrs. Chudleigh so bang in the middle of Silsbury High Street. I don't know whether I can have her up for libel, but I've a jolly good mind to!'

Harding was not paying very much attention to this speech. He bowed to Mrs. Chudleigh. 'Good morning,' he said. 'Won't you sit down?'

'Thank you,' she replied, taking the chair lately vacated by Francis. 'It is perfectly true, what Geoffrey says. I consider Mrs. Halliday a most slanderous woman, and immediately I heard what she had to say I saw that it was my clear duty to come straight up to the Grange to find you! I must say, I'm not in the least surprised at her spreading such a wicked scandal, for I mistrusted her from the moment I set eyes on her.'

'Did you, Mrs. Chudleigh? But I think you were going to tell me where and when you saw Mr. Billington-Smith on Monday, weren't you?'

'I am just coming to that, if you will allow me to speak, Inspector. And I may mention that had I ever dreamed that Geoffrey could be suspected of having – murdered – his father I should have told you that I had seen him when you called on me the other night. But I am glad to say that I am not in the habit of suspecting people of crimes, and such a notion literally did not cross my mind.'

'I quite understand,' said Harding. 'And where was it that you saw Mr. Billington-Smith?'

'I saw him walking down the footpath across Moorsale Park, just beside the lake. I was on my way home from this house.'

'Do you mean that you met him, Mrs. Chudleigh, or that you saw him from a distance?'

'Considering that I was on the road, and he in the park I could hardly have met him, Inspector. But if you are hinting that I was mistaken in thinking it was Geoffrey whom I saw, I beg to state that I am not as weak-sighted as *that*!'

'In which direction was he walking, Mrs. Chudleigh?'

'He was going home, and I thought at the time that he would be late for lunch, for I happen to know Lady Billington-Smith always has lunch at one o'clock, and it must have been quite ten-to when I saw him because I know it takes just under half an hour to walk from the Vicarage to the Grange, door to door, and I was certainly home by one o'clock, if not earlier. So *that* would mean that it must have taken Geoffrey at least twenty minutes to get home from that particular point, because of the hill.'

Harding drew out a pencil from his pocket, and opened his notebook. 'I see. And you say this was at ten minutes to one? You mentioned a lake: that might give one rather a wide latitude. Can you place the exact spot rather more definitely?'

'I suppose you are going to see for yourself? No doubt you are only doing your duty, but I am not in the habit, strange as it may seem, of *prevaricating*. However, you can hardly mistake the place, since it was just where the arm of the lake stretches down to the right-of-way. If you like I will take you there myself.'

'Thank you very much, but I don't think I need trouble you to do that,' said Harding firmly.

She gathered up her handbag and gloves, and rose. 'Then I think I will be getting home. Please tell Lady Billington-Smith that I was *sorry* she did not feel equal to seeing me, Geoffrey. Good morning, Inspector!' She favoured him with a stiff little bow, and walked out of the room, escorted by the grateful Geoffrey.

'It's a frightfully lucky thing you saw me,' he confided, on the doorstep. 'I mean, I had had a row with Father, and I suppose it did look rather black, really.'

'I am only sorry that I didn't think to tell the Inspector sooner,' said Mrs. Chudleigh, buttoning up her gloves. 'No doubt had I been Mrs. Halliday I should have. You must have had a dreadfully worrying time.'

'Well, as a matter of fact, I did, rather,' admitted Geoffrey. 'It's all been absolutely ghastly, because after the way she treated me I simply didn't want ever to set eyes on Lola again, and here we've been cooped up in the same house, and everybody thinking I'd broken it off just as a blind.'

'Oh, have you broken it off?' said Mrs. Chudleigh. 'Well, I'm sure that's very trying for you, Geoffrey, but you know I can't help feeling that Miss de Silva is *hardly* the kind of girl to make a good wife for you. Not that I have anything against her, but she seemed to me a most callous, immoral young woman, and I should not be at all surprised if I heard that she was no better than she should be.'

Geoffrey looked a little doubtful at this terrific pronouncement, and said: 'Oh well, I don't know about that, quite, but she's utterly destroyed my faith in women.'

'And I'm sure I don't wonder at it!' said Mrs. Chudleigh.

Geoffrey, having finally seen his saviour off the premises, hurried back to the terrace, where Fay and Dinah were sitting. Francis was also with them, lounging in a basket-chair. 'I say, have you heard?' Geoffrey demanded. 'Mrs. Chudleigh saw me on Monday, and it absolutely clears me! Isn't it simply marvellous luck that she happened to catch sight of me?'

'Too, too marvellous!' agreed Francis. 'My poor ass, nobody's interested in your movements any longer. Attention is now concentrated on my unworthy self.'

Fay stretched out her hand to her stepson. 'Oh, Geoffrey, I'm so glad! I always knew you couldn't possibly have done such an awful thing, but it's splendid that you've found an alibi. Only Francis has been telling us – no, I can't bring myself to repeat it. It's too revolting!'

'Yes,' drawled Francis, 'it's all very shocking, Geoffrey. Truth will – in all probability – out, so you may just as well hear it now as later. I was in this house at eleven-thirty on Monday for the express purpose of abstracting one hundred and thirty pounds from Uncle's safe. And what is more, I did abstract it.'

'What?' said Geoffrey, staring. 'You were *here* that morning? Then—'

'Not so fast, dear cousin. I said I was here at eleven-thirty. You will all of you find it very difficult to prove that I murdered Uncle Arthur. The problem that is really interesting me is whether you and Fay can prosecute me for theft, or whether I, as a principal legatee, should have to prosecute myself? You do see my point, don't you?'

'You seem to me to be quite shameless!' said Fay, in a low, disgusted voice.

'I am,' said Francis, settling himself more comfortably in his chair. 'Quite shameless.'

CHAPTER SEVENTEEN

CONTRARY to Sergeant Nethersole's expectations, Harding did not busy himself that afternoon in attempting to disprove Captain Billington-Smith's story. This task he left to his subordinate, who, however, could not but feel that it should have received more minute attention. He ventured to say that he was surprised the Inspector didn't make more of the story, which, to his mind, made it look very much as though they had discovered the General's murderer.

'Sergeant,' said Harding, 'haven't all the stories we've listened to done that?'

In a manner of speaking I suppose they have, sir,' admitted the Sergeant. 'You don't make more of this one than the rest?'

'No,' said Harding. 'Frankly, I don't. Between Guest, Halliday, and Francis Billington-Smith, there isn't a penny to choose. They are all three of them strong suspects. Each one of them had a motive, large or small, and any one of them might be capable of committing murder. The fact that Billington-Smith was on the premises at eleven-thirty doesn't exonerate either of the other two; it only adds to the list of the people who might have murdered Sir Arthur. And the most important clue in my possession, that mysterious piece of paper, doesn't seem to have any bearing on any one of them. I am convinced, Sergeant, that if I can find out to whom that unfinished message refers I shall have solved this case.'

The Sergeant rubbed his chin. 'You do set great store by that bit of writing, sir.'

'Yes, in default of any other clue, I do. All the time I've been working on this case, trying to weigh the evidence of the principal suspects, I've again and again found myself brought up short by something unexplainable. In the case against Halliday, why were those papers thrown into the basket on top of that cheque? In the case against Guest, where the murder, if he did it, must have been thought out and performed in cold blood, the manner of it seems to be fantastic. In the case against Francis, if he was at the Grange as early as eleven-thirty, what kept him on the premises until after Halliday's interview with Sir Arthur? Why, if he had already robbed the safe, did he murder Sir Arthur?

'When you put it like that, sir,' said the Sergeant slowly, 'it does look as though there's something in what you say. You mean you think we're on the wrong track altogether?'

'The case doesn't quite fit any of the people in it,' said Harding. 'I've had all along a feeling that I am missing something, and the conviction that it has to do with the message we found on the General's desk grew stronger with every statement I listened to.'

'Have you got a theory about it, sir?' asked the Sergeant, interested.

'It's flattering it to call it a theory, Sergeant, but there is an idea in my head.'

'Ah, a hunch, as you might say,' nodded the Sergeant.

Harding laughed. 'Yes, if you like. It seems to me a pretty far-fetched one, but I'm going to see if I can't follow it up. Where, exactly, is Mrs. Twining's house?'

The Sergeant's blank gaze focused on his face. 'Mrs. Twining? he repeated. 'Could I take a look at that writing, sir?'

'Certainly, you can,' said Harding, extricating it from his pocketbook.

The Sergeant sat and studied it for a time in silence. Then he said: 'I don't see it, sir. I'm bound to say I don't see it.'

'Don't see what?'

'What we took for an H might be a W,' pursued the Sergeant. 'To me it looks like an H, but there you are. But what about that E and the R, what's more? No, sir, I don't see how you make it out to be Twining, and that's a fact.'

'But I don't,' said Harding. 'I get T H E R E out of it, and I have a notion that Mrs. Twining might be able to tell me what those letters mean. Where does she live?'

The Sergeant, rather chagrined, gave the necessary directions and handed back the paper. Harding put it away, and went off in search of Mrs. Twining.

Blessington House was situated about three miles from the Grange, and was a low stone building set in a charming garden. The Inspector was lucky enough to find Mrs. Twining at home and, upon sending in his card, was taken at once to a sunny, chintz-decorated room at the back of the house. Mrs. Twining was writing letters at a marquetry bureau there, but she rose as Harding entered, and said with a faint smile: 'Good afternoon, Inspector. What is it I am to do for you?'

'Nothing very much,' Harding answered. 'I ought to apologize for bothering you, when it is quite my fault that I have to!' He took several folded sheets from his pocket. 'I stupidly forgot to ask you to sign the statement you made to me on Tuesday. Would you mind? – your full name, of course.'

She took the papers, her delicate brows a little raised. 'Another statement to sign?' she asked.

'I'm afraid so,' he smiled. 'These things have to be done, you know.'

'Why, certainly,' said Mrs. Twining, a hint of amusement in her voice. She glanced through the statement and moved back to the bureau and sat down. Dipping a large quill pen in the ink-pot she wrote in a flowing hand across the bottom of the last page, 'Julia

Margaret Twining.' Then she blotted it carefully and held it out to Harding. She still seemed to be rather amused. 'There you are, Inspector.'

He took the statement and looked at the signature before folding the document up again.

'You did say my full name, didn't you?' said Mrs. Twining.

'I did,' replied Harding, returning the statement to his pocket.

'Such a nuisance for you to have had to come all this way for so little,' she remarked. 'Is that really the only thing you wanted?'

'As a matter of fact it isn't,' said Harding. 'Partly I came to see you in the hope that you, who knew Sir Arthur for a great many years, may be able to throw a little light on something which frankly puzzles me.' He took out his pocket-book, but before he opened it he glanced up from it and added: 'By the way, I have some news which I think will please you. Information has been laid with me that looks like providing an alibi for Geoffrey Billington-Smith.'

She inclined her head courteously. 'I am very glad to hear it,' she said. 'Not that I ever imagined that Geoffrey had killed his father.'

'You are very fond of him, Mrs. Twining, are you not?'

'Did I give you that impression?' she inquired.

'Decidedly,' Harding said with a smile. 'Was it a false one?'

'Oh, no!' she answered. 'Not false. I am fond of Geoffrey, as one must be of a boy one has known from his infancy. He has many faults, but I ascribe most of them to his upbringing. His father neither understood him nor liked him.'

'It was unfortunate for him that his mother left Sir Arthur,' remarked Harding.

'Very,' said Mrs. Twining in a dry voice. 'Perhaps had she been wiser, less impetuous, things would have happened differently. But she was young and in love and married a man who— Well, it is all ancient history now, and not worth discussing.'

'Were you intimate with her, Mrs. Twining?'

She reflected. 'Oh – intimate! She was a school-friend, and I suppose you may say we were fairly intimate. Why do you ask me that?'

'Only because I somehow or other got the impression that you came to live in this district to be near Geoffrey. I wondered whether you had done so for his mother's sake.'

She straightened the blotter on the desk. 'I do not know what can have given you that impression, Inspector. I lost sight of his mother many years ago – when she deserted Sir Arthur, in fact. I chose the district because, having lived abroad all my life, I have scarcely any friends in England. I did not see eye to eye with Sir Arthur, perhaps, but I had known him a long time, and to settle where he had already formed acquaintances to whom he could introduce me seemed a natural thing to do.' She looked up and saw him watching her, not suspiciously, but with a kind of grave sympathy. 'The fact that I had known his first wife and was fond of her son may have influenced me a little,' she said. 'I'm afraid, however, that I have not done very much for Geoffrey, except occasionally to talk Sir Arthur into a better humour on his behalf.'

'Sir Arthur seems to have had more respect for you than for most of the people he knew – judging from what I have been told,' commented Harding.

'When one has known a man for a great many years,' said Mrs. Twining easily, 'one does acquire a certain influence over him. You must forgive me, Inspector, but is my residence in this district the matter which you said was puzzling you?'

'No,' replied Harding. 'That isn't it.' He opened his pocket-book and took from it the half-sheet of notepaper with the word 'There' scrawled across it. 'This, Mrs. Twining, was found on Sir Arthur's desk, under his hand, on Monday.'

She cast a quick glance up at him and took the paper. She did not speak for several moments, but presently she said in a level voice, not raising her eyes from the paper. 'I don't quite understand. You say this was found on Sir Arthur's desk—'

'I believe it to have been written after he was stabbed, Mrs. Twining. Does it convey anything to you?'

Her eyelids just flickered, another woman less self-controlled, he suspected, might have winced. 'No,' she said deliberately, and held the paper out to him. The look of amusement had vanished from her face. 'It conveys nothing to me. I am sorry.' She watched him fold it again and put it back in his pocket-book. She seemed to hesitate on the brink of speech, and finally asked: 'Do you feel it to be of importance, Inspector?'

'I don't know, Mrs. Twining. I had hoped that you might be able to enlighten me.'

'It appears to be a very ordinary word, of no particular significance,' she said. 'The start of a sentence, I imagine.' She rose, and repeated: 'I am sorry. It is a pity Sir Arthur had time only to write that one word. Is there anything else you wished to ask me?'

'Nothing else,' Harding answered. 'I'm afraid I've taken up your time to no purpose.'

She moved over to the bell and pressed it. 'Not at all,' she said politely. 'I only regret that I am unable to help you.' She glanced fleetingly towards him. 'What is your own theory, Inspector? Or have you none?'

'No doubt it is, as you say, the start of a sentence,' he replied.

The butler came into the room, holding open the door. Harding took his leave of Mrs. Twining and went away, back to the police station at Ralton, where he found the Superintendent and Sergeant Nethersole awaiting him.

The Superintendent was in a mood of profound disgust and greeted Harding with the information that the whole case had gone to glory.

'What's happened?' asked Harding, rather abstractedly.

'You sent the Sergeant on here to make inquiries along the road to Bramhurst. Well, we've just had a report from Laxton,' answered the Superintendent.

'Oh, yes! Captain Billington-Smith's movements. He's ruled out, is he?'

'It looks precious like it,' said the Superintendent gloomily. 'Young Mason, of Mason's Stores there, states that he passed the Captain's car on his motor-bike at twelve-fifteen on Monday morning, just short of the village. He says the Captain was changing a flat tyre, which is why he happened to notice him.'

'How far from the Grange is Laxton?' inquired Harding.

'That's just it,' said the Superintendent, 'it's eighteen miles, and you can't make it less. I've been working it out, but it's not a bit of use, Mr. Rarding, no matter how fast he drove. He couldn't have got back from there to the Grange and still reached Bramhurst at one-thirty. No, the bottom's been knocked out of the case, and that's all there is to it.' He leaned back in his chair and tucked his thumbs in his belt. 'Which brings us,' he announced, 'back to that 'Alliday.'

His tone implied that he was prepared to expatiate on the subject, but the telephone suddenly buzzed at his elbow, and he was obliged to answer it. He became entangled immediately in what appeared to be an involved conversation with some person unknown, and Harding, seizing his opportunity said: 'I'll come back later, Superintendent,' and escaped, closely followed by the Sergeant.

'You didn't think it was the Captain, did you, sir?' said the Sergeant, outside the station.

'No, the time didn't fit. I'm going up to the Grange now. And I'd better test that alibi of young Billington-Smith's while I'm about it. Come along, Sergeant, and you can direct me to this lane that leads from the Grange to Lyndhurst village.

The Sergeant climbed into the car. 'Right, sir. You drive to Lyndhurst and we'll go on to the Grange that way, if you're agreeable. That'll save you having to turn to come back again to the Grange, which you might have a bit of difficulty over, it being what you'd call narrow, that lane.'

Neither being of a talkative disposition, there was little conversation on the way to Lyndhurst. The Sergeant asked Harding what he wanted to do at the Grange, and on being told that the Inspector wished to obtain more precise information on the subject of Mrs. Twining's movements on Monday morning, merely nodded and relapsed into meditative silence.

The lane in question led into the middle of Lyndhurst village, immediately opposite the church. A few cottages were huddled together at the top end, but these continued for only a few hundred yards. Beyond them Moorsale Park lay on both sides of the lane, behind somewhat untidy hedges.

'Precious little money to spare up at the Park, if what they say is true,' confided the Sergeant. 'The Squire's got half the house shut up, so I heard, and the place beginning to go to rack and ruin. Steady, sir, you want to stop just beyond the bend.'

Harding slowed the car down, and drew up to the side of the lane. The Sergeant stood up and looked over the hedge. 'There's the lake, sir. You can see for yourself.'

Harding got out of the car and walked over to the other side of the road, and craned to see over the hedge. As Mrs. Chudleigh described, a narrow arm of the lake ran down to a footpath that had been worn across the smooth turf.

'If she saw Mr. Billington-Smith there, which you tell me she says she did,' pursued the Sergeant, 'it's about twenty minutes' walk from the Grange. You might do it in less, but it's uphill, steady, all the way. It lets him out all right, to my mind, sir.' He noticed that the Inspector was slightly frowning, and inquired if there were anything wrong.

'I was only thinking that the hedges seem to be rather high,' said Harding, coming back to the car.

'You're right,' agreed the Sergeant, sitting down again. 'I'm friendly with the head-keeper, and he was telling me they've cut down all expenses something cruel. 'Tisn't only the hedges that have been let grow wild. Seems a shame, doesn't it, sir?'

'Yes,' agreed Harding, setting the car in motion again. 'But what I don't quite understand is how Mrs. Chudleigh contrived to see Billington-Smith on the other side of the hedge. I'm six foot, and I could only just see over the top of it.'

'Perhaps she was on her bicycle, sir,' suggested the Sergeant, having thought about it for a moment. 'Come to think of it, she would have been, most likely.'

'She bicycles, does she?' Harding's frown deepened. 'That's a point we'll go into. For if Mrs. Chudleigh was cycling home I no longer like the look of young Billington-Smith's alibi. She fixed ten-to-one as the time of her seeing him, because she knows that it takes about half an hour to walk from the Grange to the Vicarage. What she forgets – if she was cycling that day – is that it wouldn't take anything like that time to cover the distance on a bicycle.'

The Sergeant nodded slowly. 'That's so, sir. More likely she'd have seen him a good ten minutes earlier, or more. That's what happens when you get ladies giving evidence about time. It's a queer thing, but I've very often noticed that women never have any notion of time. You've only got to wait for your wife to go upstairs to get her hat on to see that. Well, you aren't a married man, sir – leastways I've got an idea you're not – but if ever you do happen to get married you'll see what I mean. And if your good lady don't keep you hanging about a quarter of an hour, and then stand you out she was only upstairs a couple of minutes – well, she'll be different from mine, sir, that's all.' With which misogynistic pronouncement the Sergeant folded his arms across his chest, and brooded silently till the car drew up at the Grange front door. Then, as he climbed out, he gave the result of his meditations. 'But if that was so, sir, and supposing Mr. Billington-Smith to have come back here unbeknownst and murdered the General, he'd have got here round about five to one, by my reckoning, and run slap into Mrs. Twining coming to fetch the General for his cocktail.'

'Yes,' said Harding. 'He would.'

'Well, but that goes and upsets it, doesn't it, sir?'

Harding did not answer, and before the Sergeant could repeat his remark Finch had opened the front door.

Harding stepped into the hall. 'Finch, when Mrs. Chudleigh called here on Monday morning, was she walking, or on her bicycle?'

'Mrs. Chudleigh, sir? She was on her bicycle,' replied the butler.

'Are you sure of that?'

'Oh yes, sir. Mrs. Chudleigh had propped her machine up against the porch, and I thought at the time that it was very much in the way of anyone coming in. I cannot say that I care for bicycles myself, sir. What I should call troublesome things, if you take my meaning.'

The Inspector stood slowly pulling off his driving gloves, his eyes, with the hint of a frown in them, fixed on the butler's face. Then, just as Finch, rendered slightly nervous by this hard, unseeing stare, was about to ask if anything were wrong, he turned away, and laid his hat and gloves down on the table. 'Is Miss Fawcett in?' he asked abruptly.

'I believe so, sir. I will go and see.'

'Ask her if she can spare me a moment in the morning-room, will you?' said Harding. He went up to the study door and opened it.

The Sergeant coughed. 'I take it you won't be needing me, sir?'

'No,' replied Harding, 'I shan't. What I want you to do, Sergeant, is to take a stroll in the garden and have a chat with the under-gardener if you can find him. Ludlow we know to have spent Monday morning in the kitchen garden, but the other man seems to have been pottering about all over the place. Try and get out of him whether he was in sight of the front drive any time between twelve and one, and find out if he saw anyone either approaching or leaving the house during that time. If it was only the butcher's boy I want to know of it.'

Miss Fawcett, entering the morning-room, ten minutes later, found it empty, and was conscious of disappointment. Since she had sought refuge from Camilla Halliday's conversation in the spinney at the bottom of the garden it had taken Finch some time to find her. Apparently Inspector Harding had lost patience and departed.

'Damn!' murmured Miss Fawcett, wandering aimlessly towards the fireplace. Looking up, she caught sight of her own disconsolate face in the mirror. She regarded it with some severity. Look here, my girl,' she said sternly, 'you're getting maudlin about this police-man. Pull yourself together!'

'Which policeman?' inquired an interested voice behind her.

She spun round to find Harding standing in the long window, watching her. For once the redoubtable Miss Fawcett was clearly at a disadvantage. 'I've – I've lost my heart to the Sergeant!' she said wildly.

'I'm sorry. I hoped it was to the Inspector,' returned Harding with simple directness.

Miss Fawcett, blushing furiously, retreated to the door. Harding stepped into the room. 'Please don't go!' he said. 'I ought not to have listened to you, or to have said that. I apologize.'

Miss Fawcett, who wanted to make a calm and sensible reply, said something quite incoherent and subsided.

Inspector Harding said haltingly: 'When I see you I keep for-getting I'm here – purely professionally. I've no right to – I ought to know better than to—' He broke off, evidently feeling that he had embarked on a hopeless sentence.

Miss Fawcett, observing his flounderings, recovered the use of her tongue and was understood to say, though in a very small voice, that she quite understood.

'*Do* you?' said Inspector Harding, grasping the edge of the table. '*Do* you, Dinah?'

Miss Fawcett nodded, and began to trace invisible patterns on the table with one forefinger. 'Well, I – well, I think I do,' she replied carefully. 'When you aren't being professional – I mean – well, any-way, I quite understand.'

'As soon as I've done with this case,' said Inspector Harding, 'there's something I'm going to ask you. I've been wanting to ever since I set eyes on you.

'More – more cross-examinations?' inquired Miss Fawcett, with a noble attempt at lightness.

'No. A very simple question requiring just "Yes", or – or "No", for an answer.'

'Oh!' said Miss Fawcett, sketching another and more complicated pattern on the table. 'I don't think I should dare say "No" to – to a policeman.'

There was a moment's silence. Inspector Harding let go of the table-edge. 'It's no use!' he said, advancing upon Miss Fawcett. 'I *have* tried, but there are limits to what can be expected of one!'

Sergeant Nethersole, whose search for the under-gardener led him up the path at the side of the house, passed the morning-room window, and, not sharing Mrs. Chudleigh's scruples, looked in. The sight that met his eyes had the effect of bringing him up short, staring. Then, for he was a tactful man, he withdrew his gaze from the spectacle of Miss Fawcett locked in Inspector Harding's arms, and tiptoed cautiously away.

For quite twenty minutes after he had gone the conversation between Miss Fawcett and Inspector Harding had no bearing at all upon the problems that might have been supposed to engross the Inspector's attention, and was not remarkable for any very noticeable degree of intelligence or originality. It seemed, however, to be an eminently satisfactory conversation from their point of view, and might have been continued for an unspecified length of time, had not Miss Fawcett chanced to ask Inspector Harding if he realized that if no one had murdered the General they might never have met.

Recalled to a sense of his duties, Inspector Harding put Miss Fawcett firmly away from him. 'Sit down in that chair, Dinah, and pretend I'm the Superintendent, or the sub-human detective who came about the plated entrée dishes,' he said, and resolutely retired to a chair on the other side of the table.

'Oh, do you remember that?' asked Dinah idiotically.

'I rem— No!' said Harding with emphasis. 'You must help me. I'm here strictly on business. There are things I want to ask you.' He eyed Miss Fawcett across the table. 'It isn't helping to look at me like that,' he said uncertainly. 'It only makes me want to kiss you again.'

'Pretend I'm Camilla,' suggested Dinah. 'Oh, and do you know, she thinks I'm making a dead set at you? She told me so at lunch. I didn't, did I?'

Inspector Harding cleared his throat. 'Miss Fawcett,' he said severely, 'I want you to carry your mind back to the morning of July first, please.'

'All right,' said Dinah, willing to oblige, 'but if you go and fasten the murder on to someone I don't want you to, I shan't marry you. I don't mind you arresting the Hallidays, or the gardener, or Lola – though I'm developing quite an affection for her, as a matter of fact – but—'

'You are wasting my time, Miss Fawcett.'

'Sorry!' said Dinah hastily. She folded her hands in her lap. 'Go

197

on, what have I got to remember? I'll do what I can for you, but I seem to have gone addled in the head all at once.'

'It's important, Dinah, so do try! Did Mrs. Twining come to lunch on Monday by chance, or by invitation, or what?'

'All three,' replied Dinah. 'Pseudo-chance, so that Arthur shouldn't think it was a put-up job, and invitation because I invited her; and *what,* because of the row about Lola. She was at the fatal dinner-party on Saturday, and so she'd seen what was likely to happen. She rang up on Monday to hear the latest news, and when I told her that it was all pretty grim, she said that she thought she'd come over and see what she could do with Arthur.'

'Did she seem to be worried about the situation?'

'N-no, I don't think so. Rather amused. To tell you the truth, I've never been able to make her out, quite. She's always cool and cynical, the sort of person you wouldn't expect to care two pins for anybody, but she really has taken a lot of trouble on Geoffrey's behalf. Of course, I know he's the sort of youth who appeals to sentimental matrons, but she isn't sentimental in the least. You can understand people like Mrs. Chudleigh falling for him, but not Mrs. Twining. She's too caustic.'

'Does she give you the impression of being very fond of him?'

'Well, she does and she doesn't. Funnily enough I asked her that very question on Monday – I mean, whether she *was* very fond of him. She said she wasn't, but that she'd known him for so long she took an interest in him, or something. She and I had gone to find Fay – it was when she first arrived – and I was asking her what Geoffrey's mother was like.'

'Were you? What did she say?'

'Nothing much, except that whatever she – Geoffrey's mother – had done that was rotten she'd had to pay for. Which rather snubbed me, because I'd said I thought it was rotten of his mother to have deserted him.'

'She said that, did she? Do you know anything about the General's first wife, Dinah?'

'No, that was why I asked Mrs. Twining. Even Fay never dared mention her to Arthur. Skeleton in the cupboard, you know. There isn't even a snapshot of her that I've ever discovered.'

'You don't by any chance know what her name was?'

'No, of course not. Arthur expunged her from the records, so to speak. Why do you want to know?'

Harding held up an admonitory finger. 'I'm asking the questions, not you,' he said.

'Ha!' said Miss Fawcett, kindling. 'Well, make the most of this interview, Detective-Inspector Harding.'

'You can take it out of me as soon as I'm through with this case,' promised Harding. 'Let's come back to Mrs. Twining. When she went to the General's study how long was she away?'

'I don't know exactly. Quite a few minutes – somewhere between five and ten, I should think, because when she came back and told us Arthur had been murdered, I wondered why on earth she hadn't come back at once. Though, when I came to think it over, I saw it was much more like her to pull herself together first. I wish I knew what you were driving at. Kindly note the way I've phrased that. Not by any means a question, you perceive. Just a remark thrown out at random.'

'Was she wearing gloves?'

'Yes, frightfully expensive ones,' replied Dinah. 'People of her generation nearly always do, only hers aren't the fat-white-woman-whom-nobody-loves kind at all.'

Harding sat back in his chair. 'What on earth are you talking about?' he asked patiently.

'You know!' said Dinah. ' "Why do you walk in the fields in gloves, missing so much and so much?" Mrs. Chudleigh wears that kind of glove. Mrs. Twining's are just part of the general ensemble, not glovey at all. And they were ruined, too, because she'd touched Arthur's body, and one of her hands was all stained with blood. It was beastly.'

'Which one?' Harding asked.

Dinah screwed up her eyes, as though trying to focus something. 'The right one,' she replied, and suddenly stiffened. 'John!'

'Well?'

'You must be mad!' gasped Dinah. 'It isn't possible!'

'Someone did it, Dinah.'

'Yes, but – but it's too fantastic! I see what you're driving at, but—'

He got up. 'I can't discuss it with you, darling. Will you sit tight and say nothing to anyone? I may be on a wrong track altogether.' He looked at his wrist-watch. 'I must go now,' he said. 'I shall see you tomorrow, I hope – late-ish.'

When he stepped out into the porch presently he found the

Sergeant seated in the car, reading a folded newspaper with the air of one who expects to be obliged to kick his heels indefinitely. He said briefly: 'Sorry to have been so long, Sergeant. Did you find out anything from the gardener?'

'No, sir, not a thing.' The Sergeant stowed his newspaper away, and coughed. 'I ought to mention, sir, that happening on Captain Billington-Smith, and him questioning me, I took the liberty of informing him that he was pretty well cleared.'

'I'd forgotten about him,' said Harding, getting into the car and pressing the self-starter. 'Quite right, Sergeant.'

'Yes,' said the Sergeant. 'I had a notion it might have slipped your memory, sir.'

Harding glanced at him suspiciously, but the Sergeant was looking more wooden than ever. 'You having other things to think about, sir, as you might say,' he added.

Harding changed the subject. 'I'm dropping you in Ralton, Sergeant, and going on up to London as soon as I've picked up my suitcase,' he said.

The Sergeant was betrayed into an unguarded exclamation. 'Lor', sir, you're never throwing the case up?'

'No, of course I'm not. I shall be back tomorrow, sometime. I'm going to find out what was the name of the General's first wife, and what became of her.'

'Ah!' said the Sergeant deeply. 'I was wondering what was in your mind, sir. But what about Mr. Billington-Smith and his alibi?'

'I'll attend to that tomorrow,' replied Harding.

It was late that evening when he reached London, and after garaging his car he went straight to the small flat he owned overlooking the river. His man, warned by telephone of his arrival, had prepared a meal for him, and he sat down to this at once, and while he ate, read over the précis he had written of the case. Then he studied the notes he had jotted down that day, and made an alteration in the original time-table. His man, coming into the room with the coffee-tray, found him staring straight ahead of him, an unlit cigarette between his lips and his lighter held in one motionless hand.

Jarvis set the tray down on the table and began to remove the remains of supper. 'A difficult case, sir?' he inquired.

Harding looked at him. 'I'm a fool,' he said.

'Oh, I wouldn't say that, sir,' replied Jarvis encouragingly.

'Not only a fool, but a damned fool,' said Harding. 'The thing's been staring at me in the face, and I've only just realized it.'

'Ah well, sir, better late than never,' said Jarvis. 'Will you be wanting me any more tonight?'

Shortly after five o'clock on the following afternoon, Inspector Harding's car drew up once more before Lyndhurst Vicarage, and the Inspector and Sergeant Nethersole got out. The Sergeant, who had been lost in thought all the way from Ralton, said slowly: 'I wonder if she saw Mr. Billington-Smith at all?'

Harding rang the front-door bell. 'Yes, I think so, undoubtedly.'

The Sergeant sighed, and shook his head. 'In my opinion,' he said, 'it's a bad business. A very bad business, and I don't mind admitting to you, sir, that I don't half like it.'

'No, I don't like it myself,' replied Harding. He turned, as the parlourmaid opened the door. 'Mrs. Chudleigh?'

The parlourmaid, who, in spite of his quite innocuous behaviour on the occasion of his first visit, seemed still to regard him with trepidation, stood back to let him enter the house, and said in a gasp that she would tell the mistress he wished to see her.

Inspector Harding, however, had no intention of being left in the hall again, and followed the maid to the drawing-room at the back of the house.

She opened the door. 'It's the police, m'm!' she announced breathlessly.

Mrs. Chudleigh, who was seated at the writing-table in the window, looked sharply round. When she saw the Inspector she rose, but she did not come forward to meet him. 'That will do, Lilian,' she said, dismissing the servant. 'Good afternoon, Inspector. Dear me, Sergeant Nethersole as well? May I ask what you want with me now?'

'Mrs. Chudleigh, I am here on a very unpleasant errand,' Harding said gently. 'I have a warrant for your arrest for the murder of your first husband, General Sir Arthur Billington-Smith. I must warn you that anything you say now may be taken down in writing and used in evidence.'

A queer, twisted smile curled her lips. 'I have been expecting you,' she said. 'I was warned. I've written it all out. It's in that drawer. You'll find it.'

Her hand was in the pocket of the cardigan she wore; she withdrew it, and raised it quickly to her mouth. 'Look out, sir!' cried the Sergeant, plunging forward.

He was too late; as he seized her wrist he saw her face convulsed. She fell forward, and a little bottle dropped to the ground, and rolled a few inches across the flowered carpet.

The Sergeant dropped on his knee beside her, and felt for her heart. He raised his eyes to the Inspector's face. 'She's dead, sir.'

Harding nodded. 'I know.' He came forward, and picked up the empty bottle, and sniffed it. 'Cyanide of potassium,' he said, and looked down at the dead woman. 'It's better like this, Sergeant.'

The Sergeant, who had been staring at him with something approaching a frown in his eyes, suddenly lowered his gaze. 'Maybe you're right, sir,' he said. 'I hadn't properly thought of it, but I don't know but what I agree with you.' He paused, and got up from his knees. 'She was too quick for us, sir,' he said deliberately. 'That's how it was.'

CHAPTER EIGHTEEN

'THIS is the full confession of me, Theresa Emmeline Chudleigh. I am perfectly sane, and what I shall write now is the truth, nor am I ashamed of it.

'I killed Arthur Billington-Smith with the dagger that was lying on his desk. I did not set out to do it, but now that it is done I know that I would do it again. I am not sorry. He was a cruel and a wicked tyrant. He ruined my life, and he would have ruined my son's life. What I did I did for Geoffrey's sake. It is the only thing I have ever been able to do for him, and I am proud of it.

'I have been warned that a piece of paper has been found with the start of my name scribbled on it in Arthur's handwriting. That is why I am setting down this confession, for if the police come to arrest me I have made up my mind to take poison.

'When I left Arthur Billington-Smith twenty years ago, I ran away with a man whose name I shall keep back, since he is dead now, and it cannot have any bearing on what I am going to write. He had promised that we should be married as soon as Arthur had divorced me, but there was another woman, and no doubt she was more attractive than I was. I do not think there is anything to be gained by my going into that. Even now, as I write, all that I went through at that time comes back to me and makes me almost glad that I have not much longer to live in this world. My family disowned me, and I am sure I do not blame them, for there was a dreadful scandal. I was very ill, and when I grew better I went right away where no one would know me. I called myself Miss Emily Lamb. Lamb was my maiden name; I thought it was common enough to attract no attention, and so indeed it proved. That enabled me to make enough to live on. It was through my work, when I was secretary to a charitable institution in the East End of London, that I met Hilary. I should like to say that whatever I had suffered was made up to me by him, and though he will say that in the eyes of God we were not married, I hope no one will deny that I have been a good wife to him. On that point my conscience is quite clear.

'I have been married – I say married, for I have never shared Hilary's prejudice against the remarriage of divorced persons – for ten years, the happiest years of my life. I was neither young nor pretty when we first met, for mine was the type of prettiness that fades quickly. I *was* pretty once, though that is neither here nor there. But he was not the sort of man to want mere beauty in his wife, and when we had known one another for just a year, he asked me to marry him.

'I did marry him. I have no doubt that a great many people will blame me for what I did, but I have never been one to care what others said, and I do not propose to change now. I never told Hilary that I was a divorced woman. To this day he does not know it. There is only one person who knows who I am. She has continued to be my friend throughout, and although she is a worldly, and sometimes, I fear, frivolous woman, I am grateful to her.

'It was chance, and not any design of mine, that brought Hilary to this parish. I would have preferred any other in the whole world, but it was necessary for Hilary's health that he should go into the country, and we could not pick and choose. I had, however, no fear of Arthur recognizing me. He had not set eyes on me for sixteen years, and I hope I am not so vain that I do not realize how much I have aged. When I left him I had literally masses of *perfectly natural* golden hair, and not a line on my face. A severe illness, and worry, turned my hair grey, and the false teeth which I am obliged to wear quite altered the shape of my mouth. I must say, it amused me to find that my successor, the present Lady Billington-Smith, was not at all unlike what I was in my young days.

'I have had to live as Arthur's neighbour for four years now. I do not know how I have been able to do it. I hope that time has improved *me*; it had not affected him. He was just the same; I was thankful that Hilary's scruples forbade him visiting the Grange more often. I could not have borne it. His second wife is, I fear, a weak, foolish woman. I have never had any sympathy for her: she should have known better than to have married a man old enough to be her father.

'I do not propose to discuss my son. His faults I lay at Arthur's door. No, I am not sorry I killed Arthur. I am, on the contrary, glad.

'I visited the Grange on Monday on purpose to discover what Arthur meant to do about Geoffrey's unfortunate entanglement. When I found that he had disowned the boy, I knew that a clear duty lay before me, and I did not shirk it. It was time that I made myself known to Arthur, for although he had divorced me I am still Geoffrey's mother, and have a right to concern myself with his future.

'I left the terrace at 12.30 on Monday. I would not permit Arthur's wife to accompany me. I knew that Arthur was in the study, and I chose to approach it from the garden so that people should not know I had gone to see him, a circumstance they must have thought peculiar. I wish to say that I had no intention of killing him. No such thought had so much as crossed my mind. I meant only to plead with him on Geoffrey's behalf. Julia Twining had promised to do what she could, but I had no faith in her power of persuasion. I thought if I threw myself on Arthur's generosity, perhaps, after so many years, he would listen to me.

'He was writing at his desk when I entered the room. I went in through the front windows. He was surprised to see me; I could see he was in one of his evil moods, though he was polite enough to me, in a surly fashion.

'When I told him who I was he did not at first believe me. He thought I was mad. When I convinced him he said, "*You* Theresa? *You* Theresa?" and burst into one of his loud, ill-bred horse-laughs.

'I did not mean to quarrel with him. I thought I had sufficient control over myself. Perhaps if he had not laughed as he did, I could have kept my temper. And yet I don't know.

'I am not going to recount what passed between us. But I do most solemnly assert that I tried to remain calm, that my only object was to intercede for Geoffrey. I had not realized, even with my knowledge of Arthur, that he hated the boy. I saw it then, of course. I cannot bring myself to write down the things that he said. His taunts at me I hope I could have borne with equanimity. What he said of Geoffrey – wicked, venomous sneers, on purpose to wound me – no mother could have borne.

'We did not talk for long, I think not more than ten minutes. I saw that I had only done harm; he would not listen to me. He told me I could go, and pretended to ignore me, and to go on with his work.

'I was standing beside his chair with my hand laid on his desk. I implored him to be reasonable. He laughed again, that jeering laugh I knew so well. I cannot explain what happened to me. It was all over in a flash. Every wrong I had suffered at his hands, all that past misery and bitterness came up before me, and there he sat, prosperous, self-satisfied, mean to the soul, revenging himself on my child— It is no use; I can't describe it. The knife was by my hand. He was not even looking. I snatched it up in a moment's fury, perhaps I should say madness, and struck him with it. If I were asked I could not say whether I meant to kill him. I think I did, at that moment. Anyway I am glad now that I did. People will say that I am a murderess. I am sure I do not care what they say.

'He fell forward over the desk. The blood spurted from the wound in the neck. Some of it spattered my sleeve. I put my scarf over it, and ran out of the room. My knees were shaking. I could hardly grasp what I had done.

'I got on my bicycle and rode home. There was blood on my gloves. I burned them in the kitchener when the servants had gone to bed.

'I thought no one would ever find out. I thought the police would suppose the murderer to have been some unknown person from outside. It did not occur to me that my action would put others in danger, even Geoffrey. When the Inspector came down from London I began to be afraid. He was not like our local police. He saw too much. He found out things about every one. I knew then that in the end I should have to come forward. Naturally I should not permit even such creatures as that designing Mexican or Mrs. Halliday to bear the blame of what I had done.

'That is all that I have to say, except that it is true that I saw Geoffrey just as I described. I have known since I told the Inspector that I saw Geoffrey at ten to one that he would find out the truth.'

Major Grierson laid the last sheet down, and dabbed violently at his nose. 'Shocking! Shocking!' he said. 'Poor soul! I do not know when I have been so – er – upset. One should not say it, but really, Harding, one cannot but be – er – glad that she ended it as she did.'

The Superintendent said sourly: 'I ought to have gone myself. Of course, I suppose Mr. Harding will explain to them up at the Yard how he came to let a thing like that happen. I only hope he doesn't get dropped on for it.'

'Come, come – er – Superintendent! Mr. Harding could not have suspected her of concealing poison about her – er – person.'

'Ah, that's where it is, sir,' said the Superintendent loftily. 'You have to be prepared for things like that. That's what I could have told the Inspector. However, it's for him to write his report as he sees fit.'

Harding got up. 'You're quite right, Superintendent, and I think it's time I started to do it.'

The Chief Constable followed him out. Before he got into his car he said, glancing momentarily at Harding: 'I'm not – er – asking whether you meant to let it – er – happen as it did. I can only say that I am – er – thankful. A terrible case! Quite appalling! I trust you won't get into – er – trouble, Harding.'

'Not very serious trouble, sir, I think. I'm leaving the Force in any case.'

'Indeed? Well, I must say I am glad to – er – hear it. Now what about that meeting of ours? Can I – er – persuade you to come out and dine – er – tonight?'

'Thanks very much, sir, but I'm afraid I can't manage it tonight,' said Harding. 'Some other time, if I may.'

'My dear fellow, it won't take you all the – er – evening to write up your report!' expostulated the Major.

Harding reddened slightly. 'No, of course not, but I've got to go up to the Grange this evening, sir – and—'

'To the Grange? But what in the – er – world for?' asked the Major, bewildered.

'Oh, just to clear up a – a small matter arising out of the case,' said Hilary.

The 'small matter', with whom he had previously held a somewhat protracted conversation over the telephone, met him on the doorstep of the Grange when he drove up shortly before nine o'clock. She expressed a desire to be informed whether he was on duty or off.

'Off,' said Inspector Harding, demonstrating the truth of this statement by taking the lady into his arms.

Miss Fawcett protested feebly. 'Suppposing somebody were looking?'

'I don't mind if there are dozens of people looking,' said Inspector Harding brazenly.

Miss Fawcett tucked her hand in his arm in a companionable way, and proceeded to stroll with him into the garden. 'I'm glad it's all over,' she said. 'I'm awfully sorry for Mrs. Chudleigh, though I can't say I ever liked her. Still, one can't be surprised at her having got curdled and bitter. Mrs. Twining's here. She's been telling us the whole story. She came on here from the Vicarage. She says Mr. Chudleigh is quite dazed. It's ghastly for him. I wish you needn't have found it out, John, though naturally I'm proud of you for having been so clever.'

'Clever?' repeated Harding. 'Did you say *clever*? I ought to have been on to it two days ago.'

'Well, I think it was distinctly bright of you,' said Dinah. 'What did put you on to it?'

'The bicycle. If Mrs. Chudleigh left this house on her bicycle at twelve-thirty she would have been home by twelve-forty-five. Only if she had been walking could she have seen Geoffrey where she did at ten to one. Either she was lying, and never saw him at all, or she left here considerably later than you all said she did. That discrepancy in the time was what finally put me on to her. What originally gave me the idea of the General's first wife was that slip of paper, coupled with something Geoffrey said. Do you remember finding me with *Chambers's Dictionary*, in the morning-room? You asked me if I was doing a crossword. I was looking up the proper names beginning with T.'

'What, not the More Common English Christian Names?' asked Dinah. 'Did you find Theresa? I thought they only had names like Abijah and Eusebius and Sophronia.'

He smiled. 'There were rather a lot like that, and I must admit I haven't often met an English person called Tryphosa, or even Polycarp. But I found Theresa all right. It was the only one that would fit the letters I had, too. That was what put me on to Mrs. Twining – a very false trail. Then I went with the Sergeant to check up on Geoffrey's alibi, and I found that Mrs. Chudleigh had been on her bicycle that morning. Even then I didn't tumble to it, though I began to be suspicious. It wasn't till I had time to think it over that it dawned on me – and then it seemed to me to be almost incredible. It took the records at Somerset House to convince me I hadn't stumbled on to a mare's nest, so I'm afraid I was anything but bright, darling.'

'If you hadn't been bright about it,' said Miss Fawcett firmly, 'You'd still be nosing round after all the really suspicious people here who might have done it. Lola, for instance. Oh, by the way, did I tell you she'd heard from her agent – not the one who came here but another one? She's been offered an engagement at some theatre or other, and she's tremendously pleased about it. In fact she told Geoffrey at tea-time that he mustn't be unreasonable and expect her to marry him at once, so there seems to be a fair chance for him to be able to wriggle out of the betrothal.' She paused, and peeped up at him. 'Which reminds me, I don't know whether you want to wriggle out of yours, but—'

'No, thank you, I don't,' said Harding.

'Well, that's rather lucky,' confessed Dinah, 'because I have just mentioned the matter to the rest of the party. Camilla looked awfully sick. She hinted that you'd been pretty matey with her.'

'I was,' said Harding. 'I paid her fulsome compliments. That's how I got her to talk.'

'It is quite evident to me,' said Miss Fawcett with decision, 'that it is time you left off being a detective.'

They had reached the lawn at the back of the house, and were wandering towards the terrace steps. In the drawing-room the lights had been turned on. Dinah sighed. 'I suppose we shall have to go in. Every one's wanting to see you in a human light. I think I shall have to introduce you, because you haven't met any of them socially yet. Can you stand up to a lot of congratulations, do you think?'

'I'd much rather stay out here with you,' he confessed, 'but we'll go in if you think we ought to.'

So Miss Fawcett, still with her hand on his arm, led Inspector Harding into the house to be introduced.